JANET DAILEY

Calder Grit

ZEBRA BOOKS
KENSINGTON PUBLISHING CORP.
www.kensingtonbooks.com

ZEBRA BOOKS are published by

Kensington Publishing Corp.
119 West 40th Street
New York, NY 10018

All Kensington titles, imprints, and distributed lines are available at special quantity discounts for bulk purchases for sales promotion, premiums, fund-raising, and educational or institutional use.

Special book excerpts or customized printings can also be created to fit specific needs. For details, write or phone the office of the Kensington Sales Manager: Kensington Publishing Corp., 119 West 40th Street, New York, NY 10018. Attn. Sales Department. Phone: 1-800-221-2647.

ZEBRA BOOKS and the Z logo Reg. U.S. Pat. & TM Off.

First Kensington hardcover edition: March 2022
First Zebra mass market paperback edition: February 2023
ISBN-13: 978-1-4201-5101-5
ISBN-13: 978-1-4967-2751-0 (eBook)

10 9 8 7 6 5 4 3 2 1

Printed in the United States of America

CHAPTER 1

Blue Moon, Montana
July 4, 1909

*H*ANNA STOOD NEXT TO HER STERN-FACED FATHER, ONE foot tapping out the beat of the polka. Couples whirled around the rough plank floor to the music of the old-time accordion band. She would've given anything to join them. But Big Lars Anderson had already turned down three cowboys who'd asked to partner his daughter. Hanna would've said yes to any of them, just to get out there and dance. But Big Lars had made his position clear. Those rough-mannered men from the ranches, even the polite ones, weren't fit company for an innocent girl.

As if being guarded like a prisoner wasn't bad enough, her mother had forced her to dress like a twelve-year-old, in a white pinafore, with her long, wheaten hair in two thick braids. But even the girlish costume couldn't hide the breasts that strained the bodice of her gingham dress. She was almost seventeen years old, with a woman's body and a woman's mind. When would her parents stop treating her like a child?

As the music flowed through her limbs, Hanna gazed at the deepening sky, where the sun was just setting behind the rugged Montana mountains, turning the clouds to ribbons of flame. It was so beautiful. How could she complain after such a glorious day—a celebration of America's freedom in her family's new home?

As she breathed in the fresh, free air, her memory drifted back to the tiny apartment in the New York slum, where she'd helped her mother tend the babies that just kept coming. Her father had worked on the docks, barely making enough to keep food on the table. When her older brother, Alvar, had turned fourteen, he'd gone to work there, too. In the desperation of those years, the American dream that had brought her parents from Sweden had been all but lost.

But then the news had traveled like wildfire through the tenements. Thanks to the passage of the new Homestead Act, there was free land out west. All they had to do was get there on the train, build a cabin, farm the land for five years, and it would be theirs, free and clear.

Now the dream had come true. Hanna's family and their neighbors had claimed their parcels of rich Montana grassland. The fields had been plowed; the wheat was planted and growing. On the anniversary of America's independence, it was time for friends and neighbors to celebrate an Independence Day of their own.

The festivities had begun earlier that afternoon with picnicking, races, games, and now a dance, with fireworks to end the day. It was the homesteaders, like Hanna's family, who'd planned the event; but the whole town, as well as the folks from the big cattle ranches, had been invited. That included the woman-hungry bachelor cowboys who'd shown up hoping to dance with the daughters of the farm families.

So far, the cowboys hadn't had much success. The immigrant fathers had guarded their girls like treasures. They wouldn't trust rough-mannered ranch hands anywhere near their precious girls.

But the girls, even the shy ones, were very much aware of the men.

"That cowboy is looking at you." Hanna nudged her friend Lillian, who stood on her left. Lillian, an auburn-haired beauty, was only a little older than Hanna, but she was already married, which made all the difference in the way she was treated.

The cowboy in question stood on the far side of the dance floor. He was taller than the others, with black hair and a hard, rugged look about him. Hanna knew who he was— Webb Calder, son of the most powerful ranch family in the region. And yes, he was definitely looking at Lillian.

"Does he know you?" Hanna asked.

Lillian shrugged and glanced away, but not before Hanna had noticed the color that flooded her cheeks. She was married to Stefan Reisner, a humorless man even older than Hanna's father. Lillian wasn't the sort to play flirting games with men. But it was plain to see that Webb Calder had made an impression on her.

As if to distract Hanna, Lillian gave a subtle nod in a different direction. "Now *that* cowboy, the one in the blue shirt and leather vest. He was just looking at *you*."

Hanna followed the direction of her friend's gaze. Something fluttered in the pit of her stomach as she spotted the rangy man standing at the break between the wagons that surrounded the dance floor. He was hatless, his hair dark brown and thick with a slight curl to it. His features were strong and solid, and there was pride in the way he carried himself—like a man who had nothing to prove.

But even though he might've been looking at Hanna earlier, he wasn't looking at her now. His gaze scanned the dance floor and the watchers who stood around the edge. He started forward. Then, as if he'd been called away, he suddenly turned and left.

* * *

Blake Dollarhide swore as he made his way among the buggies and wagons toward the open street. The Carmody brothers, who worked at his sawmill, had been warned about picking fights with the homesteaders. But with a few drinks under their belts, the two Irishmen tended to get belligerent. If they were making trouble now, Blake would have little choice except to fire them. But before that could be done, he'd probably have to stop a fight.

With the dance on, Blake had hoped to get a waltz or two with pretty, blond Ruth Stanton, whose father was foreman of the vast Calder spread, the Triple C Ranch. It was no secret that Ruth had her eye on Webb Calder, who would inherit the whole passel from his father, Chase Benteen Calder, one day. But there was no law against Blake's enjoying a dance with her. He might even be lucky enough to turn her head.

Taking anything away from Webb Calder would be a pleasure.

Ruth had been free for the moment. Blake had been about to cross the floor and ask her to dance when he'd heard shouts from the direction of the street. A quick glance around the dance floor had confirmed that the brothers weren't there. Dollars to donuts, the no-accounts had started a brawl.

Blake broke into a run as he spotted the trouble. The two Carmody brothers, small men, but tough and pugnacious, were baiting a lanky homesteader who'd probably left his friends to find a privy. The confrontation was drawing an ugly crowd.

"Pack your wagon and go back to where you came from, you filthy honyocker." Tom Carmody feinted a punch at the man's face. "We don't need you drylanders here, plowin' up the grass to plant your damned wheat, spoilin' land what's meant for cattle. Things was fine afore the likes of you showed up. Worse'n a plague of grasshoppers, that's what you are."

"Please." The man held up his hands. "I don't want trouble. Just let me go back to my family."

"You can go back—after we show you what we do to squatters like you." Tom's brother, Finn, brandished a hefty stick of kindling. Readying a strike, he aimed at the homesteader's head.

"That's enough!" Blake's iron grip stopped Finn's arm in midswing. A quick twist, and the stick fell to the ground. Finn staggered backward, clutching his wrist.

"I warned you two about this," Blake said. "I'm sorry to lose two workers, but I can't have you stirring up this kind of trouble. Any gear you left at the mill will be outside the gate."

"Aw, they was just funnin', Blake." Hobie Evans, who worked for the Snake M Ranch, was the chief instigator against the homesteaders. He'd probably goaded the Carmody brothers into targeting the lone farmer, hoping others would join in and give the poor man a beating to serve as an example.

"Don't push me, Hobie. This is a peaceful celebration. Let's keep it that way." Blake glanced around to make sure the farmer was gone and his tormentors had backed off. "Before I had to come out here, I was planning to dance with a pretty lady. For your sake, you'd better hope she's still available."

Blake strode back, past the wagons that ringed the dance floor, intent on seeking out Ruth. But in his absence, something had changed. Webb Calder was on the dance floor with the pretty, auburn-haired wife of one of the farmers. Ruth was on the sidelines, looking stricken.

Blake nudged the cowboy standing next to him. "What's going on?" he muttered.

"Webb got Doyle Petit to talk the drylanders into lettin' us dance with their women. My guess is, soon as this dance is over we can start askin' 'em." The young cowboy grinned. "I got my little gal all picked out—the one in white, with the yellow braids. She's right next to that big farmer—he's her pa. See her?"

"I see her." Blake gave the girl a casual glance. She appeared to be a child, almost, in her white pinafore, with her hair in schoolgirl braids. But then he took a longer look and the bottom seemed to drop out of his heart. He swore under his breath. She wasn't a child at all, but a stunning young woman with an angel's face and a body that even the girlish pinafore couldn't hide.

"Ain't she somethin'?" The cowboy asked. "What do you think?"

"I think you'd better be damned fast on your feet," Blake said. "Otherwise, somebody else might get to her first."

Somebody like me.

As the music faded, Webb Calder escorted the pretty redhead back to her husband. A few words were exchanged. Then Webb turned back to the waiting cowboys. "All right, boys. You can invite the young ladies to dance. But remember your manners. Any Triple C boys not on their best behavior will answer to me."

There was a beat of hesitation. Then the eager cowhands broke ranks and walked across the floor to ask the fathers' permission to dance with their daughters. Blake had decided to hang back and let the lovestruck cowboy enjoy a dance with his dream girl. But when he looked across the floor, he saw that someone else had already claimed her.

Seen from behind, the girl's escort was almost as tall as Blake, but a trifle broader in the chest and shoulders. He was dressed in city-bought clothes, his chestnut hair neatly trimmed to curl above the collar of his linen shirt.

Blake mouthed a curse. As usual, his half brother, Mason, had seized the advantage and run away with it.

Whirling blissfully around the dance floor, Hanna gazed up at the man who held her in his arms. The smile on his handsome face deepened the dimple in his cheek. His green eyes reflected glints of sunset.

"You looked like an angel, standing there in your white dress," he said. "Do angels have names?"

"My name's Hanna Anderson, and believe me, I'm not an angel," she said. "Just ask my parents."

He chuckled. "But you're an angel to me because you just saved me from a very boring evening. So that's what I'll call you—my angel."

Hanna had never heard such flattering talk. Who was this charming stranger? Certainly not a cowboy. He was too well dressed and too well spoken for that. "I'm Mason Dollarhide," he said, answering her unspoken question. "I run the Hollister ranch south of town. It may not be the biggest spread in Montana, but it sure is the prettiest. Almost as pretty as you."

"Now you're playing games with me," Hanna said. She wasn't a fool. But after what seemed like a lifetime of scrubbing, tending, washing, mending, working in the fields like a man, and never being made to feel attractive or desirable in any way, she let his words wash over her like the sound of sweet music.

Missing a step, she stumbled slightly. His hand, at the small of her back, tightened, drawing her so close that she could feel the light pressure of his body against hers. Heat flashed through her like summer lightning, making her feel vaguely naughty. Did he feel it, too?

"I would never play games with a precious girl like you." His voice had thickened. "I'd wager you've never even been kissed. Have you?"

"That's none of your business," Hanna said, although she hadn't been kissed, except by a neighbor boy when she was ten.

He chuckled. "Feisty little thing, aren't you?"

"I just don't like people forming ideas before they know me, that's all," Hanna said.

The music was drawing to a close, but his hand—smooth, with no calluses—didn't release hers. "I'd like to get to know you better, Hanna," he said. "Why don't we walk a little, where we don't have to raise our voices over the music?"

Hanna glanced back over her shoulder. Her father was talking to Lillian's husband. Lillian was nowhere in sight. Neither was the rugged cowboy who'd danced with her. Hanna felt the gentle pressure of the stranger's hand against her back, guiding her off the floor. She didn't resist. Nobody would miss her if she stepped out for a few harmless minutes.

They made their way among the wagons. He stopped her next to an elegant-looking buggy that was parked outside the circle. "This is my buggy," he said. "Get in. I'll take you for a ride."

He offered a hand to help her up, but she stopped him. "No. I can't go for a ride with you."

"But why? It's a beautiful evening. And I've got the slickest team of horses in the county."

"You don't know my father. He'd punish me, and he'd probably find a way to damage you, too. He's a good man, but you don't want to cross him. Let's just stand here and talk."

"All right." He nodded, leaning against the buggy. "So, is your mother here, too?"

"No, she took the wagon home early with my brothers and sisters. I wanted to stay for the dance, so my father remained with me. We were planning to ride home with a neighbor."

"I could offer you both a ride. Maybe if he got to know me, he'd let me see you again. I'm not one of those cowhands that might take advantage of a sweet girl like you. I've got my own ranch—at least it'll be mine when my mother passes away."

"Don't bother asking. My father would never accept." Hanna was beginning to feel uneasy. What if her father were to catch her out here, alone with a man? "I'd better go back before he comes looking for me."

She turned to go. Mason blocked her path. "Wait." His hand cupped her jaw, tilting her face upward. "Lord Almighty," he murmured. "Angel, I feel like I just stepped into heaven. You're the most beautiful thing I've ever seen."

Hanna's heart broke into a gallop as he bent closer. His lips were almost touching hers when an angry voice shattered the spell.

"Damn it, Mason, let that girl go. Her father's fit to be tied. If he finds her out here with you, he'll skin you alive!"

Hanna turned. The tall cowboy she'd noticed earlier, the one with the blue shirt and leather vest, stood a few feet away from them. "Get inside and find your father, miss," he said. "You can claim you went to the privy. If he asks, I'll tell him I saw you coming from that direction. Meanwhile, I need to have words with my brother, here."

Hanna gasped, shocked that a man would mention bodily functions to her. But at least he'd come up with a good excuse for her father. Hot faced, she fled back toward the dance floor, weaving her way among the buggies and wagons. That was when a cry went up from somewhere out of sight.

"*Fire!*"

Turning, Hanna saw a distant column of smoke rising against the twilight sky. The prairie was burning.

CHAPTER 2

"COME ON!" AS THE FLEEING GIRL VANISHED FROM sight, Blake leaped into his brother's buggy, yanking Mason in behind him.

"What the hell—?" Mason sputtered.

"My horse is tied at the saloon. There's no time to get him." He grabbed the reins and released the brake. Around them, people were piling into buggies and wagons, some already racing toward the fire.

"It's my rig, damn it! I'll drive!" Mason snatched the reins away and slapped them down on the backs of the two matched sorrels. The buggy shot ahead, careening around a wagonload of settlers.

A narrow column of gray smoke rose to the west—a grass fire, judging from the color. Not too big yet, Blake calculated, but in this torrid July weather the dry prairie grass could flame up like tinder. Uncontrolled, the fire would race across fields and pastures, destroying everything in its path, including animals, homes, and even human lives.

Some of the settlers looked confused, maybe not understanding what needed to be done. But when they saw the ranch folks and townspeople rushing with breakneck urgency toward the smoke, they joined in. A prairie fire was everybody's problem.

The buggy swung off the road and cut across the open grassland, jouncing over the rough ground. Blake could see the fire now, and the burned skeleton of the tar paper shack where it must've started. Coming closer, he could smell the acrid smoke and hear the hiss and crackle of burning grass.

Fires didn't start themselves. Blake had his suspicions about who'd set this one. But nothing mattered now except putting out the blaze. And with no source of water nearby, that was going to be a dangerous challenge.

By the time Mason pulled the team up behind the wagons and buggies, Webb Calder had already taken charge of fighting the fire. The men he'd ordered into a line were beating back the flames with horse blankets and anything else that could be found. Those without blankets flailed at the flames with shovels or scraped away the grass to act as a firebreak.

Grabbing a wool blanket out of the back of the buggy, Blake vaulted out and raced to join the line. The smoke reddened Blake's eyes and stung his throat as he beat the fire's encroaching edge. The shortness of the grass kept the flames low, but the heat was searing, the fire spreading before the wind as fast as a man could walk. The dry blankets were losing the battle with the licking flames. Only water had any chance of quenching them before the blaze burned out of control.

Now more settlers were arriving. The men and older boys jumped off the wagons to fight the fire with whatever they had.

Some of the wagons carried water barrels that had been filled in town. As Webb began shouting orders, the women on the wagons took the blankets one by one, wet them in the barrels, and returned them to the men. As Blake passed his blanket up into a waiting pair of hands, his eyes met those of the girl he'd caught with Mason—the girl with the golden braids.

Her indigo eyes were reddened from the smoke. Stray locks of hair clung to her flushed face. Her white pinafore was wet and smeared with soot from handling the charred blankets. But even so, with smoke swirling around them, Blake was struck by her innocent beauty.

For an instant, their gazes met and held. There was a flicker of recognition before she turned away, dunked the lower part of the blanket in the water barrel, and passed it, still dripping, back down to him. Grasping it, he raced back to the fire.

The water-soaked blankets made a difference, but the flames were still burning. Glancing down the line, Blake glimpsed Hobie Evans and the Carmody brothers beating at the fire. If somebody had started it, Blake's money would be on those three. But of course they'd be here, helping, to avoid any suspicion.

Webb Calder moved up and down the lines, stepping in where help was needed. Webb's father, Benteen, who was well into his fifties, was on the fire line, too. Overcome by smoke, he suddenly doubled over, coughing. Webb seized his father's shoulders, guided him away from the flames, and left him with Ruth Stanton, who'd come in the buggy with Benteen's wife. Blake was grateful that his own parents and sister had left the celebration and gone home early. His father, Joe, was younger than Benteen, but even he had begun to show his years.

By the time the fire was out, the fighters were filthy and staggering with exhaustion. The homesteader who'd lost his house and most of his wheat crop stood apart with his wife and children, gazing at the destruction. The woman was in tears, the little ones wailing.

Damned shame, Blake thought as he walked back toward the buggy, keeping an eye out for his brother. His eyes were red and sore from the smoke, his clothes filthy, his good boots charred. Neighbors would help the family rebuild their shack and see that they had food and clothes, but it was too late in the season to plant and harvest a new wheat crop. And no wheat to sell meant no money.

Blake had nothing against the recent settlers. Their arrival had been a boon to the town and to his family's lumber business. The drylanders bought cheap green boards to frame their tar paper shacks, while the high-quality, seasoned lumber from the Dollarhide sawmill went to build solid homes and new businesses in the growing community.

Joe Dollarhide, Blake's father, had seeded his fortune with his own early land grant and the wild horses he'd broken and sold in Canada. Now the family business combined land, cattle, and lumber. The lumber mill was Blake's responsibility, and he had ambitious plans for it—new sources of timber and more efficient ways to get logs to the mill, as well as the construction business he wanted to start. In this fast-growing town, there was money to be made. And Blake was determined to rake in his share of it.

Blake's father tended to measure his family's wealth against the Calders, who ruled like Montana kings in their big white mansion. The Triple C had more land and more cattle than all the other ranches combined. But with the beef market in a slump, the Calders could barely afford to pay their hired help. Ranchers all around Blue Moon were having to let their cowhands go. Some, like Mason's friend, Doyle Petit, had even sold off their grazing land to the wheat farmers.

But the Calders were different. If they were struggling financially, they refused to show it. They carried themselves with pride, gave generously to the community, and refused to complain in public or to sell so much as an acre of their land. Despite the rivalry between his father and the patriarch of the Calder family, Blake had nothing but respect for Benteen and Lorna Calder.

Their son Webb, however, was a different story—a story that had started back when Webb, the biggest boy in the one-room school they'd shared, had bullied the smaller Mason so cruelly that on some days, the younger boy would go home in tears. When Blake had tried to interfere, Webb had given him a black eye and a nosebleed. Of course, neither of the brothers told their teacher or their parents. There was nothing more shameful than a snitch.

All three were men now. Blake would bet that Webb Calder wouldn't even remember how he'd tormented the smaller, weaker Mason. But Mason had neither forgotten nor forgiven.

Blake found Mason waiting in the buggy. He'd lost track of his half brother while the fire was raging, but the dust that coated Mason's clothes, and his dirt-streaked face suggested that he'd been helping to shovel a firebreak.

Mason grinned. "Good thing you showed up. I was just about to drive off and leave you."

"You know better than to do that, little brother." Blake hauled his tired body onto the buggy seat. "But I'll tell you what. When we get back to the saloon, I'll buy you a drink."

"Done. I've got a powerful thirst. I may need more than one." Mason swung the team in an arc and headed the buggy back toward town. The homesteaders' wagons departed in the opposite direction, leaving men behind to make sure the fire didn't flare up again. Blake found himself scanning the crowd for the girl in white, but he didn't see her. Not that it mattered. Why should it? He didn't even know her name.

Driving back toward the road, they passed the Calder buggy. Webb was driving the matched bays, with Ruth beside him on the front seat. Benteen, looking pale and drawn, sat in the back with his wife.

Mason slapped the reins to get ahead, leaving the Calders in a cloud of dust—something Blake wouldn't have done, but he'd long since learned that Mason had his own way about him.

"Webb was quite the hero boy today," Mason said as he slowed the team down. "He was strutting around like the biggest rooster in the coop."

"He did all right." Blake didn't much care for Webb either, but, unlike Mason, he kept his opinions to himself. The Dollarhides didn't need enemies—especially enemies as powerful as the Calders.

"Hell, it's not like we don't know how to fight a fire," Mason said. "We all knew what to do. We didn't need Webb to boss us around. I think he was mostly doing it to impress that sodbuster's redheaded wife."

"The one he was dancing with." It wasn't a question.

"That's right. The pretty one. Webb was all over her at the dance, and with her husband right there. If Webb had got his teeth kicked in, it would've served him right." Mason maneuvered the buggy back onto the dusty, rutted road. "And poor Ruth, having to stand there and watch. Her face said it all. A classy girl like that deserves better than Webb."

"If I could convince her of that, she could have me."

Mason chuckled. "You and half the other single men around here. But did you see the goings-on back at the fire?"

Blake shook his head. "I guess I was in the wrong place. Or maybe I was too busy fighting the fire to notice."

"You'd have noticed if you'd been there. It happened when the fire was almost out. As the wind changed, the fire started toward the wagons. The redhead—the wife—tried to stomp it out, and her skirt caught on fire. Webb tackled her and rolled her on the ground to put it out."

"Was she hurt?"

"It didn't look all that bad. But then Webb scooped her up in his arms and started for his buggy. That old man she's married to stepped right in front of him and snatched her away. He looked mad enough to kill. And of course Ruth saw it all."

"Ruth needs to show Webb the door and give the rest of us a chance," Blake said.

"But she won't. She wants to be a Calder. And she's got Webb's mother backing her. Hey, brother, there are other good-looking ladies out there—like that little angel with the golden braids. She's the one I've got my eye on. I just need to find a way around her father."

"Good luck with that." Remembering those innocent eyes, Blake felt a stab of something he didn't fully understand. The thought of Mason with that girl, winning her with his usual charm, then most likely breaking her heart, made him want to grind his teeth.

"How's your mother?" Blake asked, changing the subject.

"Fine. Spinning her little webs as usual." Amelia Hollister Dollarhide, Joe's first wife, had inherited her father's ranch and expanded it into her own empire. Blake, the son of Joe and his second wife, Sarah, was a year older than Mason. There was a story behind that incongruity. But most people either understood or knew better than to ask questions.

"And how's Dad doing?" Mason asked. "I've been meaning to come up to the house and see him."

"He's slowed down since that stallion broke his leg this spring. But otherwise he's doing all right. And Sarah's the same. They miss you. You know you'd be welcome anytime."

"Sarah was like a second mother to me. You can tell her I said so. But I didn't see our little sister at the dance. I was looking forward to watching the cowboys battle to lead her to the floor."

"Kristin isn't much for socializing—or cowboys. She's got her own way of thinking, whatever that is. But she misses you, too. We got used to having you around in the old days. Now it seems everything's changed."

"I know." Mason pulled the buggy up alongside the saloon, where Blake's buckskin horse was still tied to the rail. "Mother's grooming me to take over the ranch—a waste of time if you ask me. She'll probably live to be a hundred, and she won't let go of the reins as long as she's got breath in her body. Her only ambition for me is that I marry a rich woman. Do you know any of those around here?"

Blake chuckled. "Only your mother. Now what do you say we get that drink I promised you?"

* * *

The Andersons' nearest neighbor, Stefan Reisner, paused his wagon outside the shack that was Hanna's family home. His wife, Lillian, lay in the wagon bed with wet cloths on her blistered legs. The burns would heal, but she was in pain. Stefan was anxious to get her home. He was stopping only to drop off Hanna and her father.

Hanna had ridden in the wagon bed next to Lillian, cradling her friend's head and giving her sips of water. "I could stay with her the rest of the way," she said. "It's not that far to walk home."

"I can take care of her." Stefan sounded almost angry. "Just get out so we can go."

Big Lars had already climbed off the rear of the wagon. As Hanna moved back to join him, he turned and held out his huge hands to help her to the ground.

"I'll come to see you, Lillian," Hanna called as the wagon rolled away. Stefan didn't look back. She hoped he wasn't angry at Lillian. It wasn't Lillian's fault that her skirt had caught fire or that Webb Calder had been there to save her.

As Hanna walked toward the house with her father, she could smell the rabbit stew cooking in the kitchen. Her mother came rushing outside, wiping her hands on her apron. "We saw the smoke. Are you all right?" Inga Anderson had been a pretty girl in her youth, but twenty years of work, worry, and childbearing had aged her before her time. Her blond hair was streaked with gray, her face creased, her body shapeless beneath her worn gingham dress.

"We're fine. I'll wash up." Big Lars was a man of few words. Walking to the barrel, he filled a tin dipper with enough water to splash the soot off his face and out of his sparse, light brown hair.

"And you." She looked Hanna up and down, shaking her head. "I was hoping that pinafore could be passed down to Britta, at least. But it'll never come clean. We might as well tear it up for rags. Why can't you be more careful, Hanna? We don't have money for nice clothes. We need to make them last."

Hanna untied the sash of the pinafore and slipped it off, uncovering the threadbare calico dress beneath. She could see that the pinafore was ruined. And new clothes cost money the family didn't have. "I'm sorry, Mama," she said. "I needed to wet down blankets so the men could fight the fire. The blankets were dirty. What could I do?"

"I suppose you could've taken the pinafore off and put it out of the way. But that might be asking too much of a young girl with other things on her mind." Inga held up the pinafore, examined the soot stains, shook her head again, and rolled it into a ball. "So, did you have a good time at the dance?"

"It was . . . all right."

"And did you behave yourself?"

"Of course, Mama." Hanna knew better than to talk about the handsome, well-dressed man who'd almost kissed her. As for the news about Lillian's accident and the rancher who'd rescued her, that would be best passed on by her father.

"Let me wash up, and I'll set the table." She dipped enough water into a shallow basin to get her hands and face clean. Her hair would have to be brushed clean at bedtime.

Mason Dollarhide.

Hanna's lips shaped his name as she set the table with the tin plates and the few chipped, mismatched dishes that had been salvaged from their old home. When Mason Dollarhide had told her his name, he'd mentioned that he had his own ranch, so he wasn't one of those common cowboys her mother had warned her about. She wasn't fool enough to think she was in love, or that she had any future with such a man. But the memory of his pretty words caused her pulse to skip a little.

What if he had kissed her? Would his lips have felt like warm velvet touching hers? That was how she'd imagined her first kiss. There next to his buggy, with his hand tilting her face toward his, she'd been ready to let it happen. But then the other man had come—his brother—and sent her running back to her father like a scolded child, her face burning with shame.

"Hanna, didn't you hear me?" Her mother's voice broke into her musings. "I said, go outside and call your brothers and sisters to supper. For heaven's sake, what's got into you?"

With a sigh, Hanna obeyed. Daydreaming was a waste of time, she admonished herself. Her life was here with her family, plowing and planting, washing and mending, tending the animals and the younger children—all for a future in this land where nothing was won except by hard work. For now, at least, she would have to put away her secret longings and try to be content with her lot.

Blake and Mason had enjoyed two whiskeys each and were about to leave the saloon to go home and clean up when Mason's friend, Doyle Petit, walked up to their table and sat down without an invitation.

"Doyle." Blake gave him a nod. He didn't especially like the young man who'd inherited his father's cattle ranch and sold every stick and pebble of it to the wheat growers. Doyle was awash in money—some of which he'd spent on the county's first automobile. He was keen to make more, even if it meant taking advantage of other people's bad luck.

Blake pushed his chair back from the table. "You're welcome to stay and visit with my brother. But I was just about to climb on my horse and head home."

"But I came in to talk to you, Blake." Doyle's clothes were spotless. When the fire had needed fighting, he'd clearly been somewhere else. "Stay a minute," he said. "I've got a business proposition for you. I'll buy you a drink while you listen."

Blake sighed. He already knew what his answer would be, but it wouldn't hurt to know what Doyle had on his mind.

"All right. But I've already had enough to drink. Just keep it short." He left his chair pushed clear of the table, to make his getaway easier when he decided he'd heard enough.

Settling back in the chair, Blake waited for Doyle to begin his pitch. Four cowboys who'd been at the fire were sitting at the table behind him. They were talking and laughing, making a lot of noise, but Blake willed himself to ignore them. He didn't plan to be here much longer.

"Here's what I'm thinking, Blake," Doyle said. "You sell a lot of cheap green lumber to those drylanders. But it's a long drive for their wagons, out to your sawmill. I aim to start a lumber business here in town—buy the lumber from you, haul it to a lot I've staked out behind the general store, and sell it at a profit. I'm betting the drylanders will be glad to pay a little extra for the convenience. Mason thinks it's a great idea. You even said so. Didn't you, Mason?"

"I did. But it's not up to me. It's up to Blake."

"So what do you think so far, Blake?" Doyle asked.

Blake shrugged. "As things stand now, you can buy all the lumber you want from me, Doyle. And once you've paid me, I don't care what the hell you do with it. So what do you need me for?"

"Just this. If we're partners, you can give me a better deal on the lumber and lend me one of your wagons to haul it. That way we can sell it cheaper, sell more, and still make a profit."

"A profit for you, not for me. No thanks, Doyle. I'm not interested. You can buy all the lumber you want, but not at a discount." Blake shifted in the chair, preparing to stand.

"No, wait." Doyle took a small notepad and a pencil out of his vest and began scribbling. "I've thought this all out. Let me show you some figures."

As Blake waited, knowing it was a waste of time, bits of conversation from the cowboys at the neighboring table broke into his awareness. He'd seen them come in, and he recognized a couple of them. They worked for the Calders.

"Can't say I think much of them sodbusters, but glory hallelujah, they brought some good-lookin' gals with 'em." The speaker was a big, bearded man named Sig Hoskins.

"I'll say," another cowboy responded. "That redhead's a pretty one. But it looks like Webb Calder's already staked his claim to her, even if she's married to that old geezer."

"Hell, that won't stop Webb. When he wants somethin', he goes after it."

"Webb can have her," Hoskins said. "The one I want is Yellow Braids. Now there's a fine little filly for you."

Blake had been listening idly while Doyle scribbled on his pad. But the mention of Yellow Braids caught his full attention. He glanced at Mason. Either his brother hadn't heard or he didn't care.

"I'll bet you that little filly ain't never even been rode." Hoskins's voice rose above the buzz of conversation and the clink of glasses. "Twenty bucks says I'll be the first one to get up her skirt. Anybody want to raise me?"

Blake's blood had begun to boil. Forgetting Mason and Doyle, he stood up, turned around, and grabbed Hoskins by the front of his vest.

"Take this for your twenty bucks, you sonofabitch!" he muttered. Then his fist slammed into the cowboy's jaw.

Letting the man fall, he turned away, stalked outside to his horse, and rode off into the dusk.

Hanna bowed her head while her mother said grace. The prayer included words for the Gilberg family whose home and wheat field had been destroyed by the fire. Tomorrow Hanna would be sent trudging across the fields with a basket of food—as much as Inga could spare, and then some—as well as a bundle of hand-me-down clothes for the little ones, clothes she'd put aside from her own children.

At dawn, Hanna's father and older brother, Alvar, would gather their tools and any scraps of building material they could find to set up a shelter for the family. Others would do the same. It was what good neighbors did—and who could say which of them would be struck by the next disaster?

The stew, made from the skimpy meat of a rabbit Alvar had snared that morning, along with some vegetables from Inga's garden, was a treat for the hungry family. Served with plenty of fresh biscuits, it was just enough for the seven of them. The parents ate sparingly to make sure there would be plenty for the children. Alvar, barely eighteen, and Hanna did the same. The younger children, Britta, almost thirteen, Axel, ten, and Gerda, eight, filled their plates. There would have been one more child at the table, but the baby boy, born after Hanna, had only lived a few days. Much as Inga loved her blue-eyed, flaxen-haired brood, Hanna knew that her mother still mourned the little one she'd lost.

The children ate in silence, as was the custom. But for the parents, the evening meal was a time to catch up on the events of the day.

"I was talking with Stefan on the way home from the fire," Big Lars said. "He told me that somebody found a broken lantern in that burned shack. That means the fire was started on purpose while the family was in town."

"Are you sure?" Inga had gone pale. Hanna knew what her mother was thinking. If she and the children hadn't gone home early, with Alvar driving the wagon, their place could have been the one that was burned.

"That fire didn't start itself, Inga. Some cowboys at the dance almost beat up Ole Hanson. They left after a man stopped them. Ole thinks they might have gone to start the fire. Those cowboys hate us. They blame us for the bad cattle market. It isn't true, but they don't care, as long as they've got somebody to punish."

"We could be next," Inga said. "Anybody could be. And maybe next time it won't be just a fire. They'll start hurting people, even killing them."

The younger children had stopped eating. They were staring at their mother.

"We'll just need to keep our eyes open," Big Lars said. "Keep the shotgun loaded and handy. Watch for any strangers coming around. If you see anybody you don't know, assume they're an enemy."

"So the cowboys and ranchers are our enemies now?" Hanna asked, thinking of the handsome man who'd almost kissed her.

"Yes," her father said. "We can't trust any of them. Remember that."

CHAPTER 3

*I*N THE WEST, THE LIGHT HAD FADED FROM THE SKY. HERE and there, the first stars emerged among the wispy clouds. The evening breeze carried the odors of smoke and charred earth—or was it his own hair and clothes that Blake could smell as he rode? After fighting the fire, he was too tired to wonder.

His horse needed no guiding. The ten-year-old buckskin gelding knew where to turn onto the rutted wagon road that led across the pastures and wound up the bluff to the sprawling log home at the top. Blake could lose himself in thought, knowing the trusted animal would take him home.

Tonight, he had enough on his mind to keep him occupied all the way. He flexed his hand, feeling the soreness as he closed his fingers into a fist. He'd prided himself on being a man who could hold his temper. But that Calder cowboy betting that he could take a young woman's innocence—probably by rape—had lit his already-short fuse. When his fist had crunched into the bastard's jaw, it had felt damned good.

How many men had looked at her golden hair, big, corn-flower-blue eyes, and womanly figure and wished for the same thing? Right now, Blake wanted to punch them all, including Mason.

Strange that a girl he'd barely met, with a name he didn't even know—a girl he'd never see again except in passing—could rouse that pitch of emotion.

But right now he had even more urgent concerns than the girl.

As the road began its winding ascent, Blake could see the edge of the moon rising over the eastern hills. A coyote howled from the top of a ridge—a lonesome sound but one he'd grown up with and had come to love. It was the sound of home.

He thought of the family who'd lost everything—the man's desperate look, the wife's tears, and the wails of the young children. He could only hope that someone had taken them in tonight.

He had little doubt that Hobie Evans, the Carmody brothers, and maybe a few of their friends, had started the blaze. But if that was true, Blake asked himself, didn't that make him partly to blame?

If he hadn't left the dance to stop those hooligans from tormenting the lone homesteader, and if he hadn't fired the brothers for their part in it, the disaster might never have happened. The man could have fought, fled, or called for help. Everything might have turned out differently.

Tomorrow the sawmill would be idle, awaiting a new shipment of logs. In the morning he would load up a cart with enough spare wood to frame a new shack, and take it to the site of the burned home. He couldn't do anything about the wheat crop, but at least he could help the family rebuild, and maybe ease his conscience.

Ahead, at the top of the road he could see the rambling log house that Joe Dollarhide had built for his family. It

wasn't as grand as the Calder mansion or as elegantly finished, but the rugged design was more functional and pleas-
ing to the eye; and its sweeping front porch commanded a
view that had no equal.

In the stable, Blake rubbed down his horse, left it with
food and water, and walked back to the house. His parents
and sister would have seen the smoke from here and would
be wondering what had happened. If they were waiting to
eat, he could tell them about the fire over dinner.

There were things he wouldn't be telling them, of course.
His mother despised gossip, having been a target herself as a
young, unmarried mother. So he wouldn't mention Webb
Calder's possible involvement with a married woman. And
because he knew better than to criticize Mason to his father,
he wouldn't mention the scene with the girl in the white
pinafore. But the fire and his suspicions about Hobie and the
Carmodys were fair game for dinner talk.

As he mounted the porch, the door flew open. Kristin, his
seventeen-year-old sister, stood framed in the lamplight. Tall
and slim, with her father's dark hair and her mother's earnest
violet eyes, she was a stunning beauty. Men might have been
swarming around her, but she was a loner, spending most of
her time at home, riding her horse, tending the stock, or
reading her mother's treasured books.

"Thank goodness you're here!" She hurried toward him.
"Mother wanted to wait dinner for you. But don't go in yet. I
need to talk to you first."

An arm's length away from him, she halted. "God's gar-
ters, Blake, you smell like a burning barn! Mother won't let
you in the house. Go wash up at the pump. Your hair, too.
And take off that smelly shirt. I'll get you a fresh one from
inside. Come on. We can talk after you clean up."

Ignoring her unladylike language, Blake stripped off his
shirt, followed her back to the pump, and let her work the
handle while he used a sliver of soap to wash his hands, face,

and hair and splash the sweat off his chest and shoulders. The water was cold, but the night breeze was warm as he waited for her to bring his clean shirt. By the time she returned minutes later, his skin was dry.

"So what is it you wanted to talk about?" he asked as he worked the buttons.

"No details yet. But I'm going to make an announcement tonight. It's something I've thought about long and hard. I don't know how Mother and Dad will take it. But it would help to know that you'll support me."

"And you won't tell me what you're going to say?"

"You'll know soon enough. So can I count on you?"

"Why should I say yes when I don't even know what you're thinking?"

She nudged his ribs. "Because you're my big brother. That's why."

He laughed. "I guess you've got me there. Come on, let's go inside."

Even for her own small family, Sarah Foxworth Dollarhide liked to set an attractive dinner table—the good china and silver plate, white linen tablecloth and napkins, and even a small vase of wildflowers. And she'd drilled her children on proper etiquette. "I want to be sure that you can eat with anyone—even the president—and not embarrass yourself," she was fond of saying.

The years had been kind to his mother, Blake reflected as he viewed her across the table. Her light brown hair, worn in a simple bun, was touched with silver at the temples. Her calm violet eyes were creased at the corners. Her energetic body was only a little stouter than he remembered from her younger days.

Sarah and her husband were close to the same age. But Joe Dollarhide's face had been weathered by sun and wind.

His hair was iron gray, and he'd walked with a cane since last spring, when a fall from an unruly stallion had broken a bone in his leg. But the fire still burned in his fierce, blue eyes.

"Did you see Mason at the dance?" Joe always asked about his other son. Growing up, Mason had spent days on end with his father's family. But Mason had moved on. These days he rarely came by the house.

Blake dished up a mound of mashed potatoes and drowned it in gravy. "I did see Mason. We rode to the fire in his buggy and had a drink in the saloon afterward. Doyle Petit came by. He plans to start selling lumber in town. When he asked me for a discount, I almost laughed in his face."

"I never thought much of Doyle. His father was a good man, but Doyle's selling the ranch must have him turning over in his grave." Joe paused to survey his family around the table. One chair was empty. Blake knew that the sight of it pained his father. Still, Joe had insisted that the chair be kept waiting in case Mason dropped by. "Anything new with Mason? Any plans?" he asked.

"Not that he mentioned. He's just helping his mother run the ranch." As if Amelia needed help with anything.

"We saw the smoke," Sarah said, changing the subject. "How bad was the fire?"

"We got to it before it spread out of control. But it burned a sodbuster's shack and most of his wheat field. I'm pretty sure the fire was set. And I've got a good idea who set it. I had a run-in with Hobie Evans and the Carmody brothers at the dance. They were looking for trouble. After I stopped them from beating up a homesteader and fired both the Carmodys for it, I'm guessing they lit out to make more mischief."

"You fired the Carmodys?" Joe speared a slice of roast beef. "Too bad. Good workers are hard to come by. Now you'll be shorthanded."

"I know. But they were always grumbling. They'd have made trouble sooner or later." Blake glanced at Kristin, wondering if she was waiting for a chance to speak. She gave him a slight shake of her head.

"I have a suggestion for you," Joe said. "Those immigrant farmers are strong and ambitious. Some of them might even have skills you could use, like carpentry. And I'm guessing they could all use extra money. If you let them know you're hiring, you might find some good workers."

"I'd have to make sure they could get along with the men I've already hired. But that's not a bad idea," Blake said. "I'll give it some thought." He'd be going out among the wheat fields tomorrow to deliver that load of scrap wood. Maybe the man who'd lost his house and field would be interested in a job.

In the brief silence, Kristin cleared her throat. "Listen, everyone, I have an announcement to make."

"We're all ears, honey," her father said. "As long as you're not planning to run off with some snake oil salesman."

"Believe me, that's the last thing on my mind." She turned toward her mother. "Mom, I know the story of how you almost got to be a doctor, but then you couldn't go to medical school because you were going to have Blake."

"Then you know I've never been sorry," Sarah said. "Being a mother has been the best thing that ever happened to me—that, and marrying your father."

"But you had a dream, and no matter how hard you worked to make it come true, it never did. I have the same dream. And nothing's going to stop me from making it happen. I want to become a doctor."

There was silence around the table. Blake suppressed the urge to break into applause. Kristin was smart and ambitious. She deserved to spread her wings and make something of her life. But what would her parents say?

Looking at his father, Blake could imagine what Joe might be thinking. Years ago, he'd met a young girl with a dream. He'd fallen in love with her. And that love—the love that created his son—had destroyed her dream forever.

How could he deny his daughter the same dream, even if it meant losing her?

It was Sarah who finally spoke. "You couldn't do that here. Where would you go? Have you thought about it?"

"I know you've still got family in Kansas," Kristin said. "You've mentioned a cousin who's a college professor. If I could stay with his family and go to school for my premed training, that would be perfect. I could keep house for my room and board, or even get a part-time job to help out with expenses. Or I could find some other way. I only know that whatever happens, whatever I have to do, I'm not giving up."

Sarah's gaze met her husband's. Slowly, with a look of sadness, he nodded. "Very well, I'll write to my cousin," she said. "The worst he can do is say no. But all this is going to take time, Kristin. The application process and other arrangements could take months. There's no way you'll be able to start school this fall. Maybe by winter semester, or more likely spring, everything will be in place, and then only if all goes well. But at least you'll have time to make sure it's what you want."

"I'm already sure," she said. "Time isn't going to change my mind."

"Well, all right then," Joe said. "But I can already feel how much I'm going to miss you."

Eyes sparkling, she glanced around the table. "You mean you aren't going to try to talk sense into me?"

"Kristin," her mother said, "if this is what you really want, trying to talk you out of it would be a waste of breath. But know that this will be the hardest thing you've ever done. We'll support you any way we can, but in the end, it will be up to you."

"And what do you have to say about my decision, big brother?" she asked.

Blake gave her a grin. "You're going to be a wonderful doctor, sis!"

Jumping out of her chair, Kristin danced around the table, hugging each of her family members. It was a happy moment. But Blake glimpsed the veiled sorrow in his parents' eyes. They had wanted her to stay close, to marry and raise her future family here in Montana. Now, when she left home, it would most likely be for good.

The moon had climbed to the peak of the sky. Its rays silvered the stalks of growing wheat as they rippled in the night breeze—so fragile and holding so much hope.

The tar paper shack that sheltered the Anderson family was bigger than most. But finding room for seven people to sleep was still a challenge. The parents slept on their makeshift bed at one end, behind a quilt that was hung each night from the ceiling. The three younger children, Britta, Axel, and Gerda, shared a blanket laid on the rough plank floor with a single quilt to cover them. It was left to Alvar and Hanna to fit wherever they could. For Hanna's older brother, on these warm summer nights, that meant sleeping outside in the wagon.

Even without Alvar needing space, comfortable sleep could be little more than a hope. Wide-awake, Hanna lay wedged between Britta and the wall, with the frayed edge of the blanket between her and the floor. The day's lingering heat was stifling; her father's snores a steady drone in her ears. Alvar was the lucky one—sleeping in the fresh night air with the stars overhead. A girl wouldn't be allowed to sleep outside. That would be both unsafe and improper.

But surely Hanna could sneak out long enough to get some air. Getting caught would mean a scolding. But anything would be better than lying here like a sardine in a tin, too miserable to sleep.

Squirming backward, she eased away from her sister, rose to her feet, and tugged the hem of her cotton nightgown down to cover her legs. There was no need for shoes. Her feet had been toughened by a summer of working in the wheat field and the yard.

The makeshift door was a flap of cowhide nailed to the top of the frame. Pushing past it, Hanna stepped out into the night.

In the yard, she took a moment to fill her lungs and let the breeze whisper through her hair. Overhead, the Milky Way spilled a glorious trail of stars across the sky. The wheat field rippled like a silver sea in the moonlight. *So beautiful,* she thought. If only she didn't have to go back inside.

"What are you doing out here, Hanna?" Alvar, still in his work clothes, had come around the far side of the wagon. At eighteen, he was almost as tall as his father, his lanky frame still filling out with muscle. Fair and blue-eyed like the rest of the family, he was so handsome that women turned to stare at him on the street. But he was surprisingly shy, as if unaware that he looked like a young Norse god. Even if he'd been homely, his ready smile and gentle manner would have won hearts. Hanna adored her older brother.

"Couldn't you sleep?" he asked her.

"Not in there." She glanced back toward the house. "Please don't make me go back in yet. It's so lovely out here."

"I'm not going to make you do anything. But you might get in trouble if Papa catches you out here in your nightgown."

"I know. But it isn't fair. I'm almost seventeen. Mama and Papa treat me like a baby—or maybe a prisoner. And it's just because I'm a girl."

"They only want to protect you."

"That's easy for you to say. You can do what you want, but they'll be in charge of me until I get married. And being a wife instead of a daughter won't make much difference. Look at Lillian. Stefan watches every move she makes."

"And that's not what you want?"

"To be controlled by a man? No. I want to be free, to make my own choices. But Mama and Papa will do their best to make sure that doesn't happen."

Alvar pointed out the path of a falling star as it streaked across the sky. "What would you do if you were free? Have you thought about it, Hanna?"

"Some. I'd get more schooling if I could. Or maybe I'd go to a city somewhere and get a job."

"Remember those girls in New York, the ones who worked in the sewing factories for long hours and miserable wages? If they stopped sewing to rest their hands or even go to the necessary, they'd be fired. And their boss was a man. Do you think those girls were free?"

"You're not making me feel any better, Alvar. Oh—look! Another star!" She watched the trail of light fall and vanish. "What about you? Is this place enough for your whole life?"

Alvar was silent for a long moment. "I know Papa would like it to be enough. He expects me to stay and work the land, help him build a bigger house, then raise my own family here when the time comes. You girls, he figures, will get married and leave. But Axel and I—we're the ones he expects to stay and build this farm into something a man can be proud of—his legacy."

"So you're not free either."

"Is anybody? Think about it."

"What would you do, Alvar, if you could choose anything?"

"Travel." He answered without a moment's hesitation. "There's a whole, exciting, mysterious world out there. I would maybe get a job on a ship, and see it all—China, India, South America, Africa . . . I always wanted to see elephants and lions, and the Pyramids . . . all of it." The emotion in his voice told Hanna how fervent his desire was.

She looked up at him, noticing the way the moonlight etched the beautifully sculpted planes of his face. *Oh, Alvar, if I had the power, I would tell you to forget this place and just go,* she thought.

"Maybe someday you'll get the chance," she said. "You never know what might happen in your life."

His chuckle sounded forced. "I know what will happen in your life if you don't get back in the house. I need to get some sleep, too. In the morning, Papa and I will be taking the wagon over to help the Gilbergs rebuild their house. It's a shame we can't save their wheat crop, too."

"I know. Mama is going to send me over there with some food and clothes. But she won't have it ready in time for me to ride with you. I'll have to walk. But I don't mind. It's nice having a little time to myself."

"Good for you. Now get going."

Hanna hurried back to the house. As she slipped through the doorway, she happened to glance back. Alvar was standing where she'd left him, still gazing up at the sky.

The sawmill was located at the mouth of a box canyon on the lower part of the hill—the same canyon that Joe Dollarhide had used to trap and pen wild horses in the early days of the ranch. When the horses were gone, he'd cut trees from his land and used the creek to power a saw. The Dollarhide Lumber Company had grown from there.

Fenced and gated to prevent theft, the site was quiet this morning. There was no one inside except a solitary old man named Garrity who was paid to keep an eye on the place and care for the team of Belgian draft horses used to pull the lumber wagons and drag the uncut logs where they needed to go.

While Garrity hitched the team to the smaller of the two wagons, Blake loaded as much useful-sized scrap wood as he could fit into the bed, along with several twelve-foot lengths of green board sturdy enough to support a roof.

"So when do you figure we'll be startin' up again, Boss?" Garrity was a grizzled former army veteran who'd lost a leg fighting the Cheyenne. He lived on-site in a cozy cabin on the far side of the creek, which he shared with a big, shaggy mutt named Custer, who earned his keep as a watchdog.

"The logs should be on tomorrow's train," Blake answered, hoping he was right. The need for lumber was unending, but with most of the nearby timber long since harvested, finding a steady supply of straight, solid logs, thick enough for cutting into boards, was an ongoing challenge. With hauling distances getting longer and freight prices going up, he was always searching for ways to meet the demand. A big load of logs, hauled by rail on a flatcar and dumped next to the tracks, could keep the sawmill busy for several weeks. But getting the logs from there to the mill was an operation in itself.

"If you've got that supply list ready for me, I'll stop by the store on my way back here," Blake said to the old man.

"Got it right here." Garrity pulled the half-crumpled paper out of his vest. "If they got any of them peppermint sticks, I sure would appreciate a couple of 'em."

"I'll see what I can do." Blake swung onto the wagon seat and picked up the reins. Minutes later they were out of the gate and heading down the wagon road.

For a loaded wagon, moving over rough ground, the trip from the sawmill to the site of yesterday's fire would take the better part of an hour. Blake took his time, enjoying the cool morning air that would turn hot by midday. Beyond the rolling grassland, the wheat fields spread patches of lush green carpet. Pretty as the growing wheat appeared, cattle ranchers like the Calders hated the sight. For every acre that was plowed up and planted in wheat, an acre of rich Montana grass was lost—grass that had taken years, if not centuries, to form a deep root bed in the perfect soil. Where the wheat grew, the grass would never return. And when the wheat crops failed—which was sure to happen in a dry year—there would be nothing left on the land but weeds and dust.

Blake understood. But he also understood change and

progress. Blue Moon's growth was providing jobs, goods, and services for people in search of a better life. Sooner or later, the cattle barons would have to accept that.

The warbling call of a meadowlark roused Blake from his musings. He expected to be getting close to the site of the fire. But when he scanned the horizon for the remains of the burned shack or maybe a sign of people who'd come to help, all he saw was a distant blue dot, moving away from him, at an angle. As he urged the team ahead, narrowing the distance between them, he could make out a woman on foot wearing a light blue dress and broad-brimmed straw hat. She was carrying what appeared to be a large basket over one arm and a bulky sack slung over her shoulder. She moved awkwardly, as if she might be injured or lame.

Whatever she was doing out here, the lady could probably use a ride. At least she might be able to point him in the direction of the burned-out property. But before he could get close enough to call out to her, she vanished from sight behind a grassy knoll.

Hanna had twisted her ankle stumbling into a badger hole. Every step she took shot pain up her leg, but resting would only waste time. She needed to get the basket of food and the bundle of clothes into the needy hands of the Gilberg family. Papa and Alvar would already be at the burned-out farm with the wagon. If she could make it that far, she'd be all right. She could wait and return home with them. But right now she had no choice except to keep walking, no matter how much it hurt.

Pausing a moment, she looked around her. If she had some kind of stick to use as a cane, it would ease the weight on her ankle and help her balance. But where could she find anything useful in this sea of grass?

Coming from the north, the direction of the Calder ranch, she spotted two riders. Hanna judged them to be a half mile off, but they appeared to have seen her. They were coming straight toward her, riding fast through the yellow grass.

She remembered what her father had said last night—that cowboys were the enemy. But she had nowhere to run or hide. She could only hope the pair would have decent intentions. Either way, she was injured, with a heavy load and no place to run. All she could do was keep moving, with a silent prayer on her lips.

As the riders came closer, she could hear them talking and laughing. She couldn't make out words, but their raucous tone told her enough. She was in trouble.

Hanna was innocent in terms of experience. But she had helped deliver her mother's last two babies, and she knew where babies came from. A friend of hers in the city had been gang-raped by some street boys. Hanna had held the girl afterward while she cried. She knew what could happen if these cowboys were the kind of men her parents had warned her about.

As they pulled their horses up in front of her, cutting off any chance of escape, she faced them, frozen with terror but determined not to show it.

The bigger of the two men, dark, with a dirty-looking beard, grinned. "Well, ain't this my lucky day! It's little Yellow Braids, out here all alone. I reckon I'm about to win that bet I made. Give me a hand with her, Lem. Then you can have a go."

"I'll hold 'er down, Sig. But you gotta promise me." Lem, a weasel-faced little man, smiled, showing a gap where his front teeth had been.

Hanna's knees quivered beneath her skirt. Her heart was pounding like a sledgehammer, but she glared up at the mounted men and spoke in a level voice.

"Touch me, and my father will kill you."

The big man laughed. "Feisty little thing, ain't ya? But I don't see your father anywheres around here. And I don't think he's gonna come onto the Calder ranch lookin' for us."

He dropped the reins of his piebald horse and swung out of the saddle. "Take it easy, gal. My buddy and me, we's just lookin' for a little fun. We won't hurt you none. Hell, you might even git to like it. Most women do."

The small man had dismounted as well. As the two moved toward her, grinning, Hanna backed away, holding her burdens in front of her like a shield. But she had nowhere to go. And as hard as she might struggle, she couldn't fight off two men. She could scream, but there was no one close enough to hear her. She was trapped.

CHAPTER 4

BLAKE WAS APPROACHING THE KNOLL WHERE THE WOMAN in blue had disappeared. From the far side, he could hear the faint mutter of voices—men's voices, punctuated by laughter. At this distance, he couldn't make out words, but his instincts screamed trouble.

Maybe he was wrong. Maybe the woman had met some friendly neighbors or helpful cowboys. But after what he'd heard in the saloon, he couldn't assume any woman was safe out here alone.

Urging the horses to a trot, he drove the team as fast as he dared. On rough ground, with the wagon full of loose wood, there was always a risk hitting a bump and losing his cargo or worse, breaking an axle. But that was a chance he'd have to take.

As always when he hauled cargo, he'd stowed his rifle under the wagon bench. Guiding the horses with one hand, he reached down, picked up the gun, and laid it across his knees. With luck, he wouldn't need it. But his danger senses told him otherwise.

As he came around the low end of the rise, Blake could

see what the landscape had blocked from his view—about thirty yards away, two men had the woman down on her back with her skirt and petticoat pulled up. One crouched at her head, pinning her hands and shoulders. The other was kneeling between her straddled legs, undoing his belt as she struggled and twisted.

With no time to lose, Blake fired the rifle over their heads and slapped the reins on the backs of the horses. The wagon shot ahead, rumbling over the ground. Keeping the reins between his knees, Blake cocked the rifle, aimed high, and fired again. He was a good shot, but between the jouncing wagon and the danger of hitting the woman, he couldn't risk aiming lower. He could only hope the gunfire would scare the bastards off.

Leaving their victim, the two men sprinted for their horses. By now Blake was close enough to recognize them. They'd been part of the gang at the next table in the saloon. The big, bearded one was Sig Hoskins, the man Blake had punched. The other man was his sidekick, a little toady named Lem.

By the time Blake could pull the team to a halt, the two men had mounted up and were fleeing for their cowardly lives. But this wasn't over, he vowed. Once he let the Calders know what their cowhands were up to, the pair would be jobless. He might even be able to talk the newly hired sheriff into jailing them. Either way, he would see to it personally that they weren't welcome in Blue Moon.

He watched them long enough to make sure they weren't coming back. Then he turned his attention to the woman.

By now she'd scrambled to her feet and was brushing the dust and grass off her clothes. She'd found her straw hat and jammed it down on her head, low enough for the brim's shadow to hide her face. The basket and bundle she'd been carrying lay in the grass, the contents partly scattered. So far he hadn't heard her make a sound.

Leaving the rifle in the wagon, Blake swung to the ground and started toward her. Her voice stopped him.

"Don't you come near me!" The hoarse whisper rose from the depths of terror and humiliation. She might be on her feet, but she was still paralyzed with fear.

He went no closer. "Don't be afraid," he said. "I'm a friend. I won't hurt you."

She shook her head. *"You're one of them."*

"No, you're wrong," he said. "I'm not like those men. Did they hurt you?"

"Not in the way you mean." She kept her gaze lowered, refusing to look at him. The hat brim shadowed her features, but she sounded young, and her figure was small-waisted. A girl.

"Where's your family? I can take you to them."

She didn't answer.

"I can't just leave you. You won't make it anywhere on foot. What were you doing out here alone?"

Again there was no answer.

"I'm going to gather up your things and put them in the wagon," he said. "Then I'll wait until you're ready to come and get on board. All right?"

She hesitated, then gave him a slight nod. At least he was making progress. "What's your name?" he asked.

"Hanna." The name was a whisper. "Hanna Anderson."

"Well, Hanna, you can call me Blake." He kept his voice low. "I realize that you're probably scared of me—hell, after what you've been through, I don't blame you. But I give you my word I won't hurt you. Now let's pick up your things and get you out of here."

Blake walked over to where the basket and the stuffed flour sack had been flung. Children's clothes lay strewn on the dry grass, along with loaves of bread, some boiled potatoes, a slab of bacon wrapped in cheesecloth, some dry beans tied in a kerchief, and a precious, unbroken jar of blackberry preserves. He dropped to a crouch and began reaching out for the scattered items, then putting them away.

"I'll do it." A slender hand, suntanned and callused, invaded his vision. He felt a shock of recognition as he looked up into stunning blue eyes below the brim of her hat. But it wasn't the eyes that riveted his attention. It was the ugly bruise that purpled her face below the left cheekbone.

She read his dismay. "They hit me because I wouldn't stop fighting them. I kept on anyway, for as long as I could." She began replacing the spilled food in the basket, brushing away any traces of dirt. Pausing, she looked directly at him. "I know you, don't I?"

"You might."

"At the dance. I was with your brother. You came out to warn us."

"That's right. And I saw you again at the fire when you wet down my blanket." Blake had finished stuffing the clothes back into the flour sack. He waited while she finished filling the basket. "You won't have to worry about those men. I got a look at the bastards. I know who they are, and I'm going to make sure they pay."

"My father and my brother will make sure. I won't be able to keep this from them when they see my face."

Her words set off warning bells. Blake could picture a bloody feud of vengeance and countervengeance between settlers and the ranching families. It could start from a spark like this incident and spread like a prairie fire. He had to stop it now.

"Keep your father and brother out of this, Hanna. If they get involved, there'll be no end of trouble. Your family could lose their house, their farm, and even their lives. Let me deal with those men. I'll talk to the Calders and to the sheriff. At the very least, you'll never see them again."

"You should be saying this to my father, not to me."

"I plan to." Blake picked up the basket and the bundle, carried them to the wagon, and stowed them under the bench. "Now let's get you home."

"Not home. I was taking these things to the family whose house was burned. My father will be at their place. Take me there."

"Fine. Since that's where I'm headed with this load of wood, you can guide me."

"It's about two miles east of here. You won't have any trouble finding it."

"Thanks." He turned, waiting for her to follow him. Standing now, she took a few careful steps, then stumbled. Pain flashed across her bruised face. She pressed her lips together, then shook her head. "I'll be all right. Just a twisted ankle."

Blake remembered then that he'd seen her limping. That would've made her easy prey for the monsters who'd almost raped her.

"Let me help you." He strode to her side and scooped her up in his arms. She didn't resist him, but he could feel the tension in her rigid body as he carried her to the wagon and lifted her onto the bench. Only then did he notice the smears of greasy dirt and the missing buttons on the bodice of her faded gingham dress. The memory of those men, touching her with their filthy hands, would stay with her for a long time. He probably should have asked her permission before picking her up.

It wouldn't hurt to check her ankle. It could be sprained or even broken. But the intimacy of taking off her high-topped boot and touching her leg might put too much of a strain on her. Soon she would be with her family. They could look at her ankle and do what was needed.

As he took his seat on the wagon, she shifted to the end of the bench, widening the distance between them. Blake understood. The girl had been through a hellish experience. He couldn't blame her for being nervous and distrustful with a man she barely knew.

It wouldn't do for him to appear too friendly. He kept his eyes fixed ahead as he drove the team, giving her a choice. She could talk to him or be silent.

*   *   *

Hanna fingered the tender bruise on her cheek. Given a few weeks, it would heal and fade. But the memory of those two cowboys holding her, their dirty hands groping her body, their faces leering down at her, would be part of her forever.

Blake had arrived in time to save her from rape. But she'd come so close and been so scared—not just scared, but angry. She'd kicked and punched and clawed as they seized her. But the two men had pinned her down, laughing as she struggled.

Now that she was safe, she'd expected to fall apart—to cry and shake with relief. What she felt instead was an icy numbness, as if some part of her still needed to believe that nothing had happened.

Sooner or later the numbness would wear off and she would begin to feel again—to feel the rage, the terror, and yes, the shame of being touched by those horrible, filthy men, in places where only her future husband should have the right to touch her.

Until her emotions began to thaw, there was nothing to do but behave as if everything were normal—to talk and listen, even try to smile. Anything to keep the unspeakable memory from flooding her senses and pulling her under.

She forced herself to speak. "Your brother told me his name was Mason Dollarhide. Are you a Dollarhide, too?"

He nodded. "Mason and I have the same father but different mothers. It's a long story."

"He said something about his mother's ranch. He wasn't just feeding me a story, was he?"

"No need to. Mason's mother owns the Hollister Ranch, south of town. My family owns the Dollarhide Ranch on that hill above town, along with the lumber mill."

"I take it Dollarhide is an important name in these parts."

"*Important* is just a word. It's what's behind it that counts."

"Yes, I suppose so." She nodded, feeling the pain in her bruised cheek as she tried to smile. "But I'd like to know more."

Blake knew she was just making conversation—doing her best to hold herself together and keep the black thoughts away. Fine. He didn't mind going along with that.

"If you want important, the big name in these parts is Calder," he said. "Benteen Calder drove the first herd up here from Texas before I was born. He and his men laid claim to every parcel of land they could get their hands on, and all of it became the Triple C, for Calder Cattle Company."

"So they came here as homesteaders, just like us."

"That's right. And until they built that grand white house on the bluff, Lorena Calder kept house in a shack that was no fancier than the ones your people live in. Some people resent the Calders, but everything they have, they've earned."

"That's all we want," Hanna said. "Just to make our own way on the land, like the Calders did."

The Calders had arrived with more than two thousand head of Texas cattle. But Blake decided against reminding her of that. "Benteen is still running the outfit, but he's grooming his son, Webb, to take over. You might've seen them both at the fire. Webb was the one giving orders. Benteen was the older man who had to be taken back to his buggy."

"I did see them," Hanna said. "There were two women in the buggy, an older one and the pretty blond girl I saw at the dance. Is she Webb Calder's wife?"

"Not yet." *And not if I can help it.* Blake gave the girl a sidelong glance. Even with that ugly bruise on her cheek, she was pretty—even prettier than Ruth Stanton. But she was young. Too young for him, and too young for Mason. Worse, she was a *honyocker,* one of the sodbusters who were so hated by the ranching people. They were a clannish bunch who stuck to their old ways. By this time next year, Hanna Anderson would probably be married to some rednecked farmer and be carrying a baby in her belly. Damned shame.

Hanna watched the yellow prairie roll past, knowing that every turn of the wagon wheels carried her closer to the inevitable moment when she would have to face her father and explain what had happened. Would he blame her? Would he have a woman examine her to make sure she was still a virgin—maybe even marry her off at once to Ulli Swenson, the forty-year-old widowed neighbor who'd already asked for permission to court her?

Family honor was everything to a man like Big Lars, who had little else. And nothing was more vital to that honor than the virtue of his wife and daughters. What would he say to her? What would he do?

With uncertainty gnawing at her stomach, she forced herself to continue the conversation with the man who'd saved her.

"And what about the Dollarhide family?" she asked. "How did you come to be here? There must be an interesting story behind that."

"There is," he said. "My father, Joe, signed on with Benteen Calder as a wrangler, but one night he got lost in a stampede. After Benteen left him for dead, his life took a whole different turn, and not a good one. All he wanted was to get even with the boss for leaving him."

"And did he get even?"

"In a way, but not the way he planned. He'd learned to handle horses, and in the end, it was the horses that saved him. He made it to Montana and married a rancher's daughter who became Mason's mother. After they parted ways, he married my mother, Sarah, and built his own empire. That's the story."

"What happened with Benteen Calder? Did they ever settle things between them?"

"Dad and Benteen made their own peace. But you could never call them friends—respectful rivals, maybe, but not friends."

"And his son, Webb? Where does he stand with you?"

"Webb and I have our own differences—pretty much like our fathers do. And Mason likes him even less than I do."

"So the feud goes on."

"I guess you could call it that." Blake chuckled, showing a dimple in his cheek. He wasn't as handsome as Mason or as smooth. But he had his own rough-hewn appeal. Not that either man should be of any interest to her, Hanna reminded herself. As her father would say, they weren't her kind.

Talk faded as they came within sight of the burned property. From a distance, Blake could see several men working with rakes and shovels to clear the spot where the shack had stood. A few yards away, a shelter for the family had been rigged using a wagon and a piece of canvas. Two other wagons, with their teams still hitched, stood nearby. Beyond them, the trampled wheat field lay black under the blazing sun.

Some of the men were familiar. Hanna's father, Big Lars, was easy to spot because of his size. The younger, blond man working alongside him could be the brother Hanna had mentioned. He recognized the property owner, a small, nervous man. Blake had seen the two other men in town and remembered the older one from the dance. Stefan Reisner—that was his name. He was married to that pretty auburn-haired woman Webb had been twirling around the dance floor.

As the wagon rumbled closer, the men stopped work and turned to look. Beside him, Hanna seemed to shrink into herself. She lifted one hand to cover the bruise on her cheek.

Blake couldn't blame her for feeling self-conscious. She might even be worried that she'd be blamed for what had happened.

"What do you want me to do?" he asked in a low voice.

"Stop here and get my father." Her voice was unsteady. She took a breath. "Ask him to come to me."

Blake nodded and climbed out of the wagon. As he walked toward the group of men, he could feel their eyes on him—the suspicion, the hostility. Did they think he'd done something to Hanna? Or was this just how they looked at strangers?

"Mr. Anderson?" He spoke as soon as he came within hearing.

"Ja?" Big Lars stepped forward, his flinty gaze darting from Blake to his daughter in the wagon. "What is it?"

"Your daughter's been hurt. She needs to talk to you."

Big Lars brushed past Blake and strode back to the wagon. From where he stood, he could hear snatches of their emotional conversation. But he could only tell that Lars was angry and Hanna was weeping.

At last, with Hanna still in tears, Lars turned back to Blake. "Hanna tells me you saved her from those men. I owe you my thanks, but we take care of our own. We will find those cowboys and make them pay."

"Did Hanna tell you what I said about that?"

"She did."

"So you know you could risk starting a war?"

"We can't let men like those have their way with our women. For honor and safety, we must teach them a lesson."

"Let me talk to the sheriff—" Blake began, but Lars cut him off.

"The sheriff won't help us. We are not the ones paying him."

"Then all I can do is ask you to think before you act. If you take the law into your own hands, there could be bloodshed on both sides—and more fires."

Glancing around, Blake noticed that the other men had left their work and gathered close enough to hear what was being said. They didn't look friendly. Maybe they thought he was threatening them.

"Look." He gestured toward the loaded wagon. "I own the lumber mill. I brought you some spare wood for the house. Help me unload it, and I'll be on my way."

A short, pugnacious man stepped forward. Blake recognized him as Franz Kreuger, the most outspoken of the farmers. "Take your wood back where it came from," Kreuger snapped. "We'll do for ourselves. We don't need charity from your kind."

Blake felt his temper rising. "I've hauled the wood this far, and I'm not taking it back. If you're too muleheaded to use it, you can damn well set it on fire." He strode to the back of the wagon, lowered the tailgate, and began pulling boards out and dropping them onto the ground.

"For God's sake, Kreuger." It was the owner of the property who spoke. "We need this wood. Without it we won't have enough lumber for the house."

"He is right, Franz. Ve vould be fools not to take this gift." Stefan Reisner stepped forward and began pulling more boards off the wagon. Two others joined him. With help, the wood was soon unloaded.

Hanna hadn't tried to climb off the wagon or asked anyone to help her down. She sat huddled on the bench, holding the basket and bundle she'd brought. She had put on a brave face while Blake was bringing her here. But whatever her father had said to her, his words had crushed her spirit.

Blake took the basket and bundle from her and handed it to one of the men. "It's time for me to leave," he told her. "I'll get your father to help you down and see to your ankle."

When she looked at him, he saw the tears welling in her eyes. "Please," she whispered. "I don't want to stay here. I want to go home to my mother."

"You're sure?"

"They're all looking at me. Please."

"I can take you, but only if your father agrees to it. Do you want me to ask him?"

She nodded.

Blake took Lars aside. "Your daughter's been through a bad time. She wants her mother. I can take her home, but only with your permission."

Scowling, Lars looked past Blake to where Hanna sat huddled on the wagon bench. "You can take her, *ja*, but not alone. Only if her brother goes with you. Do you understand?"

"Yes." Blake needed no explanation. Hanna's reputation had already been compromised. To her father's way of thinking, the family's honor was at stake.

Lars beckoned to the tall young man who stood nearby. Father and son exchanged a few words in Swedish before turning toward Blake.

"This is my son Alvar," Lars said. "He will go with you now. He can work at home for the rest of the day."

"I'm pleased to meet you, sir." The young man extended his hand. He was tall like his father, with wheat blond hair showing beneath his straw hat and blue eyes that shone with intelligence. His handshake was firm but restrained.

Blake returned the greeting. "Let's go, then," he said.

The relief on Hanna's face when her brother climbed onto the wagon was like the sun coming out. Alvar hugged her, his tone comforting as he spoke a few words to her in Swedish. Once they'd settled into their places, with Hanna on one side of him and Alvar on the other, Blake took the reins, turned the wagon around in a wide circle, and started back the way they'd come.

"I'll need you to guide me," he said to Alvar. "How far is it to your place?"

"About three miles. It won't take long. For now, just keep heading west." Alvar's English was good, with only a slight accent. His words and speech patterns were somewhat book-ish, suggesting that he'd done his share of reading. "I'm not aware that anyone thanked you for the wood. Allow me to thank you now. It was kind of you to bring it."

"I just wanted to help," Blake said. "In a way, I feel re-sponsible. Yesterday I fired two men who worked for me. They might've been the ones who started the fire."

"And my sister?" His voice hardened. "Was it the same two men who attacked her?"

"No. They were different men."

"So you recognized them." It wasn't a question.

"Yes."

Sitting next to Hanna, Blake felt her body stiffen.

"My father will want to know their names and where to find them," Alvar said.

"He won't get that information from me, Alvar. And you know why. If you and your father punish those men, you could go to jail. Or worse, you could start a war that could get people killed, including your own family."

"Do you have a daughter?" Alvar asked.

"No, but I have a sister. If anybody tried to hurt her, I'd feel just the way you do. But I wouldn't go after them my-self. I'd use the law to punish them."

Is that true? Blake asked himself. *What if it was Kristin those bastards tried to rape? What would you do?*

He knew what his father would do. Joe Dollarhide would kill any man who laid hands on his daughter. And so would Big Lars Anderson.

"The law won't help us," Alvar said. "And if we don't do something, our girls and women will become fair game. If you won't give us the names of those men, we'll find out some other way."

"Then I wish you luck. But I won't be part of this. I won't be responsible for what's liable to happen if your people take the law into their own hands."

"Are you defending those men?"

"I don't give a damn about those two bastards. My concern is what their friends, and the ranchers, could do to your families. You'd be giving them an excuse to drive you off the land."

Alvar didn't reply. Blake could only hope he'd given the young man something to think about. But it was the father who'd have to be convinced.

By now, the July sun was climbing the peak of the sky. The heat-seared grass crumbled under the wheels of the wagon. Blake could feel the warmth of Hanna's body resting lightly against his side. Her womanly fragrance crept into his senses. His arousal came unbidden. He cursed himself as he struggled to ignore the male urge. This girl, with her air of sensual innocence, was not for him.

Until now, Hanna had stayed silent—perhaps she'd been taught not to interrupt when men were talking. But now she spoke up.

"Why do they hate us so much—the cowboys and ranchers? We're good, honest people. We don't want to take anything from them. All we want is the chance for a decent life—the same thing they wanted for themselves when they came here."

Blake took a moment to come up with a reply that might satisfy her. "What they really hate is change. They've built a good life here with the ranches and the grass and the cattle. And they never planned on things being any different. Then the new laws and the railroad brought people like your family—good folks but with different ways, like digging up the grass to plant wheat. Then there've been other troubles, like the big drop in beef prices. That has nothing to do with your people, but the ranchers are losing money and laying off men—men who are looking for somebody to blame."

"So they blame us," Hanna said. "That's not fair."

"It isn't fair," Blake said. "But it's pretty much the way of things."

"What about you?" Alvar asked. "You just delivered a

load of free wood to our neighbors. But I can't believe you'd side with us against the ranchers. So where do you stand?"

"I'm on the side of anybody who buys Dollarhide lumber," Blake said. "My father still runs a few hundred head of cattle, but the lumber is our main family business. We can't afford to choose sides."

"And what about your brother?" Hanna asked.

He should have expected the question, Blake told himself. Still, her mention of Mason rankled him. "Mason's mother owns her own ranch, and she's brought him up to take over. He's a cattleman, through and through."

A cattleman who'd rather chase women and race his horses than get dirt under his fingernails. Blake didn't finish the thought out loud. The hands-on management of the Hollister Ranch was mostly done by Ralph Tomlinson, Amelia Dollarhide's longtime foreman and lover.

Alvar cleared his throat, as if he'd been working up the courage to say something important. "You mentioned that you'd fired two of your workers. Does that mean you'll be hiring more?"

"Not right now. But when the log shipment we're waiting for comes in, I'll be needing more help. Why? Are you interested?"

"I would be," Alvar said. "Now that the wheat's growing, my father can manage without me on the farm. And we could use the money to get us through till harvest. I've never worked in a sawmill, but I could learn what to do."

Blake remembered his father's suggestion about hiring the homesteaders. Alvar impressed him as a strong, willing young man who would get along with the other workers. "Come see me at the mill when we're up and running again," he said. "No promises, but we'll see if you can do the job."

"Alvar!" Hanna leaned past Blake to look at her brother. "What would Papa say? You know that he wants you to stay and help him on the farm. He wants to build a new shed and put up more fences."

"But I'd be doing this for the family," Alvar said. "Sheds

and fences won't put food on the table or buy shoes for the young ones, or winter feed for the horses. We're going to need money. And I can help Papa in my spare time. I'll talk to him. He'll understand."

A few minutes later the tar paper shack that Hanna and her brother called home came into sight. Three younger children—two girls and a boy, as fair-haired and handsome as their older siblings—were outside doing chores. A tired-looking woman was hanging the wash on a makeshift clothesline strung from the house to a pole in the ground. There was no shade, no trees or flowers, nothing to soften the harsh setting.

Alvar jumped to the ground before the wagon came to a full stop. The woman dropped the shirt she was hanging into the basket at her feet and hurried toward him.

"Alvar, what is it?" Her eyes were wide with alarm as he came around the wagon to help Hanna. "Is it your father? Is he all right?"

"He's fine, Mama. But Hanna had an accident and hurt her ankle. She can tell you what happened." He lifted his sister down from the bench and set her gently on the ground. "Mr. Dollarhide here was good enough to give us a ride home."

"Thank you." The woman looked up as she wrapped a supporting arm around her daughter. "You've done us a great kindness. I'm sorry I can't invite you to stay for lunch."

"I was glad to help. I'll be on my way now. Ma'am." He touched his hat brim, clucked to the team, and moved on. He wouldn't have accepted her invitation even if it had been offered. But the good woman's air of painful pride had touched him. Maybe she didn't have enough food after the generous gift to her neighbors. Or more likely, she'd been warned not to deal with strangers. Whatever the reason, he couldn't help feeling sorry for her lot. Heaven had blessed her with a bounty of beautiful children, but clearly not much else.

Within minutes Blake had left the sad little homestead

behind and turned his thoughts back toward more urgent matters. By now, Big Lars and his friends could already be plotting their revenge on Hanna's attackers. Blake had sworn not to get involved. But as the only outsider, he knew it would be up to him to stop the war that was sure to follow.

However, he couldn't do it alone. Whether he liked it or not, he was going to need the help of the Calders.

CHAPTER 5

B LAKE HAD PLANNED TO RETURN TO THE SAWMILL BY WAY of Blue Moon, pick up supplies, return the rig to Garrity, and ride his buckskin horse out to the Calder ranch. But twenty minutes after leaving the Anderson place, his plans changed.

Checking the horizon, he spotted a rider coming at a diagonal from the direction of the homesteads that lay to the north. Even from a distance, Blake recognized the tall black gelding and the broad-set shoulders of the man in the saddle. It was Webb Calder.

At first he thought Webb might be trying to catch up with him. But after a moment's watching, he realized that the Calder heir had cut off in a different direction, as if to avoid him.

Based on what Blake already knew, Webb's behavior made sense. He remembered seeing Stefan Reisner with the other men at the homestead where he'd dropped off the wood. There'd been no sign of Reisner's pretty young wife, who'd suffered burns when her skirt caught fire. And now here was Webb, coming from the direction of the Reisner place and behaving as if he didn't want to be seen.

Webb's secret love life was none of his business, Blake reminded himself. But he did have urgent business with the Calders. Catching up with Webb now would save time—maybe enough time to prevent a tragedy.

Decision made, he swung the team to the right and headed after Webb at a speed that sent the empty wagon bouncing and flying over the rough ground. As soon as he got within range, Blake started shouting, hailing Webb by name. Webb reined up, turned, and trotted his black horse back to meet the wagon.

"What are you doing out here, Blake?" Webb's eyes were narrow slits below the brim of his Stetson.

"Just making a delivery." Blake knew better than to ask Webb the same question. "But I was planning to find you later. There's trouble brewing, and I need your help to stop it."

Webb exhaled. "I'm listening."

"It concerns two of your hands—Sig Hoskins and the one called Lem. This morning I stopped them from raping one of the homesteader girls." He told Webb the rest of the story.

"I know the girl you mean," Webb said. "Pretty little blonde. I noticed her at the dance. Damn, it's lucky you showed up when you did."

"Another minute and I'd have been too late," Blake said. "Even so, the girl got a bad scare and a bruised face where they hit her. When I left them, her father and his friends were talking revenge. I tried to reason them out of it, but they were in no mood to listen. To their way of thinking, if they don't make an example of those two men, none of their women will be safe—and they're probably right."

"And what can I do about that? If they didn't listen to you, they sure as hell won't listen to me."

"You can make sure Hoskins and Lem are headed out of the county. Otherwise, you know what's bound to happen. There'll be blood, and there's no telling where it will end."

"I hear you." Webb's voice was flat, his expression unreadable. "But there's nothing I can do. My foreman fired those two galoots last week for drinking and fighting. He told them to get their gear and clear out. They could be any-where."

"Well, I know where they were this morning when they attacked an innocent girl. And Hanna—the girl—told me they mentioned hiding out on the Calder ranch. Is there any place they might've holed up?"

"We have a couple of empty line shacks. I'll have my men check and clear them out if they're there. But beyond that, I've got a ranch to run. I can't be responsible for two men who don't work for me anymore."

And will you be responsible if the next woman attacked is the one you can't seem to leave alone? The thought passed through Blake's mind, but he kept it to himself.

"I know this isn't what you want to hear," Webb said. "But those sodbusters should've had better sense than to come here, where they weren't welcome. Any trouble they might have, they pretty much bring on themselves. If they want to keep their women safe, maybe they shouldn't let them go wandering around on the prairie by themselves."

Blake had never cared for Webb Calder. But he had never disliked the man more than he did at that moment. "I've taken enough of your time, Webb," he said. "I hope nothing comes of this situation. But if it does, don't say I didn't warn you."

With that, he flicked the reins and drove away. He didn't bother to look, but the fading sound of hoofbeats told him Webb Calder was headed back to his kingdom.

As he drove toward town, Blake's curses purpled the summer air. A war between the cattlemen and the home-steaders would cause bloodshed and heartache on both sides. But in the end, the sodbusters would lose—and if they cleared out, the cattlemen would win. Maybe that was why Webb Calder didn't seem to care what might happen. Maybe all the ranchers felt that way, even his brother.

Let it go. It's not your problem, Blake tried to tell himself. But the memory of Hanna's haunting eyes, reflecting shat-tered trust, stayed with him as he drove into Blue Moon. He could talk to Sheriff Potter. But despite what he'd told Lars Anderson, Blake knew that the authority of the newly hired lawman didn't extend beyond the town. There were no laws on the open range except the ones commonly understood, and enforced, by the people who lived there—and that enforcement included hangings.

As he pulled the wagon into the side lot next to the general store, another thought struck him. With luck, Hoskins and Lem would have the good sense to stay hidden or leave. But what if Big Lars and his friends were to find the cowhands and carry out their revenge—be it beating, maiming, or even killing the cowboys?

What then?

Only two outsiders—Webb Calder and Blake himself—knew about the planned vendetta. Blake had no wish to report the settlers and cause them more trouble. But what about Webb? He had no sympathy for the newcomers. He'd even hinted that he wouldn't mind seeing them driven off the land. And if Stefan Reisner were to be caught and punished with the others, Webb would have access to Reisner's wife.

The war Blake was struggling to prevent would work in the cattlemen's favor—especially Webb's.

Damn! Blake's hand doubled into a fist. He'd set out to keep a tragedy from happening. But so far, his meddling efforts had only made the situation worse.

He took his time, giving his anger a chance to cool as he climbed down from the wagon and hitched the team to a post. It didn't help to see that right across the street the frame of a shedlike building was going up. On it was a sign—*Petit Lumber Company.* So Doyle was already expanding his business. And Blake didn't recognize the green boards that were stacked under the roof. Maybe Doyle had struck a deal to get his lumber somewhere else, like Miles City. Good for him. Today, Blake had more urgent concerns on his mind. But his thoughts were about to turn in a different direction.

As he rounded the corner of the general store, he was distracted by the sight of a familiar buggy drawn by two handsome bays. The driver—a man Blake recognized as one of the longtime Calder hands—sat dozing on the front seat, a rifle propped against his knee.

If Lorna Calder was inside, Ruth Stanton, who was like a daughter to Benteen's wife, would likely be here, too. With luck, he might get a word with her. Given Webb's recent behavior with a married woman, which he'd made no effort to hide, Ruth might be ready to turn to someone else.

He walked inside, holding the list Garrity had given him. Ollie Ellis, the proprietor, greeted him with a smile. "What can I do for you, Mr. Dollarhide?"

"I'll need everything on this list." Blake held out the crumpled sheet of paper with Garrity's labored printing on it.

"Of course." Ellis was familiar with the old man and his ways. "And I take it Mr. Garrity would like a couple of peppermint sticks. I'll include them, free of charge."

"That's right kind of you. Take your time." Blake was already scanning the crowded store, with its shelves of merchandise breaking up the space to form aisles. He could see Lorna Calder looking at some fabric. But she was alone. Maybe Ruth hadn't come with her after all.

Then he caught sight of Ruth on the far side of the store, where the kitchen supplies were kept. Dodging a cluster of drylanders, he made his way toward her.

It wasn't easy to get time with Ruth. She lived with her widowed father on the Triple C, where she taught at the small school for the ranch children. When she wasn't teaching, she was often with the Calders. People who knew the family assumed that one day she and Webb would marry. But the years had passed, and it hadn't happened. Now that Webb was behaving in a way that no woman should tolerate, the time might be ripe for Blake to get Ruth's attention. Maybe he could even ask her to go for a ride or a picnic.

"Hello, Blake." She looked up as he approached. Her blond hair was caught back in a prim bun and topped by a smart straw bonnet that shaded her pearlescent skin. Her eyes were pale blue, her smile as gentle as her voice.

"Surprise," he said, wishing he had Mason's way with pretty words. "I didn't expect to see you here."

"I didn't really plan to shop today." She took a bottle of vanilla off the shelf and laid it in her basket. "But it's Webb's birthday tomorrow, and I'm baking him a special cake, his favorite. When I read the recipe, I realized I didn't have everything I needed. So Mrs. Calder was kind enough to accompany me here in the buggy. What brings you into Blue Moon?"

"Just picking up some supplies." Blake's hopes had faded like sunlight behind a cloud. He was just making conversation now. "I saw you at the dance. I meant to whirl you around the floor a time or two, but then you know what happened."

"Yes. The fire. I hope that poor woman who got burned is all right. Thank goodness Webb got to her in time."

"I hope she's all right, too." *Damn Webb Calder*. Blake wished he could take Ruth aside and tell her how callously she was being treated by the man she plainly loved. But something told him that she already knew. She was hanging on in the hope that Webb would come to his senses. Ruth deserved better. But to her, that didn't seem to matter. Webb Calder was the man she wanted.

"Your order's ready, Mr. Dollarhide." Ollie Ellis's voice broke into a conversation that had become awkward. "I'll put it on your account."

"Thanks. Good luck with that cake, Ruth." Blake tipped his hat to the ladies, carried the box of supplies out to the wagon, and headed out of town. Rainless clouds had drifted over the sun, darkening the day to match his mood. A raven scolded him from a stump at the side of the road.

Wasted time—so far that was all his efforts had amounted to. But he'd brooded enough, Blake told himself. Back at the mill there was work to be done. He would throw his energy into making adjustments on the machinery and updating the inventory to have everything ready when the new, bigger logs arrived by rail. At least that would give him something to show for the day.

For the Anderson family, supper that evening was potato soup seasoned with a few slivers of bacon, along with field greens and biscuits. Hanna took only a spoonful of soup and a single biscuit, which she forced herself to eat. Her throat was so tight that she could barely swallow.

Earlier in the day, Inga had wrapped her sprained ankle with strips of flour sacking. She'd also sent the other children outside and, after hearing Hanna's story, ordered her to lie on the bed and spread her legs. Hot-faced, Hanna had protested even as she obeyed.

"Mama, I told you, nothing happened down there. The man in the wagon arrived in time to save me."

"I believe you, *kära*. But your father will ask, and I must give him an honest answer." There'd been a moment of uncomfortable probing. "*Ja*, you're fine, thank God. Sit up now. You should rest inside today. I'll give you some mending to do."

Still flushed with humiliation, Hanna had settled on a chair and taken the basket of worn stockings her mother handed her. Holding the needle to the light, she'd threaded the large eye with a thin length of yarn, worked the wooden darning egg into the first sock, and began stitching around the hole in the toe to create an anchor for the weaving.

"Mama," she'd asked as a chilling thought struck her. "What if those men had raped me? What would you and Papa do then—about me, I mean?"

Inga's hands had paused in the task of peeling a potato. "I suppose, just to be safe, you would need to get married. Then if a baby should come . . ." Her words had trailed off, the implied meaning clear.

"But what man would want me—knowing what had happened?"

"Hanna, you're a pretty girl, and young. Even if you weren't, there aren't that many girls out here for a man to choose from. Ulli Swenson is a good man and a hard worker. You already know that he's asked Papa for permission to court you."

Hanna had lowered her gaze to hide her distaste. Ulli Swenson was a grim widower with four children. The oldest, a boy, wasn't much younger than Hanna, the youngest a little girl of three.

"But it didn't happen, did it, Mama? I wasn't raped. And I certainly don't want to marry Ulli."

Inga had sighed. "*Kära,* if you're expecting a handsome prince on a white horse to sweep you up and carry you away, you're going to be sadly disappointed. We do our best with whatever life gives us. Remember that in the days ahead."

Now those words came back to Hanna as her family finished the meal and her father sent the other children outside. Feeling like a prisoner in the dock, she faced her parents across the rough plank table. She'd done nothing wrong. So why did she sense that she was about to be punished?

Lars cleared his throat. "Your mother says you were not harmed, Hanna. But you were lucky. We must make sure nothing happens to any more of our women. Tell me everything you remember about those two cowboys."

Hanna recalled Blake Dollarhide's warning about what could follow if her people took revenge. It occurred to her that she could lie about the appearance of the men and what she'd heard them say. But that could make the situation worse, especially if the homesteaders felt free to attack someone else. In any case, lying to her father was unthinkable. She told him everything.

"What are you going to do?" she asked.

"Find them first. Then we will decide."

"Is that all you need from me?" She stood and began stacking the bowls to clear the table.

"No, sit down," Lars said. "We need to talk about something else."

Something else. Hanna felt a wave of nervous nausea. Her life, she sensed, was about to change, and not for the better.

"Your mother and I have been talking," Lars said. "You're growing up, Hanna. Today already proved what can happen to a pretty girl like you. Men will look at you and want you. There could be more trouble. There could be talk. We think it's time you were safely married."

Hanna felt a sinking sensation, as if her heart had dropped into the pit of her stomach. She'd guessed that something like this might be coming. But now that the words had actually been spoken, she was stunned speechless.

"No." Her lips formed the word but no sound came out.

"Ulli Swenson is a good man, and he's got more money than the rest of us together," her father said. "He's already started building a fine cabin with a stone fireplace and wood floors. He plans to have it done before winter. Just think, you would have a real house with your own bedroom."

Not her own bedroom. Her and Ulli's.

"Your children would never be cold or go hungry," Inga added. "You can't imagine how much that can mean to a mother."

Hanna found her voice. "This is America. You can't force me to marry a man I don't love."

"There are more important things than love," Inga said. "Will love put food on your table or keep a roof over your head? Will love put clothes on your back or win the respect of your neighbors?"

"Mama—"

"Listen to your mother, Hanna," Lars said. "She is giving you good advice."

"You might not love Ulli now, but love can happen with time," Inga said. "Your friend Lillian was just fifteen when she married Stefan. Look at them now. You can see how devoted they are."

"But she wasn't forced to marry him." Hanna knew her friend's story well. "He took her in after her parents died in a fire. He was like a father to her. They married because she was growing up and people were beginning to talk. But at least they cared about each other."

Lars sighed and rose from his place at the table. "We can't force you to marry anyone, Hanna. But I will insist that you keep yourself open to the idea. Ulli wants to finish his cabin before he takes another wife. In the meantime, I've invited him to stop by and visit from time to time so you can get to know him."

"In other words, he'll be courting me."

"I suppose he will. And you are to be pleasant to him. Do you understand?"

"Yes, Papa, I understand." Right now, Hanna just wanted the conversation to end.

"Ulli will want an answer by the time his cabin is finished," Inga said. "For our family's sake, we hope you will say yes."

For our family's sake. Guilt twisted inside Hanna like the blade of a sharp knife. Of course, it would be to her family's advantage if she were to become Mrs. Ulli Swenson. Ulli had money and influence. He was becoming a leader in the small community of immigrants. The connection to his family could be useful in many ways, especially for her brothers and sisters.

Hanna barely knew the man. The thought of sharing his bed made her cringe. But in this untamed land where survival was a constant struggle, how could she allow her own happiness to rule her decision?

That night, with her father's snores reverberating through the shack, Hanna eased away from her slumbering sisters and tiptoed outside to find the one person with whom she could speak openly—the one person who would understand. At first, she didn't see Alvar, and she feared he might be asleep in the wagon. But then he stepped into sight, alert and fully dressed.

"I had a feeling you might come," he said.

"Thank you for waiting—oh, Alvar."

"I know," he said.

They stood side by side, gazing up at the Milky Way, just as they had the night before. But since then, the world had shifted for both of them.

"Have you told Papa you want to work at the sawmill?" she asked.

"Not yet. I have a feeling he won't approve. But I want to do it anyway. I need something more than plowing and planting and living for the harvest—something more than this farm. I know Papa needs me here—Axel's too small to do the work. But I don't know if I can be what he wants me to be."

He ran a hand through his thick blond hair, raking it back from his face. "Papa took me aside after he got home tonight. He said that when they go after those men who attacked you, I'm to stay behind. If anything happens to him, he wants to know that I'll be here to take care of the family."

Hanna shook her head. "I hope they never find those men. Forget that brave talk about honor—I can't stand the thought of lives being lost on my account."

"That's not how men think, Hanna." He looked down at her. "But what about you? When Papa shooed the rest of us outside, what did he and Mama have to say to you?"

"Oh—I'm to marry Ulli Swenson, to preserve my honor and improve the prospects of our family."

Alvar's breath whistled as he exhaled. "Can they make you do that?"

"No. But they can make me feel like a traitor if I don't. Ulli's cabin will be finished sometime this fall. I have until then to make up my mind. But they're expecting a yes."

Turning, she caught his sleeve. "Why can't we just run away, to someplace where nobody knows us—someplace where we can be anyone we want to be?"

Alvar sighed. "It's a nice fantasy, Hanna. But fantasies are for children. Most of us never get what we want. We just have to accept what life gives us and make the best of it."

Hanna watched a falling star streak across the sky and vanish into the darkness. Alvar was wise beyond his years. But was he right? What about men like Benteen Calder who had driven a herd of cattle up from Texas and forged an empire? He could have stayed in Texas and settled for whatever he had there. Instead he had chosen not to make do. He had seized life and fashioned it to his own purpose.

She'd met other men cast in the same mold—men like Blake Dollarhide, who had money and power and were determined to build on what they had. He'd been in her thoughts all afternoon, while she sat by the table darning socks and sewing on buttons. The image of his rugged face and fierce blue eyes had drifted in and out of her memory. She'd felt protected with him, and strangely alive. But she knew better than to think anything would come of their meeting. As Alvar had said, fantasies were for children. It was time she grew up.

"I need a favor," she said to her brother. "My friend, Lillian, was burned by the fire yesterday. I'd like to go and visit her, but after what happened this morning, I'm sure Papa won't let me go alone. Could you find the time to take me?"

"I don't see why not, as long as it's all right with Papa," Alvar said. "I'll ask him and let you know. For now, I think it's time you went back inside before somebody wakes up and misses you."

She touched his arm. "Good night, Alvar. I wish I was as wise as you are."

"I don't have all the answers, Hanna. Nobody does. You mostly have to find your own."

She left him then to steal back into the house and slip

under the edge of the quilt next to the sleeping Gerda. For the rest of the night she lay still, listening to the sounds of her family breathing as she gazed up into the darkness.

Tomorrow, if all went well, she would have a chance to talk with her friend Lillian. Although they were close to the same age, Lillian was years older in terms of experience. She knew what it was like, being married to an older man. She should be able to offer Hanna some advice.

But was Lillian happy with Stefan?

Hanna remembered watching her friend dance around the floor in Webb Calder's arms. It was as if Lillian had come to life, her eyes sparkling, her cheeks flushed, her generous mouth curved in a smile. And later, when Lillian's skirt had caught fire, Hanna remembered how Webb had swept her up in his arms and how Stefan had blocked his path and snatched her away.

If Hanna could believe what her eyes had seen, maybe her friend's marriage wasn't so happy after all.

Blake was on the platform four days later when the east-bound train came through. He cursed as the freight cars clattered past without so much as slowing down. The flatcar loaded with his logs should have arrived days ago. But there was still no sign of it. What the devil had gone wrong?

Before the railroad had come to Blue Moon, Blake had depended on ox-drawn wagons to haul two-foot-thick western white pine logs from the mountain forests of central Montana. But the need for even bigger logs, which could provide more and larger cuts with less waste, had spawned the idea of shipping three-foot logs of Douglas fir from the Oregon coast by rail. There were even bigger logs available—some as thick as a man was tall. But for Blake's purpose, they would be too heavy to transport and haul.

Blake had made the trip to Oregon, signed the contracts, and paid the money for the timber and the transport. The first couple of shipments had arrived without a problem. But the third shipment was days overdue.

It was too late in the day for a visit to the telegraph office in Miles City. He would go there first thing tomorrow, send one wire to the rail shipping agency, with a demand that they account for the missing logs, and another to place an order for two more wagonloads of the regular white pine logs.

Between the cost, the delays, and the challenge of dragging the heavy logs from the rail to the mill, using a device called a big wheel—a pair of giant wheels on an axle supporting a platform and drawn by horses—his latest idea was proving to be more bother than it was worth. Maybe after tracking down this last shipment, he'd give up hauling big logs and stick to the ones that could be brought right to the mill by wagon.

Feeling as irascible as a grizzly with mange, he mounted his horse and rode down the street to the saloon. Blake had never been much of a drinker, but right now the thought of cheap whiskey burning its way down his throat had some appeal. He'd take time for a quick drink, then head home and spend the rest of the day riding fences.

Dismounting, he glanced at his pocket watch. Sheriff Potter, a cocky little bantam rooster of a man, had made drinking against the law before 3:00 in the afternoon. But it was just past 3:00, and several horses were already tied at the rail out front. Blake left his horse next to them and went inside through the swinging doors.

Three men were seated around a table, talking and drinking. Blake's nerves prickled as he recognized them, but he ignored them and ambled to the bar. They'd paid him no attention when he walked in; but sooner or later they'd be likely to notice him. When they did, he would need to be ready for whatever they had in mind.

He paid for three fingers of whiskey and sipped it slowly, every nerve and muscle tensed and waiting. Without turning to look, he pictured them at the table—Hobie Evans and the two Carmody brothers—triple trouble. He'd bet good money they were up to no good.

From where he stood, Blake could make out only fragments of their conversation—the mention of honyockers and something about the fire. No surprise there. But then he heard something else from one of the Carmodys—something that caused the hair to bristle on the back of his neck.

". . . Say, Hobie, Sig and Lem want to know when we'll be seein' some money for this work."

Hobie's reply was drowned out by a gang of noisy cowboys who'd chosen that moment to burst into the saloon and crowd up to the bar. Blake took advantage of the commotion to blend in with the newcomers and slip out the door.

As he swung into the saddle, his mind grappled to make sense of what he'd just heard. It appeared that Sig and Lem, who'd almost raped Hanna, were in league with Hobie and the Carmodys, and that somebody was paying them to harass the drylanders, probably with the aim of driving them away.

But who would pay those men to commit crimes like rape, arson, and God knows what else?

Could it be the Calders?

CHAPTER 6

*A*FTER LUNCH THE NEXT DAY, HANNA AND ALVAR RODE
one of the draft horses across the prairie to the Reisner
homestead. They traveled bareback, Hanna behind with one
arm clutching her brother's waist and the other cradling the
towel-wrapped loaf of bread she'd baked that morning.
Alvar had brought their father's single-barreled shotgun,
which he balanced across his knees. While Hanna was visiting Lillian, he planned to hunt some birds for the pot.

The day was overcast but still simmering with July heat.
In the wheat fields that spread on both sides of the wagon
trail, green stalks rippled like the waves of an emerald sea,
beautiful in their promise of the money that would come
with the harvest and the sale of the wheat. But the parched
ground cried out for water. If rain didn't come soon, the
shallow roots would wither, leaving nothing in the fields but
dead yellow sticks. It was a worry for everyone. But Hanna's
mind was on more personal matters.

The distance to the Reisner homestead wasn't that far.
Ordinarily, Hanna and Alvar would have walked. But Hanna's
sprained ankle was still swollen and sore. She couldn't take

more than a few steps without pain. So her parents had let Alvar take her on the horse. Hanna knew they were eager for her to go, probably hoping that Lillian could talk some sense into their daughter. But it wasn't sense that Hanna wanted. It was the truth.

They rode into the yard to find Lillian hanging laundry on the clothesline. To Hanna's relief, there was no sign of Stefan. She had never felt at ease around Lillian's grim, taciturn husband, who made her feel as if she were being judged.

Without dismounting, Alvar lent an arm to help her slide down the horse to the ground. After giving Lillian a soft-spoken greeting, he tipped his hat and rode off toward the open grassland that lay beyond the wheat fields. He'd agreed to come back for Hanna in an hour.

"What are you doing, Lillian?" Hanna limped toward her friend. "Shouldn't you be resting?"

"I suppose I should. The burns on my legs still hurt. But Stefan has no clean underclothes, and the dirty ones won't wash themselves. So I do what I must."

Hanna's gaze traveled from the copper washtub sitting on an iron stand over a fire to the wicker basket at Lillian's feet and the lanky, worn, one-piece cotton union suits dripping over the line, along with socks, trousers, and shirts. "Let me help you," she said.

"I'm almost finished. This is the last one." Wincing with pain, Lillian lifted the final garment out of the basket and hung it over the sagging line. "At least they will dry fast in the heat. But look at you. You can barely walk. Stefan told me what happened. Come and sit down. I'll get us both some cool water, and we can talk."

"You can save this for supper." Hanna passed her the loaf of bread, which Lillian accepted with thanks.

"I made it myself," Hanna said. "My mother is teaching me to be a capable wife—at least she's trying."

"Oh, Hanna."

The sympathy in Lillian's voice did nothing to ease Hanna's misgivings. As Lillian disappeared into the house, she took a seat on a crude wooden bench that had been placed next to the stoop. A moment later, Lillian came outside, sat down beside her, and handed her a tin cup. The water would have come from a barrel which had to be filled in town. The settlers, including the Reisners and Hanna's family, had sunk wells, but the water in them had proven too alkaline to be of any use.

Hanna sipped the water, knowing how precious every drop was. As it cooled her dry throat, she summoned her courage and spoke.

"So you already know that my parents want me to marry Ulli Swenson?"

Lillian nodded. "There are very few secrets in our little community. People know, or at least they've guessed. And they wish you happiness—as I do, whatever you decide." Her work-roughened hand moved to rest on Hanna's. At moments like this, it was hard to believe that Lillian was barely a year older than she was.

"What's it like being married, Lillian?" she asked.

"It's about the way you'd expect. You work to take care of your husband and your home. He works to provide, and what he tells you to do, you do. Times can be hard. Sometimes you wish you could be someone else, somewhere else. But in the end you go on because you are building something important together—a family."

"And the rest—in your husband's bed?"

Lillian looked away, her eyes gazing out across the fields. "It's fine once you get used to it. Even if you'd rather not do it, it's what men need—and of course it's how you get children."

"But you and Stefan don't have children."

"No . . . sometimes it just doesn't happen."

Hanna knew better than to probe deeper. Lillian was young and healthy, but Stefan was past his prime. Maybe he wasn't able to become a father.

"Ulli has children." Lillian seemed to read Hanna's thoughts. "You should be able to have more of your own."

"But I don't love him, Lillian!" The words burst out of her, accompanied by a sob. "I can't stand the thought of being touched by him!"

Lillian squeezed her hand. As she spoke, a deep sadness shone in her eyes like the moon's reflection in a dark lake. "Then you don't have to accept him. But for people like us, the kind of love you're talking about is a luxury—like a fine carriage, a necklace of pearls, or a grand house. We might dream of it. We might want it. But in real life, we have to settle for what will allow us to survive—and what will be best for others."

"Do you love Stefan?"

"Stefan is a good man. He is kind. He works hard and takes care of me. When my parents died, I would've had no place to go if he hadn't taken me in. So yes. I am his wife, and in my own way, I do love him."

In my own way.

An image flickered in Hanna's memory—Lillian in Webb Calder's arms, smiling up at him as he whirled her around the dance floor. Was she thinking about Webb now, as she spoke?

Webb Calder was handsome and powerful. But was he a good man? Or was he just a man who felt entitled to claim what he wanted, even if what he wanted was another man's wife?

She'd known other powerful men, Hanna reminded herself, thinking of the two intriguing Dollarhide brothers. With Blake she'd felt safe and protected. But it was Mason who'd made her pulse race. When he'd bent to kiss her, she'd felt deliciously wicked and alive in every part of her body. If she were to marry Ulli, she would never feel that way again, and the thought made her want to weep.

Was that the way Lillian had felt with Webb?

"Look, someone's coming!" Lillian's voice broke into Hanna's thoughts. Shading her eyes, Hanna gazed in the direction her friend was pointing. Through the blur of heat waves, a distant horse and rider took shape.

"It's Alvar." Hanna recognized the horse. "But he wasn't planning to be back this soon."

"He's riding fast." Lillian was on her feet. "Something must have happened."

Braced for bad news, the two women waited in the yard. Lillian's hands twisted the hem of her apron. Hanna's stomach churned as Alvar rode into the yard, reined the horse to a stop, and slipped to the ground, balancing the shotgun in one hand.

"There were two men out there, past the fields." He spoke between breaths. "They started riding toward me. Then they turned and galloped away, probably because they saw the gun."

"What did they look like?" Hanna had gone cold inside, as if she already knew. "Was one of them big, with a beard?"

Alvar nodded. "The other man—he was small. We need to let somebody know."

"But we can't leave Lillian. They could come here."

"Stefan should be home soon." Lillian glanced at the sky to gauge the angle of the sun. "He went to Franz Kreuger's. But he said he wouldn't be late."

"Well, we're staying until he gets here."

"Will your family be all right?" Lillian asked.

"Papa's home, and he's got the rifle," Alvar said. "We'll stay."

They didn't have long to wait. Stefan came home, riding one of the two chestnut Belgians that the Reisners used to pull their plow and their wagon. When Alvar told him about the two men, he was incensed.

"This cannot go on! Ve have to protect our farms and our families from these animals. Tell me where you saw them, Alvar. I will go now and get the men together."

"Please, Stefan." Lillian touched his sleeve. "If you go, I will be left alone. Alvar and Hanna can't stay and protect me. They need to go home."

"But those men—"

"They were riding away when I last saw them," Alvar said. "Going after them will waste time and leave your families unprotected. If those men want to make trouble, they will come back. You can make plans to be ready for them."

Stefan's shoulders sagged. To Hanna, he looked old and tired. "All right. I vill stay with my vife for now. Tell your father I vill see him tomorrow."

"I will tell him everything," Alvar said. "Come on, Hanna. we need to go."

Hanna ran to Lillian and hugged her. "I'll come back again soon," she said.

Lillian returned her embrace. "Come anytime you need to talk."

Alvar sprang onto the tall horse. Hanna held the shotgun and passed it up to him before he pulled her up behind. She straddled the broad back, her skirt and petticoat bunched around her knees. Back in New York City, she'd seen elegant ladies riding sidesaddle in the park. But she knew better than to think she would ever have what they had. Lillian was right. Some things were out of reach for people from poor families like hers. But did one of those things have to be love?

The sunset streaked ribbons of flame across the sky as they headed for home, the colors fading to purple and indigo when they rode into the yard. To Hanna's surprise, there were two saddle horses outside the house. Her pulse skipped as she recognized Blake Dollarhide's rangy buckskin and saw Blake talking to her father. They both turned as Alvar reined up and helped Hanna slide to the ground.

"I saw those two men out on the range, the ones you're looking for," Alvar said, dismounting. "They rode toward me, like they were up to no good. But when I made sure they saw the gun, they headed away."

"Does Stefan know?" Lars asked.

"He knows, and he's hot to go after them. But we talked him out of leaving his wife alone."

"Then he'll need to hear this," Blake Dollarhide said.

"Those two bastards aren't working alone, and they didn't just come across Hanna by accident. There's a gang of them out there, at least five men, including the ones who set the fire. Somebody's paying them to stir up trouble, so you and your neighbors will pull up stakes and leave."

"Somebody's paying them?" Alvar stared at his father and the other man. "But who?"

"Somebody with money," Blake Dollarhide said. "I've got my suspicions, but no proof, so I'll leave it at that. But anybody who goes after that pair will be up against a band of armed thugs who won't care how much blood they shed. Until they're stopped, my advice to you, and to men like Stefan, would be to stay home, protect your families, and have a plan in place for when they make more trouble, because they will."

"I understand," Lars said. "I can't promise we'll follow your advice, but I will spread the word among our families. Then we will decide what to do."

"You might not have much time." With that warning, Blake Dollarhide mounted his horse and turned to go.

"Wait!" Alvar said. "If we don't fight those men, how can we stop them?"

"Find out who's paying them and stop the money. That's what I'll be working on. If you learn anything useful, get word to me at the mill."

As Hanna watched Blake Dollarhide ride off into the twilight, the second saddle horse, a handsome grulla tied to a post, caught her attention. As she turned, a man stepped out of the shadows next to the house. Clad in a white shirt and gray waistcoat, he was short, with thinning hair, a slight double chin and a belly that overhung his belt by a couple of inches. In Hanna's eyes, he was neither handsome nor ugly, neither bright nor stupid. Just ordinary. As ordinary as a potato.

"Hello, Hanna, my dear." Ulli Swenson's smile showed a discolored front tooth. "You look surprised. Didn't your parents tell you that they'd invited me to dinner?"

* * *

Mason Dollarhide paused to check the mirror before leaving his room to go downstairs. Ordinarily he didn't take such pains with his appearance. But today was a special opening of the Blue Moon Bank, in which he was a partner with his friend Doyle Petit and a fat, oily-tongued easterner named Wessel who'd arranged the original sale of land to the homesteaders. The other two partners had put up most of the money, but by virtue of his mother's owning the property where the bank was to be built, Mason had been included in the business.

He'd never been that keen on wearing a suit and sitting behind a desk, but as both Doyle's and Mason's mothers had pointed out, there was a lot of money to be made, especially by offering high-interest loans to the drylanders for seed, equipment, animals, and improvements to their homesteads. Mason couldn't argue with that.

Today, three weeks after the July 4 dance and the prairie fire, there would be another celebration. This one, sponsored by the bank and designed to lure the drylanders into town, featured fiddle music, free barbecue, and a welcome speech by Doyle, extolling the services a bank could provide for its customers.

Mason's job would be to mix with the crowd, handing out brochures, making friends, and answering questions, something he did well enough. But what he was hoping for was to see that pretty little blonde he'd met at the dance. What was her name? Hanna, that was it. Hanna Anderson. With luck, he might even get her alone long enough to collect that kiss he'd been about to claim before Blake had interrupted them.

Just imagining the taste of those innocent lips and the feel of that curvy little body pressed against his was enough to heat his blood and strain the buttons on his trousers. Mason considered himself a gentleman. He would never force a woman. But there were other, more enjoyable means of persuasion. The right words and a few kisses, and he would have sweet Hanna right where he wanted her.

He came downstairs to find his mother waiting in the parlor. Now in her mid-forties, Amelia Hollister Dollarhide was still a stunning woman, her flame-colored hair untouched by gray and her waist as slim as a girl's. She was dressed in an airy mint-green summer gown that matched the color of her eyes.

Looking him up and down, she smiled. "You look like a right proper businessman," she said.

"I'm glad you approve. Why don't you come to town with me and join the celebration?"

She laughed, a brittle sound, like the tinkle of the glass wind chime that hung over the porch. "Please, don't even ask."

"Whatever you say. I know you don't mingle with the peasants. But I wanted you to know that you'd be welcome."

Amelia smiled. "I understand. But my answer is still no."

Mason wasn't surprised. When Amelia wanted to shop, dine, or do business, she went to Miles City or took the train to St. Louis, where she had friends and family. If she had no social life in Blue Moon, that was by choice.

His invitation had been nothing more than a gesture. Amelia understood that as well as he did.

"Before you leave, Mason," she said, "I've been meaning to have a little chat with you."

"I really need to go." Mason had already guessed what his mother had in mind. It wouldn't be the first time she'd raised the subject of his finding a suitable wife. And by suitable, she meant upper-class and wealthy. Mainly wealthy.

"You've got time." She glanced out the front window. "Hank hasn't even brought your buggy around yet. Sit down."

Mason lowered himself to the arm of an overstuffed chair. "How many times must we have this conversation, Mother?"

"As many times as it takes. I'm not just building a legacy for myself. I'm doing it for your family, your children, their children, and on down the line."

"In other words, what you want is your own dynasty."

"Well, yes, if you want to put it that way. And as my only

child—the only one I presume I'll ever have—you have a responsibility to carry on the family line."

"You know there are other Dollarhides in the county."
Mason wasn't above needling his mother.

"Of course. But they don't count. Your brother was a bastard, born out of wedlock—you know that story. He'll probably marry some husky farm girl who can plow a field and
pop out babies like a brood sow. But it's quality we're going
for here. When I want to breed a prize stallion, I look for a
mare with a champion pedigree."

"I'm hardly a prize stallion, Mother."

"Of course not." She laughed again, that same sharp-
edged sound. "In any case, I've written my cousins to expect
the two of us in St. Louis for Christmas week. They'll be in-
troducing you to some suitable girls. I'll be returning home
after New Year's Day. You can stay on for as long as it takes
to find a proper girl and come back married—or at least engaged."

"All in good time." Mason sighed with relief as the one-
horse chaise drew up in front of the house, drawn by a sharp-
looking bay mare. He stood, brushing a crease from his
tailored gabardine trousers. "Time to go. I mustn't miss the
ribbon-cutting."

"Think about what I said," his mother called after him as
he strode out the door. "I know you like the local girls. Fine.
Do what you must with them. But don't you dare bring one
home. Our future family deserves better."

By the time Mason had reached the main road to town,
his thoughts were flying ahead. The winter season in St. Louis,
with its fine restaurants, theater, and socializing, would be
one grand, endless party. Of course, he had no intention of
finding a wife to tie him down and spoil his fun. But his
mother didn't need to know that. After all, he was her only
heir. How angry at him could she get?

Meanwhile, there was the delicious challenge of finding
sweet Hanna and getting himself between her virginal legs.

* * *

Blake wandered among the farm families and towns-people who'd shown up to celebrate the opening of the bank—or maybe just to get a helping of free food. Part of the street had been cordoned off in front of the bank and set up with a plank table, where a couple of ranch cooks, hired for the event, cut slabs of pit barbecued beef to lay on thick slices of bread. One serving was big enough for a meal, and the meat-hungry drylanders were taking full advantage.

Despite the mouthwatering aroma, Blake had resolved to pass on the food. Taking some would imply an obligation to do business with Doyle Petit's new bank, which was the whole idea behind the free feast. And Blake didn't plan to stay long—just enough to look around, see who was here and what was going on in town, and maybe have a slim chance of talking with Ruth. Not that he expected her, or any of the Calders, to be here. Folks on the Triple C could have all the beef they wanted, and they were no friends of Doyle's. Like the Dollarhides, they did their banking in Miles City. A quick glance around confirmed that Ruth hadn't come.

Blake had heard that Mason was a partner in the banking venture. The news hadn't pleased him, but Mason was his own man—or maybe his mother's man in this case, doing Amelia's bidding. Blake could see his half brother outside the bank, dressed in a suit and handing out printed bro-chures. Blake made no effort to approach him. There was nothing to say.

Keeping his distance, he scanned the crowd. With so many people in town, this could be an ideal time for Hobie Evans's gang to strike the wheat farms. In the past few weeks there'd been no fires, beatings, or assaulted women. But smaller acts of mischief—a field trampled, livestock let loose, fences pulled down—gave Blake every reason to be-lieve they were still out there making trouble. And some-body was still paying them.

If no major crimes had been committed, it was most

likely because the families were on guard. They no longer left their properties unwatched or let their women and girls go out alone.

Blake found himself looking for the Anderson family. Lars would be easy to spot because of his size. But there was no sign of him or his wife. Alvar had been hired at the sawmill after the delayed logs had arrived. He was at work today, and the younger children wouldn't be in town without their parents.

But suddenly, there was Hanna. Wearing a pink dress that appeared new, she was with a balding, middle-aged man who looked vaguely familiar. It took a moment for Blake to remember that he'd bought a load of premium, aged lumber earlier that summer. He'd paid cash and hauled the lumber away in his own wagon.

But what was he doing with Hanna—taking her arm, touching her back in a way that implied possession?

Blake studied the girl who'd woven her way into his thoughts. She seemed older somehow—maybe it was her hair, swept up, twisted, and pinned high on her head in a grown-up style. But it was her face that revealed the most. Her girlish smile was gone, replaced by a look of grim resignation.

Blake remembered Stefan Reisner and his wife, a woman young enough to be his daughter. Was he looking at a similar situation here? Was this what these people did to keep their girls in line?

The anger that welled in Blake's chest was so hot that he almost spoke out. But he checked himself. This sad affair was none of his business. He could turn away or stand here like a helpless fool and watch Hanna walk away on the arm of a man whom, for no logical reason, he already detested.

He chose to turn away.

Hanna hadn't been keen on going into town with Ulli. But after he'd invited her, her parents had insisted she accept. Her mother had even remodeled an old gown—out of style but still pretty—for her to wear.

Ulli had been to the house several times over the past weeks, conversing with her family and taking her for short walks around the property. The next logical step in their courtship would be an outing with him. The opening of the bank had provided an opportunity.

Hanna hadn't been to town since the Independence Day dance. She'd told herself that going out would do her good, even if she had to go with Ulli. He was a nice man—she had to give him that. And he was a proper gentleman in his own bland way. He'd never tried to press his affections on her and probably wouldn't until they were engaged. But the thought of being in his bed, enduring his kisses and his lovemaking, was enough to set off an attack of shudders. She didn't love him. She would never love him. But she was trapped; and she didn't know how to get free without shattering her family's hopes.

As he helped her down from the buggy, Hanna became aware of turning heads and curious gazes. Her heart sank as she realized that from this day on, she and Ulli Swenson would be regarded as a couple. It was as if the whole town had learned that they were keeping company.

She could see the tall figure of Blake Dollarhide at the edge of the crowd. What would he think, seeing her with Ulli—and why should it matter? Sensing his eyes on her, she looked down at her shoes. After a tense moment, he turned away as if he hadn't seen her.

Moving on, past the line to the food table, Ulli guided her with a hand on the small of her back. A few paces from the entrance to the bank, she could see Mason talking to people and handing out brochures. He caught her eye at once, giving her a secret smile that made her pulse flutter. Acting on impulse, she smiled back at him, then instantly regretted it. She hadn't meant to send him a message, but to Mason, it might appear that way.

"I want to stay up front to hear what Mr. Petit has to say," Ulli said. "After that, we can get some food."

Hanna scrambled for an excuse to get away from all the prying eyes. "I promised my mother I'd pick up some things at the store," she said. "The basket's in the buggy. Why don't I run my errand while you learn more about the bank? I can meet you at the buggy when I'm finished."

"Fine. Whatever you like," Ulli muttered, intent on moving forward. Leaving him, Hanna hurried back to the buggy for her mother's basket. She scanned the crowd for Blake, mostly to avoid any questions from him, but he was nowhere to be seen.

With the basket over her arm, she crossed the dusty street and hurried down the block to the store. Her mental list of items to buy was a short one—salt, thread, a length of muslin, and a jar of liniment. As she waited in line to pay, she was tempted to buy three peppermint sticks for her younger brother and sisters. But she forced herself to resist. The money she was spending wasn't hers, and her parents needed every cent. Maybe after she was married to Ulli she'd be able to treat her family.

After she was married to Ulli. Hanna's stomach clenched at the thought. Ulli was still working on his house and had yet to make a formal proposal, but her family assumed that the marriage was going to take place. After seeing them together today, the whole town would assume the same.

Even Mason.

The memory of his smile was like the touch of satin on her skin. But a memory was all she could expect to have of the most exciting man she'd ever known. As Lillian had reminded her, there were some things a girl of her station could never hope to have. One of them was the love of a man like Mason.

Hanna paid for her purchases and carried her basket out the front door. Looking to her left, down the boardwalk that lined the street, she could see people gathered around Doyle

Petit, who was speaking from the improvised bandstand. Ulli would be with them, probably intent on what was being said. There was no need for Hanna to join him. She would go back to the buggy and rest in its shade until he came to find her.

She had just turned and started down the boardwalk when a strong hand seized her arm, jerked her into the alley, and propelled her into the shadows behind a stack of wooden crates. Hanna's scream died in her throat as she looked up and saw Mason smiling down at her.

Without speaking, he drew her close, his hands molding her against him. The contact was so intimate that she gasped. Her conscience whispered that this was wrong, but she had no desire to push him away. The sensations that coursed through her body were too powerful to resist.

"Lord help me, Hanna," he murmured. "I almost died from wanting you these past weeks. And now here you are, in my arms. I must be the luckiest man on earth."

CHAPTER 7

*E*VER SINCE HER EARLY TEENS, HANNA HAD TRIED TO imagine what her first kiss would be like—the kiss that would change her from a girl to a woman. In the weeks since the dance in town, her fantasies had spun around Mason— how he would hold her, how his lips would feel, even how they would taste.

Not that she'd counted on Mason being the one to give her that kiss. It would more likely be some awkward farm boy or even Ulli—a kiss to shrug off and forget. But she'd been wrong. Mason was here, and the kiss of her dreams was about to happen.

Her heart slammed the walls of her chest as he leaned toward her. As his lips brushed hers, warm from the sun and as smooth as the skin on a horse's nose, she felt a shock of pleasure. Unbidden, she rose on tiptoe to heighten the sensation. His mouth teased her, nibbling and nipping until a compelling ache rose in the depths of her body. She whimpered, begging for more. Only then did he take full possession, crushing her lips with his, tasting and devouring. Dizzy with need, she let him, pressing close.

When his tongue slid into her mouth, tasting faintly of whiskey, she was startled. But as the tip stroked the silky inner surfaces, new sensations awakened like opening flowers. Every part of her seemed to shimmer with life. The voice of her conscience still whispered that this was not only wrong but foolish, but Hanna was beyond listening. She gave a little moan as her body responded to his mouth and to the hand that had moved to a breast, stroking the exquisitely tender flesh through her clothes.

Lost in a swirl of new sensations, she was barely aware of a faint sound, like the boom of a faraway cannon shot. In an instant it had passed. Was it only the pounding of her heart she'd heard? But it didn't matter. Nothing mattered except the here and now, and Mason's lips on hers.

Suddenly he thrust her away from him and stepped back, leaving her damp and breathless. Bewildered, she stared at him.

"We have to stop this now, Hanna." His voice rasped with emotion. "If we go on, I could hurt you, damage your reputation, even ruin your life. I care for you too much to let that happen."

Hanna lowered her gaze. Scalding shame rose in her face. Mason was right. What had she done? What had she become? When he'd pulled her into his arms, why hadn't she slapped his face and fled, as any proper lady would do?

"Are you all right?" he asked.

She nodded, hands fumbling to smooth back her hair and reposition the loose pins.

"You're a beautiful woman, Hanna," he said. "I'd give anything to love you the way you were meant to be loved. But I know you belong to another man. I saw you with him earlier. I have no right—"

"Just go." Hanna was angrier with herself than with him. How could she go back to Ulli now that she'd behaved like a wanton in another man's arms? How could she marry him, now that Mason had shown her what she'd be missing—and what she was never likely to have?

But how could she not marry the man who offered her family the chance for a better life?

Her mother's shopping basket lay at her feet where she'd dropped it. Mason picked it up and handed it to her. "You go first," he said. "I'll wait a bit, then cut around behind and come out next to the saloon. Nobody will notice."

Hot-faced, Hanna walked out of the alley, crossed the street, and returned to the place where Ulli had left the buggy. Sheltered from the sun, and from prying eyes, by the raised hood, she huddled in the seat, fighting tears and hoping no one had seen her.

Mason's kisses had awakened responses she hadn't known she possessed. Like a prairie fire, they'd blazed out of control. Even now, they were smoldering below the surface. But his words had made it clear that what had happened between them was no more than a stolen moment. Now it had ended—in the most humiliating way, with her sneaking out of the alley like a criminal. Her only choice was to get on with her colorless life, do what was expected of her, and forget it had ever happened.

She remembered her friend Lillian, and how she'd glowed with life when Webb Calder was dancing with her. Now Hanna understood that glow. She'd experienced it herself in Mason's arms. But Lillian was loyal to her husband and to their way of life. She was wise enough, and strong enough, to keep her wedding vows.

But was she happy?

Maybe that didn't matter.

"Here you are." Ulli had come up alongside the buggy. "Did you get everything you needed at the store? You took so long getting back that I was beginning to wonder where you were."

"Yes, I found everything. But I didn't hurry. I took my time." All of this was true. So why did she feel as if she'd just lied?

"Well, then, let's go and get some barbecue," he said. "I hope you're as hungry as I am."

At the mention of food, Hanna's stomach clenched. The last thing she felt like was eating. "Please go ahead without me, Ulli," she said. "I'm not feeling well. Most likely it's just the heat. I'll stay here and wait for you."

"Nonsense." Seizing her hand, he gave it a forceful tug. "What will people think if I leave you and go back alone? They'll be saying that we must've had a quarrel. Now stop acting like a child and do as I say."

Resisting would only make things worse. With a sigh, Hanna let him help her down from the buggy and lead her through the crowd to the long table where the last of the barbecue was being served. Ulli handed her a slab of bread and meat, then took one for himself, devouring it with big, hearty bites.

Hanna forced herself to take small mouthfuls and chew them. Looking to one side, she could see that Mason had returned to his place near the bank entrance. She turned away, hoping he wouldn't see her but knowing that he probably had.

"Aren't you going to finish that?" Ulli asked.

"Take it." She handed him her bread and meat and watched him wolf it down, a thin trail of juice dribbling from the corner of his mouth.

While he finished, Hanna forced herself to smile and nod at people who passed. Her feet, in their too-tight high-topped shoes, had gone numb. Her lips stung with the memory of Mason's kiss and the humiliation that had followed. Today's outing had been a miserable mistake from beginning to end. All she wanted now was to go home.

Blake had seen Hanna come out of the alley, fussing with her hair and looking as if her heart had been broken. He had also seen Mason slipping behind the store, coming out on the far side of the saloon, and crossing the street to return to the bank.

He'd held back the urge to catch up with his brother and give him the tongue-lashing he deserved. Mason would probably laugh in his face. In any case, it appeared the damage had been done. He could only hope that the girl had suffered nothing worse than wounded feelings.

He had watched Hanna from a distance to make sure she was safe. Only after she'd climbed into the buggy did he turn away, find his horse, and mount up to go back to the sawmill.

That was when he'd noticed a familiar black horse hitched outside the saloon.

So far, Blake had failed to find out who was paying Hobie Evans and his gang to stir up trouble with the drylanders. His number one suspect was still the Calders, but he had no proof. Maybe it was time he faced Webb and straight out asked him. The Calders were capable of some skullduggery, but they weren't known to be liars. If he could get Webb to talk, he might even learn something helpful.

With his mind made up, he tethered his horse to the rail out front and walked into the saloon. Webb was alone and on his feet, drinking at the bar. Blake walked up to the bar, ordered a whiskey, paid, and took a sip. Webb glanced at him, then looked away. They weren't enemies. But they weren't exactly friends either.

"Can I have a word with you, Webb?" Blake nodded toward a small empty table with two chairs in the far corner of the room.

"All right, as long as you make it short." Carrying his glass, Webb ambled toward the table, pulled out a chair, and sat down opposite Blake. "So what's this about?" he asked.

Blake gave him a quick summation of the damage that had been done to the homesteaders so far, some of which Webb already knew.

"Exactly why are you telling me this?"

"There's a gang behind all the trouble—Hobie, Hoskins, Lem, and the Carmody brothers. I heard them talking.

Somebody's paying them to make trouble so that the home-steaders will sell out cheap and leave."

"So?" Webb sipped his whiskey, studying Blake with narrowed eyes. "Do you think it's me, or my father, paying those galoots?"

"That came to mind. Your family's got money, and I know how much you hate the drylanders and want them gone. So is it you?"

Webb tilted back his chair. "Why should we throw down good money for something that's going to happen anyway?"

"Go on." Blake sipped his whiskey and waited.

"Right now, with all that wheat planted and growing, nothing's going to get those honyockers off their land," Webb said. "Let's say the weather breaks, we get some rain, and they get a decent harvest this fall. All well and good. They'll make some money and plan to grow more wheat in the spring. But none of them have ever lived through a Montana winter. In those little tar paper shanties, they're going to freeze or maybe starve, or they'll burn down their houses trying to keep warm. Oh—and the wolves. You've heard those howls at night. The packs will come down from the hills and go after any damn thing they can eat—animals, food stores, even people. My dad tells a story about some wolves that were so hungry they ate a leather harness."

Webb finished his drink and set the glass down. "I guarantee you, any of those drylanders who are still alive by spring will be ready to pack up, sell out, and leave. But if they're crazy enough to stay and plant another crop—you've lived here long enough to know what can happen—drought, storms, fire, sickness—you name it. They won't last here. All we need to do is wait. So I ask you, Blake, why should we pay a bunch of hooligans to knock over a few chicken coops, scare the women, and burn down a privy or two?" Webb pushed out his chair and stood. "I'm not sure why you felt the need to ask, Blake, but I hope you just got your answer." With that he turned away and walked out of the door.

Blake sat looking after him. Webb had done a lot of talking, and what he'd said made sense. It was true that if the ranchers didn't drive the homesteaders out, the hard conditions probably would. But Webb hadn't really answered Blake's question. Was all the talk a smoke screen to hide what the Calders might be doing? It might pay to remain suspicious.

Leaving the saloon, Blake mounted up and headed south through town. The next couple of months would be a busy time at the sawmill, supplying boards and timbers for the buildings that had to be finished before winter snows set in and the mill had to shut down. He'd hired a good crew, and they worked well enough without him, but he needed to be there in case a problem or question arose.

Passing the bank, he saw that the crowd had dispersed and a crew was cleaning up after the barbecue. The buggy where Hanna had taken refuge was gone. He could only hope she was all right.

He drove on out of town, trying to focus his thoughts on the work at the mill. But his thoughts kept returning to Hanna and the stricken expression on her beautiful face.

Damn his brother for messing around with a vulnerable young girl. Mason deserved to be horsewhipped.

Hanna didn't feel like talking. She gazed down at her hands while Ulli drove the buggy, going on about his house, which would be finished in a few weeks, about his wheat crop, and about his plans for the money the sale would bring. She imagined listening to the same one-sided conversation, in his flat, nasal voice, for the rest of her life. If anything, the thought made her feel even worse about what she'd done. Ulli was a good man, kind, honest, and responsible. If he wasn't handsome, with a glib tongue and elegant manners, that wasn't his fault. Maybe she should try harder to like him.

"Are you all right, Hanna?" His question broke into her

thoughts. She realized that they'd left the town behind and were driving across the open prairie. Heat waves shimmered above the sun-scorched landscape. Two vultures circled on the updrafts, their black wings spread against the blinding sky.

"I'm fine," she said. "Just tired, that's all."

"You aren't saying much. Is there something you might want to tell me?"

"Not that I can think of." Hanna looked away, brushing back a stray lock of hair. Her face felt hot.

Ulli took a deep breath, then pulled the buggy off the side of the trail and stopped. "Look at me," he said.

Hanna turned back to face him but still couldn't meet his gaze.

"Look at me, Hanna." His voice was calm but firm. Hanna forced herself to look into his eyes. They were pale and etched with tiny red veins.

"I saw you today," he said. "I saw you go into that alley by the store. I saw you come out, and I saw the way you looked. I didn't see the man, but I imagine there was one."

Hanna's fingers twisted the fabric of her skirt. She dropped her gaze, unable to look at him. "I'm sorry," she said. "I didn't mean for it to happen."

"You're a lovely girl," he said. "I was smitten the first time I saw you. But I should have known that you were too young and unsettled to be a wife to me and a stepmother to my children. I need a woman I can trust, a woman I can depend on to do her part." He paused, as if preparing to say something painful. "Since we've made no promises to each other, I think it would be best if we parted."

Tears welled in Hanna's eyes—tears of relief and shame. She'd never wanted to marry Ulli. But she'd disgraced herself and shattered her family's hopes. "You're a good man, Ulli Swenson," she said. "I'm sure you'll find the right woman soon. Now please take me home. There'll be no need to speak to my parents. I'll tell them what happened."

"Tell them whatever you want. If anybody asks me, we parted by mutual agreement, and anything else is no one's business."

"Thank you."

Hanna gazed straight ahead as Ulli drove the buggy toward her home. He had set her free. But even if she didn't tell her parents the truth, they would be devastated. Not only would they lose the satisfaction of seeing their daughter married to a prosperous man, they would have a rejected woman on their hands. People would wonder why, and they would talk.

She would hold up her head and make the best of the situation, Hanna resolved. Still, one question lingered, like a secret whispered in her ear.

Now that I'm free, will it make any difference to Mason?

Another mile, which passed in awkward silence, brought them within sight of the Anderson homestead. Seeing movement, Hanna shaded her eyes and gazed ahead. "Everyone's out in the yard, like they're waiting for us. Something must've happened."

By the time the buggy rolled into the yard, Hanna's pulse was hammering. Her parents were waiting, along with the three younger children. Alvar would be at work. But the sawmill was a dangerous place where anything could go wrong. Could some terrible thing have happened to her brother?

As the buggy came to a stop, Hanna sprang out and ran to her mother. "What's happened? Is it Alvar?" she demanded.

Inga's eyes were wet. She shook her head. Her gaze traveled to Ulli, who was still in the buggy. Lars was striding across the yard to talk to him.

"We just found out, Ulli," he said. "Those men, the ones we've been looking out for, they hit your place. They rode by, shot out a window, and tossed some dynamite into your new house. The explosion blew the walls apart."

Ulli had gone white. "My children—?"

"The boys were outside. They're all right. But your youngest, your little girl . . . she's gone."

How Ulli could keep from crumbling like a dry leaf in a bonfire Hanna would never understand. He had gone rigid, his knuckles white where his hand gripped the reins. "I have to get home. My children need me" was all he said before he drove away, whipping the horse with the reins.

As the news sank in, Hanna doubled over as if she'd been kicked. Sobs shook her body as tears of grief and shame washed over her. She remembered hearing the faint booming sound when she was in the alley, dismissing it as nothing. Now she knew what she'd heard. While she'd been kissing Mason, thinking only of her own pleasure, Ulli's child had died.

It was Alvar who told Blake the next day. Blake had lent him a mare to travel the distance between the homestead and the sawmill. Alvar had arrived home last night to the news of the attack on Ulli Swenson's property and the tragic death of his three-year-old daughter.

"You can imagine how people are feeling," Alvar said. "My sister is in shock. She and Ulli were courting. He was finishing his house so they could marry. But she says that's over now."

So Ulli Swenson had been the man he'd seen briefly at the homestead, and later in town with Hanna—before Mason had lured her into the alley. Blake couldn't help feeling relieved that Hanna wasn't going to marry him. But Lord, no man deserved the kind of tragedy Swenson had suffered.

"They'll be burying the little girl today. Then there's talk of riding out afterward, tracking down those men, and killing them all." Alvar shook his head. "Some of the men are saying we should've done that after the Gilbergs' house was burned. Maybe then this wouldn't have happened."

He gazed at Blake, his eyes narrowing. "I know you

meant to help us, and maybe you tried. But nothing's been done. We already know the sheriff won't do anything. What choice do we have except to take the law into our own hands, as you say?"

Blake had no reply, but that was just as well because at that moment, the first big log of the day was moved into the double rotating blades. The scream of steel biting into solid wood was loud enough to drown out any conversation.

Alvar hurried off to do his job, which was to help move a second log into place and have it ready when the first one was done. The log to be cut would be rolled onto a low metal carriage and bolted into place. The carriage, which ran on a pair of rails, would move the log through the circular saw blades.

With each pass through the blades, the log's position had to be adjusted precisely for the next cut. This was done by the most skilled of the workers, known as a sawyer. The wood was cut off in slabs, which would later be sawed into boards of the desired width and hand finished as needed.

The saw, its double blades mounted one above the other, was steam driven, the fire in the boiler fed by the scraps and strips of bark that were trimmed off the logs. The work was strenuous, hot, noisy, and dusty. Blake paid his crew well, and they earned every cent. But they also took pride in a job well done. Premium lumber from the Dollarhide mill was smoothly and precisely cut, the boards perfectly matched.

Young Alvar was off to a good start. He was strong, quick to learn, easy to like, and not afraid of hard work. Blake was especially impressed with the way his mind took in the entire process of making lumber, not just the narrow task he'd been hired to do.

With some schooling, he could have a bright future anywhere. Sometime later, Blake told himself, he would have a talk with the young man. But right now, both he and Alvar had more urgent concerns on their minds.

Ulli Swenson's sons had been outside when the raiders

showed up. The fifteen-year-old had described the men in detail. There could be no doubt of their identity. It had been Hobie Evans and his gang.

Even though they'd probably assumed that the house was empty, the death of the child was murder. And the bastard putting up the money to pay them was as guilty as the ones who'd shot out the window and thrown the dynamite.

Ulli and his fellow homesteaders deserved justice. For them, the only way to get it would be to go after the gang and put a violent end to them—which would give their enemies an excuse to drive them out, soaking the land with blood on both sides. It would be the Johnson County War all over again.

Could the carnage be stopped? But this wasn't his fight, Blake reminded himself. He did business with all sides— ranchers, homesteaders, and townspeople. He made it a rule to treat everyone the same. But this was his land, too, and his family's land. These people were his neighbors. How could he just stand back and let the tragedy happen?

The Calders were the most powerful people in the county. Blake hadn't cleared them of suspicion—but if they were behind the raids, how could they live with the death of a little girl?

When Blake had asked Webb for help, Webb had walked away. But there was one man who had the final say—the head of the family, Chase Benteen Calder. If anybody had the power to order the raiders rounded up and brought to justice, or order a halt to the violence, it was Blake's father's old rival.

After making sure that everything was in order at the mill, Blake mounted up and set out for the Calder place. A brisk wind had sprung up from the west, rippling the yellow grass and bringing a few muddy-looking clouds over the horizon. But Blake knew better than to hope for rain. He'd been disappointed too many times before.

Skirting the wheat fields, he glimpsed distant wagons, horses, and buggies all headed in the same direction. He remembered Alvar telling him that Ulli's daughter was to be buried today. Once the sad little body was laid in the ground, grief would be replaced by outrage and anger. Blake imagined a band of farmers, armed with guns and ropes, riding out on the trail of the raiders, bent on vengeance.

The raiders would have the best chance to escape if they scattered and hid separately. If they were caught together, and the shooting started, good people were bound to lose their lives.

At least Alvar wouldn't be among them. He'd told Blake that his father wanted him safe, to care for the family in case the worst happened. But others—fathers, sons, husbands, and brothers—were bound to die senselessly, and more families would be ruined.

Even after Blake rode under the high main gate of the Triple C, he had some distance to go. The Calder spread was so vast that it seemed more like a kingdom than a mere ranch, with rich grassland that could be measured not in acres but in square miles.

Here and there he saw clusters of grazing cattle, most of which would be rounded up and loaded into railway cars this fall. There were fewer of them than he remembered seeing in earlier years. Between the drought and the deflated beef market, Benteen must've sold some of them off early just to get operating cash. All the cattle ranches were hurting, which was why there were so many out-of-work cowhands hanging around Blue Moon.

The most trusted hands, some whose fathers had made the original drive with Benteen's herd, lived in nice homes on the ranch. Others stayed in well-furnished bunkhouses. These, along with the barns, sheds, warehouses, and corrals, gave the ranch's central area the appearance of a small town.

On a nearby bluff, Blake could see the mansion with its pillared front which had always reminded him of the White

House in Washington, which he'd seen as a photo in a book. As a boy, he'd visited the Calder home with his mother, who was good friends with Lorna Calder. The two women were still friends, although, over time, Sarah's marriage to Joe Dollarhide had created some distance between them. Years had passed since the last time he'd walked through the doors of the great house. He could only hope that the man he'd come to see would be at home and in a mood to listen.

It was Lorna who answered his knock. Looking fresh and pretty in a yellow summer dress, she swiftly replaced her surprised expression with a smile.

"Why, Blake, how good it is to see you. Please come in." She motioned him inside and closed the door. "How is your mother?"

"She's fine. I'll tell her you asked." Blake happened to glance past her. Ruth, dressed in pale blue, was standing at the open entrance to the dining room. She gave Blake a smile and a nod, then turned away and vanished.

"What can we do for you, Blake?" Lorna asked. "Can I get you something to drink?"

Blake pulled his attention away from Ruth. "Nothing to drink, thanks. I have business with your husband if he's available. Would it be possible to talk with him now?"

"Certainly. He's in his study." She raised her voice slightly. "Ruth, would you tell Mr. Calder that Blake Dollarhide is here to see him?"

Blake could hear the patter of Ruth's footsteps hurrying down the hall. In a moment's time she came back to the entryway. "He can see you now, Blake. I'll show you the way."

Blake already knew where Benteen's study was, but this might be his only chance to talk with Ruth. "Thanks," he said. "How've you been, Ruth? I haven't seen you in a while."

"I've been pretty busy here. There's the door to the study.

You can just go in." She turned away and went on down the hall. Ruth was pretty and intelligent, but she'd never been much for conversation. Some men liked that quality in a woman. But that was a thought for another time.

After a light knock, Blake opened the door. Benteen Calder sat behind his massive desk with a ledger spread open in front of him. He looked older than the last time Blake had seen him. The skin seemed to sag on his rugged face, and his dark hair was streaked with gray. He appeared to be tired, maybe even ill. But when he spoke, his voice was as deeply powerful as Blake remembered.

"Pull up a chair, Dollarhide. Pardon me for not getting up. The old knees are giving me hell. Might be a touch of lumbago." He cleared his throat. "So what brings you all the way out here?"

"Trouble with the drylanders. I'm hoping you can help put a stop to it."

"You don't say?" One heavy black eyebrow shifted upward. Benteen's dislike of the wheat farmers was no secret. "And why should I want to put a stop to it? As far as I'm concerned, any trouble those honyockers are having is good news."

"So you haven't heard about the dynamiting?"

"Oh, that." He scowled. "Yes, my foreman said something about it last night. Damned shame about the little girl. But there's not much I can do about that, is there? I mean, I can't bring her back to life, can I?"

Blake had never imagined he'd want to punch Benteen Calder in the face; but the thought struck him now. He forced his temper under control. "Do you know that somebody's paying the gang that dynamited the house? And that the drylanders are going out to track them down and kill them?"

"And how am I supposed to put a stop to that?"

"Did Webb tell you I spoke to him?"

"Webb and I haven't done much talking lately. But I take

it that whatever you wanted from him, he said no. And that's why you've come to me. So get to the point."

The man wasn't making it easy. "Two of those raiders used to work for you. They could be hiding on your ranch. Either way, you've got the manpower to go after them, round them up, and turn them over to the state authorities. If the drylanders get to them first, and lynch or shoot them, the bloodbath that follows is bound to get innocent folks killed. I'm trying to keep that from happening."

Benteen shook his head. "You say I've got the manpower. Hell, I'm not even paying my men, just letting them live here free until the work picks up. No cowboy who's not being paid will want to ride after those galoots. I say let the bastards go. If they're smart, they'll get away. If they're dumb enough to get caught, they deserve to be strung up. This isn't my problem. And I can't help you." He turned a page in the ledger, dismissing Blake with a gesture. "You can show yourself out."

Blake walked down the hall to the entry and let himself out the front door without seeing either Ruth or Lorna. Why had he taken the time to come out here and talk to Benteen? Why should he care about a bunch of stubborn wheat farmers—especially when no one else seemed to? Maybe he should just back off and let events take their course, come hell or high water.

As he mounted his horse, a distant sound caught his attention—the faint but unmistakable rumble of thunder. Sooty clouds were rolling in from the west. Could it really be rain, or was Mother Nature playing another of her cruel jokes?

By the time he rode under the high gate of the Triple C, black clouds had filled the sky. Lightning crackled and hissed. Thunder boomed. Recognizing the danger of being a high target, Blake dismounted and led his nervous horse.

As they reached the road back to town, the sky seemed to split open. Rain poured down like water through a broken dam. Life-giving rain that turned the road to a sea of mud and plastered Blake's wet clothes to his body; rain that would wash out the tracks of the raiders and send their pursuers racing for their shacks and wheat fields.

As the lightning moved off toward the mountains and the rain settled into a steady drizzle, Blake swung into the saddle again and rode for home.

CHAPTER 8

*T*WO WEEKS HAD PASSED SINCE THE RAINSTORM THAT HAD inundated the fields and flooded the dirt floor of the Anderson home. The sticky clay mud had dried rock hard, but the wheat was thriving. A grain office had been opened in town to handle the sale and shipping of what was expected to be a bountiful crop.

The gang who'd dynamited Ulli's house had vanished with the rain. Speculation was that once the raiders realized that they could hang for the death of the child, they'd separated and left the county. There was no more sign of them; and for now, the talk of vengeance had faded.

Ulli had sold his homestead to Doyle Petit, taken his three sons, and returned to the East. He'd told Lars, who'd driven them in the wagon to meet the train, that he had no more heart for farming and never wanted to see Montana again.

Hanna had watched the wagon disappear in the distance, feeling as if one chapter of her life had closed and a new one had yet to begin. But her old routine continued as before—long days of helping her mother with the washing, cooking, sewing, and mending, with the tedium broken only by rare trips to town for supplies.

Alvar's job at the sawmill was bringing in needed money, but he was working long hours, leaving before dawn and returning home so tired that he usually fell asleep right after supper. Hanna missed their talks. He was the only person who seemed to understand her longing for something beyond the life that fate had given her.

On an August day, not long after the first cool morning, Inga gave Hanna a shopping list that Britta had written down for her and sent her into town with the wagon. Britta would be going along. The sisters were to pick out some fabrics for fall dresses—made possible by the extra money Alvar brought home. It was a rare treat to be going into town without a parent to chaperone. And picking out cloth for new dresses made it extraspecial.

"I can't wait!" Britta, a pert strawberry blonde with freckles, bubbled as the wagon approached town. "I've been wearing your hand-me-downs all my life. I can't believe I'll finally be getting something new. You're so lucky, being the oldest girl."

"Even if my dresses are makeovers from Mama's clothes?"

"Well, at least you get to wear them before I do."

Hanna gave her a smile. She'd always viewed her sister as a child. But maybe now that Britta was growing into young womanhood, the two of them would become close.

As the wagon rolled into Blue Moon, Hanna couldn't resist glancing up and down the street for any sign of Mason—or at least his buggy. She didn't see it. But as they passed the bank, she couldn't help wondering if he was at work there. She'd told herself to forget him; but every time she came to Blue Moon with her family, she found herself searching for a glimpse of the man whose kisses had made her feel like a woman for the first time. So far, she'd seen nothing of him. She was starting to wonder if he might've left town.

She pulled up in front of the store and set the wagon brake. By the time she'd climbed to the ground, Britta had jumped out of the wagon and raced into the store ahead of her.

Hanna was tethering the horses to the hitching rail when a deep, familiar voice from behind went through her like a lightning bolt.

"Don't turn around, Hanna."

"Mason?" Her face went hot. Her pulse broke into a gallop.

"Go on with what you're doing." His low whisper thrilled her. "We don't want to cause any gossip, do we?"

Her hands shook as she finished tying the loose knot. She ached to turn and look at him, but he'd warned her against it. "How've you been? Why are you here?"

"I had to see you," he said. "I understand that beau of yours sold out and left town."

"He wasn't my beau, just a friend of my family."

"I was hoping to hear that—because I haven't stopped thinking about you. I need to see you, Hanna, someplace where we can be together and I can show you how I really feel."

Her heart slammed. "My parents—"

"You're not a child, Hanna. You're a woman—a beautiful woman who was born to be adored and worshipped." He paused. Hanna could hear him breathing.

"I know where you live," he said. "About a mile east of your homestead, there's a place where two trails cross, by an old dead tree. Do you know it?"

"Yes." Her pulse was pounding.

"If you say you can meet me, I'll wait there for you tonight—late, after everyone's gone to sleep. Can you come to me then?"

Hanna knew she should say no. But she was already plotting how she could get to the place. Walking would take too long, but she could borrow the mare Alvar used to get to work. Alvar would be asleep. He'd never know the mare was gone—and she'd have it back long before he woke up.

But what was she thinking? Sneaking out at night to see a

man, breaking every rule her parents had ever made? It wasn't just wrong; it was foolish, even dangerous.

Still, when she remembered how she'd felt in Mason's arms, trembling and alive in every part of her body, she knew that she'd risk almost anything to feel that way again.

"I need your answer, Hanna," he said.

Just then Britta came bursting out of the store. "Hanna, come on! They have some new calicos! You've got to see them!"

"Go on back inside, Britta. I'll be right there." She hesitated, torn.

"Yes or no." His voice was warm in her ear.

Hanna took a breath, feeling as if she were on the edge of a precipice. "Yes," she whispered, then hurried after her sister.

It took less than half an hour for the girls to fill their mother's shopping list and pick out three dress lengths of bright calico—green for Britta, dark blue for Hanna, and a smaller piece of light blue for eight-year-old Gerda. Hanna could sew well enough to make her own dress. Britta was learning but would need help. Their mother would make Gerda's dress. The task would keep them busy as they worked to finish the dresses before harvest time when all hands would be needed. After the wheat was reaped, threshed, bagged, and sold to the grain office, there would be a celebration with a dance—a time to show off pretty new dresses.

Britta chatted happily all the way home. Hanna lent her half an ear, but her mind was churning with thoughts of her rendezvous with Mason. The idea that he wanted to be with her had her head spinning. But what if she'd made the wrong decision? What would Mason do if she changed her mind, or couldn't get away?

After lunch they started on Britta's dress. Laying out the fabric on the kitchen table, and using a worn-out dress for a pattern, they cut the green calico fabric with the treasured scissors Inga had brought with her from Sweden and pinned the pieces together to check the fit.

Hanna could barely keep her mind on the work. The hours seemed to crawl as she showed Britta how to match the edges of the fabric and make tiny, even stitches with the needle. When the light began to fade, they put yesterday's stew and dumplings on the stove to warm, gathered up the sewing, and set the table for supper.

Lars had been helping a neighbor put up a fence, and he'd taken Axel along to fetch and carry. They came in hungry just as everything was ready. Alvar showed up so late that the rest of the family had finished and gone outside to sit in the cool twilight. His supper had been kept warm on the stove. As Hanna set the plate in front of him, he gave her a questioning look.

"Is everything all right, Hanna?" he asked in a low voice. "You look troubled."

"I'm just tired. Everything's fine," she lied and turned away. Alvar had always been able to read her. They were closer than most brothers and sisters. But tonight she couldn't tell him the truth—that a few hours from now, after the family was asleep, she was going to take his horse and ride across the pastures to be in a man's arms.

While Alvar ate his supper, Hanna poured hot water into the dishpan, added a sliver of soap, and began washing the dishes. Questions, doubts, and fears gnawed at her resolve. But one certainty emerged. Mason struck her as a proud man. If she didn't go to him tonight, there would be no second chance. Those wonderful feelings she'd known with him—the pounding of her heart, the racing of her blood, and the dizzying surge of her womanly response—could be lost forever.

Getting out of the house would be the hardest part. She would have to go to bed as usual. At night, she wore a light muslin gown over her chemise and drawers. She wouldn't be able to put on anything else without rousing suspicion. She would have to go as she was. At least Axel and her sisters were sound sleepers, and her father's snoring would drown out any small disturbance. Britta, who slept next to her, was accustomed to Hanna's getting up and wandering outside when she couldn't sleep, so that shouldn't be a problem.

The aging dun mare Alvar had borrowed to ride to work was gentle. Saddling her would take too much time, but a bridle should be enough for the short ride.

Everything appeared to be in place. Still, as Hanna put the dishes back on the shelf, her hands shook so badly that she dropped a stack of tin plates. They clattered to the floor.

"What is it?" Alvar got up and slipped his plate into the water to be washed. "Something's wrong—I can tell."

Hanna bent to pick up the fallen plates. He crouched beside her to help. "Look at me, Hanna. Whatever it is, you know you can tell me."

She met his earnest eyes—the bluest eyes of anyone in her family. Lying to her brother was like cutting her skin with a razor, but she couldn't give him a true answer. "Sorry, I've got a headache, that's all. Maybe too much sun today."

"Get some rest. Let me know if you need to talk." He stood and went outside.

She took the fallen plates from him, rinsed and dried them, and put them on the shelf. She would have to be extra careful tonight. Alvar could sense that she was up to something. He might even stay awake and stop her from leaving. For that matter, anyone in the house could wake up and end her adventure before it began.

But she needn't have worried about her family. When the time came, all went as planned. Everyone in the shack was fast asleep, her father's snores reverberating in the confined space. When Hanna eased away from her, Britta whimpered and stirred but settled back into sleep.

Alvar was still sleeping in the wagon. Outside, Hanna stole close enough to check on him. His eyes were closed, his breathing deep and even.

"Alvar," she whispered, testing him. "Alvar, wake up."

For a moment, she held her breath. But he didn't stir.

Heart drumming, she turned away and raced to the shed. The ground was rough beneath the soles of her bare feet.

Finding her shoes and putting them on would have increased the risk.

Nellie, the mare, was dozing in her stall. She didn't fight the bridle as Hanna slipped it over her head, maneuvered the bit into her mouth, and secured the buckles. Mounting without a saddle gave her a moment's pause. But with the help of an empty bucket, which she turned upside down and used as a step, she managed to scramble onto the mare's back.

Hanna took a moment to catch her breath. She was about to betray every value her parents had instilled in her. But she was answering the call of her heart. How could that be wrong?

For the first few minutes she rode at a quiet walk. Only after her home was well out of hearing did she nudge the mare to a trot. The moon was nearly full, silvering the pale grass and illuminating the wagon tracks that led to another wheat farming settlement a few miles away. The warm August wind streamed through her hair, which she'd left loose tonight instead of braiding it for sleep as she usually did.

As she'd told Mason, she knew where to meet him. It was where this wagon trail crossed another one. A long-dead tree, with gnarled limbs that stuck out like arms and crude wooden direction signs nailed to it, marked the spot. It was just a short ride from her home. Still, she couldn't help wondering why Mason would choose such an isolated setting— maybe because it was private, with no homes, no farms, no barking dogs. For a secret rendezvous, it was probably a sensible choice.

She was thinking about Mason, his arms around her, his kisses setting her on fire, when a chilling thought struck her.

What if he didn't come?

What if she found herself alone at the crossroads, waiting for a man who, for whatever reason, wouldn't be coming to meet her? She remembered the cowboys who would have raped her if Blake Dollarhide hadn't happened along. Were they really gone? Could there be others like them prowling in the dark? If anything were to go wrong this time, Blake wouldn't be there to save her.

Strange that she should think of Blake at a time like this.

But her fears fled as she saw the familiar outline of Mason's buggy silhouetted hood-up against the moonlit sky. As she rode closer, she could see Mason, standing next to it. She halted the mare a few feet from the buggy, dropped the reins, slipped to the ground, and ran to his open arms.

He caught her against him, pressing her so close that she could feel his shirt buttons through her nightgown and shift. "Thank God you're here." His breath stirred her hair. "I was afraid you might not come."

"Nothing could have kept me away." She gazed up at him, feeling beautiful and wild. It was hard to believe that this elegant man, who could probably have any woman he wanted, had chosen her, a poor farm girl with nothing to offer except her heart.

"Kiss me," she whispered, stretching on tiptoe.

His mouth came down on hers, hungry and possessive, tongue thrusting and seeking. His hands roamed her body, stroking her breasts and hips through the thin fabric, then finding their way beneath her shift to touch her skin.

She gasped as his palm slid up her spine, rounding the curve of her waist. Moving upward, he traced the edge of her breast with a fingertip. The ache that rose from the depths of her body was even more powerful than she remembered. But there was fear, too. No man had ever touched her like this— in ways that only a husband should touch her. This couldn't be right.

"Mason—" She resisted slightly, pushing herself away.

His hand remained where it was. "You're so beautiful, Hanna." His breathing had roughened. "You're a goddess. I want to worship every part of you."

His palm captured her breast, stroking the nipple until it shrank and hardened like a berry. Waves of sweet-hot sensation coursed through her body. An inner voice whispered a warning. But the words were drowned out by the pounding of her heart. She was burning like a prairie fire, out of control.

Muttering something she only half heard, he scooped her up in his arms and carried her to the buggy. As he laid her on the wide seat and fumbled with his belt, a sudden awareness jolted her. This was what he'd meant to do all along.

"Mason—" She began to struggle. "I thought we were only going to kiss—not this—"

He leaned over her, his face darkened by shadow. "It's all right, Hanna. When two people love each other, this is what they do. It'll be wonderful, you'll see."

"But—"

His kiss muffled the rest of her words, his tongue thrusting deep, his breath hot against her flesh as he pushed between her legs, giving her no chance to resist. Hanna felt his thrust go hard and deep. When he broke through, it hurt so much that she cried out.

He chuckled. "There, sweetness, it's all right. The worst is over. You've just become a woman. Now the fun can start."

But the raw pain continued, hurting every time he pushed into her. And the pain was more than just physical. By the time he grunted, moaned, and pulled away, she was in tears. What had she done?

He leaned over and kissed her again, tenderly this time. "I'm sorry if it hurt, dearest. The next time will be better, I promise. I love you, Hanna. But right now it's time to get you home before you're missed."

Mason had to help her onto the mare. She rode away without looking back, wet, sore, and blazing with shame. She should have known that Mason Dollarhide only wanted one thing. But silly, romantic fool that she was, she had let him reel her in like a hooked fish, with pretty words and kisses. She'd learned her lesson, but she'd paid a terrible price for it. She felt used. And the gift she'd saved to give her husband on their wedding night was gone forever.

Furious with herself, she dug her heels into the mare's sides and rode home at a gallop. Only as she sighted the homestead, silent and undisturbed in the moonlight, did she slow to a walk.

At the edge of the yard, she dropped to the ground and led the mare into the shed. The two draft horses were dozing. They nickered softly as Hanna removed the bridle and loosed the mare into her stall.

Turning away, she released her breath in a broken exhalation. At least she'd made it home safely, without waking her family. All she had to do now was rinse her legs and face at the water barrel and steal into the house. If anyone woke up then, she could tell them she'd gone to the privy.

"Where have you been, Hanna?" Alvar stepped out of the shadows, startling her. His gaze took in her disheveled hair, her tear-streaked face, and the way her nightgown hung off one shoulder. "I don't want to get you in trouble. I promise I won't tell our parents. But whatever's happened, don't think you have to carry it alone."

As she gazed up at him, reading the concern and brotherly love in his face, something broke loose inside her.

"Oh, Alvar, I've been such a fool!" She collapsed, weeping, against his chest.

By the first week of September, the mornings had taken on a chill. On the ranches, the fall roundup had begun. Cowhands who'd hung around town complaining about the lack of work were employed once more, rounding up cattle on the ranges, sorting them, and branding any that had been missed last spring or had shown up as strays. Cattle to be sold would be herded to the loading pens in Miles City, then prodded up chutes and into railroad cars bound for the Chicago stockyards.

There was other activity as well. The rush to get shanties and outbuildings fortified and construction done before cold weather set in had spawned an urgent demand for lumber. The crew at the sawmill was working from first light until dusk. In anticipation, Blake had ordered extra wagonloads of logs brought in and one more rail shipment of the bigger trees. Customers were hauling off the finished green boards almost as soon as they were cut. The premium cured lumber had long since sold out.

The business was doing so well that Blake planned to give his workers a handsome bonus at the end of the season, which would come when snow and cold slowed the demand for lumber and made any outdoor work an ordeal. If this fall's weather was typical, he figured they had at least a month of good weather remaining. He planned to make the time profitable.

Needing a break, he wandered out of the long, open-sided shed that covered the saw workings and the finished lumber, and into the open yard where the uncut logs were stacked. The morning was clear and bright. Overhead, a flock of geese in a V formation winged south, their cries tinged with a strange sadness.

On the open pastureland that was part of the Dollarhide Ranch, the roundup was taking place, with Blake's father in charge. Until this year, Blake had been there to help. But the sawmill had become a full-time job, and he couldn't be in two places at once. Joe Dollarhide wasn't as young as he'd once been, and his injured leg was still giving him pain, especially when he sat a horse. But he had a good crew of men who knew what to do. They would look out for him and make sure the work got done, Blake told himself.

A shout broke into his thoughts. "Boss! You'd better come quick!"

As Blake turned in the direction of the voice, he realized that he could no longer hear the saw. Racing back under the shed, he saw that something was wrong with the large log that was going through the blades. At some time in the past, an iron bar had been hammered partway into the tree— maybe to anchor a rope or tool. The saw blade had struck the bar at an angle, causing the log to splinter. The teeth of the lower blade were bent, but that was the least of Blake's concerns. A man lay bleeding on the ground next to the splintered log. A shard of wood had been driven through his trousers and into his lower leg.

It was Alvar.

Alvar's teeth were clenched against what must have been excruciating pain. Blood was oozing through his trousers where the wood had penetrated. He needed urgent help. But if the wood were simply pulled out, he could bleed to death. There was a new doctor in town, but he was apt to be out making calls. There was almost no chance of finding him and getting him here in time. Only one other person would know what to do—Blake's mother, Sarah.

"Get him as comfortable as you can. Give him whiskey for the pain—Garrity should have some. I'm going for help." Blake sprang onto his horse and set off at a gallop, out the front gate of the mill yard and up the road to the house.

Blake's mother had never made it to medical school. But before Blake's birth, she'd assisted her great-uncle, a doctor in Ogallala, Nebraska. The old man had taught her everything he knew. Although she didn't have access to the more recent tools and medicines, she had the skills of a trained doctor coupled with a woman's sensitivity. She still offered her services to her neighbors, especially as a midwife.

At the foot of the front steps, Blake vaulted off his horse and rushed inside the house. Kristin met him in the entry. "What is it?" she demanded.

"A man's hurt at the mill. We need Mother to come."

Kristin's eyes widened in dismay. "She's not here. She went to some kind of women's meeting in town. She said she might stay for lunch."

"What about you? I know you've been reading those old medical books of hers."

"Yes, but I've never—"

"You have to come. You're all we've got. Did she leave her medical bag?"

"I'll get it." She raced into the next room and came back with the black leather doctor's bag that Sarah had inherited from her great-uncle, along with a bundle of muslin wrapping strips in case they were needed.

"You'll ride with me. Come on." They hurried outside. Blake mounted and pulled her up behind him. She gripped his waist with one arm, clutching her burdens with the other, as he kicked the horse to a gallop.

Kristin had read every page of every medical book in her mother's well-thumbed collection. True, the books were outdated, but the human body and its functions didn't change. She had plenty of information in her head. But would it be enough?

As they flew down the winding road, raising their voices to be heard, what she learned about the injured man only gave weight to her worries. She'd doctored a few animals on the ranch, and even helped her mother deliver twin babies. But *this?* If she didn't do everything right—or even if she did—the man could bleed to death or lose his leg from infection.

Kristin offered up a silent prayer as the horse swung into the sawmill yard. As it jerked to a halt, she slid down the horse's flank to the ground. Clutching the bag and the wrappings, she raced for the open shed, where the small crowd of workers showed where she would find the wounded man.

Her heart dropped as she saw him.

Blake had mentioned that he was lying on the ground near the saw. But now he'd been moved onto a ragged blanket, in an open space with more light. His right trouser leg was soaked in blood. A splintered shaft of wood, as thick as Kristin's middle finger, protruded from the outer calf of his leg. Someone had tried to stanch the blood with a dirt-stained towel, but with the splinter sticking out of the wound, there was no way to apply pressure.

Kneeling, she bent over the injured man and looked into his face. He was surprisingly young, not much older than

Kristin herself, with hair the color of ripe wheat and the clearest, bluest eyes she had ever seen. His face was gray-white and beaded with sweat, his jaw clenched with the effort of keeping silent.

"Damn it, didn't anybody give him whiskey, like I told you to?" Blake had come in behind her.

"We couldn't find none," one of the men said. "Garrity was fresh out."

"It's all right," Kristin said. "There should be some laudanum in the bag. That'll help with the pain." She fumbled in her mother's doctor bag, silently praying the small brown glass bottle wouldn't be empty. Finding it, she held it up to the light. It was less than a quarter full. Her heart sank. Why hadn't she checked for more at the house?

She glanced up at Blake. "What's his name?"

"Alvar. He's one of the drylanders."

Kristin unstopped the bottle and slipped a hand under his head to raise it. "Alvar, my name is Kristin. I'm going to give you something for the pain before I treat your leg. Just take a sip."

"Y—you're a doctor?" He spoke between ragged breaths.

"Not quite. But I'm all you've got."

She tilted the bottle to his lips. Would there be enough laudanum to dull the pain? One way or the other, she would have no choice except to go ahead with the procedure.

He took it all in one sip. While she waited for the laudanum to take effect, Blake brought her a basin of water and a bar of soap. She washed her hands and shook them dry. The tools in the bag had been sterilized. But her hands could also carry germs into the wound.

Struggling to remember what she'd seen her mother do, Kristin laid the instruments she'd need on a small tray and put the wrappings nearby. With scissors, she cut away the blood-soaked fabric of his trousers below the knee. The full sight of his injury, the shard of wood sticking out of the purpled flesh, oozing blood, made her feel weak.

The young man's eyes were open. His breathing was still

ragged. There was no way to tell whether the laudanum had taken effect. But she couldn't delay any longer.

"Are you still in pain?" she asked him.

He spoke through clenched teeth. "Just go ahead and do it."

Picking up a pair of forceps, she stared down at the awful wound.

Please God, I don't even know how to start. What if I kill him? Please, please help me.

"Excuse me, miss, but could you use some advice from an old soldier?"

Startled by a gravelly voice on her left, she looked up. "Mr. Garrity? What is it you need?"

"This ain't about what I need." The grizzled old man gave her a knowing look. Kristin knew he'd lost a leg in the Indian wars and that he served as caretaker at the sawmill, but she'd barely spoken two words with him until now.

"I was a corpsman back in the army," he said. "I've pulled out more arrows and dug out more bullets than you could count in a month of Sundays. These old hands ain't steady enough to do much anymore. But if it would help, I could try and talk you through this."

"Oh, yes, please!" If the old man had sprouted wings and a halo, Kristin couldn't have been more grateful. She glanced up at Blake, who'd shooed the workers back to give her more light and space. "Get him a chair so he can sit next to me."

Blake stepped away and was back in a moment with a wooden chair. Garrity eased the weight off his crutch and settled onto it. He smelled of bacon, horses, and tobacco smoke. "This is one fine lad you've got here," he said. "I don't want him endin' up like me. You'll need this."

He reached into his ancient buckskin jacket and pulled out a knife, which he slid out of its leather sheath. Reaching out to Alvar, he thrust the sheath between the young man's teeth. "When it gets to hurtin', and it will, bite down on this. Hear?"

Alvar nodded. His eyes were half-closed, his chiseled

features beaded with sweat and rigid with pain. His fists were clenched at his sides. There must not have been enough laudanum in that bottle to give him much ease. But she couldn't wait any longer for the drug to take effect.

She'd hoped to pick out the splintered wood with forceps, but the piece was solid. It would have to be pulled out all at once.

She took a moment to swab the area around the wound with alcohol. Then she met the old man's eyes in a silent plea for his help. He nodded and spoke.

"Take a look at the angle of that splinter. Try to guess how deep it is. You pull with the angle, straight and hard and fast. Just do it. Once it's out, you've got seconds to stop the bleeding, so have something handy to sop up the blood and pinch off any vessels."

Clamps. She had two small ones on the tray. She could only hope she wouldn't need them. And the muslin wrappings were close by.

The splinter appeared to have gone in almost to the bone. With Blake holding Alvar's shoulders and another man bracing the leg, she positioned herself in a spot where she could pull straight back. Her heart was pounding. Drops of sweat streamed down her face. She noticed that Garrity was clasping one of Alvar's hands.

She gripped the splinter with both hands. "Now." Bracing, she pulled back with every ounce of her strength.

CHAPTER 9

*A*LVAR OPENED HIS EYES. FOR A MOMENT HE LAY STILL, staring up at the sturdy beams that supported the ceiling above him. His leg still throbbed—he remembered the accident, though not clearly. What surprised him was that the rest of his body was cushioned in softness. After a lifetime of sleeping on hard surfaces, the feeling was almost unearthly.

Where was he?

"So you're awake." An angel's face bent over him—violet eyes, edged with long, black lashes, creamy skin, framed by dark curls. Alvar searched his awakening memory—yes, she'd doctored his leg. At the time, he'd been in too much pain to notice how pretty she was.

He found his voice. "Where am I?"

"In our house—in my brother Mason's room, but that's all right because he doesn't stay here anymore."

When he looked puzzled, she continued. "My mother showed up after I'd finished bandaging your leg. Once she heard what had happened, she thought it best that we take you home and keep you here for a day or two.

"My mother's the real doctor in the family," she added. "After we brought you here, she disinfected your wound, stitched it up, and changed the dressing."

He shook his head. "I don't remember any of that."

"You wouldn't. You fainted from the pain when I pulled that splinter out of your leg. Before we moved you up here on the cart, my mother gave you more laudanum. You've been sleeping it off since then."

He glanced at the window. The angle of the light coming through the glass told him it was almost sundown. "My family—" He struggled to sit up as the realization hit him. "They'll be worried sick if I don't come home."

She put a light hand on his shoulder to ease him back. "It'll be all right. My brother's gone to tell them what happened. He should be getting there about now." She stood looking down at him, her face luminous in the rays of the fading sun. "I'll bet you're hungry. Would you like some soup and maybe a sandwich? It'll help you get your strength back."

"If it's not too much trouble." He really was hungry.

"No trouble at all. And I think we might have some leftover oatmeal cookies. I'll be right back." She flitted out the door.

Alvar settled back onto the pillow, feeling strangely out of place. The grand house, which he'd only seen from a distance until now, the cushiony bed, the enchanting girl—it had been generous of the Dollarhides to take him in. But his being here wasn't a good idea. It would only serve to make him see how other people lived—and to desire things he had no right to want.

A blazing sunset cast its glow over the ripened wheat fields as Blake sighted the Anderson homestead—the low-slung tar paper-covered shanty, the nearby shed that sheltered the horses and wagon, and the chicken coop that looked as if it could be blown away in a high wind.

Come winter, they were going to need a proper door to keep out the cold, a roof that could bear the weight of heavy snow, and some kind of barrier on the shed to protect their animals. He would mention the need to Lars. And when Alvar went home, he would send the boy with a wagonload of spare wood, in the hope that the big, stubborn Swede wouldn't be too proud to accept it.

He'd never meant to take the Anderson family under his wing. But after rescuing Hanna and hiring her brother to work at the mill, it seemed natural to be concerned about all of them. They were so ill prepared for this wild country where survival could never be taken for granted, and any life could be snuffed out like the flame of a candle.

They had seen him coming. The younger children, who'd been outside, were waving. One of them ran into the house. Seconds later, Lars, Inga, and Hanna came rushing outside. They would already be braced for bad news about Alvar. Why else would Blake have come here?

As he rode into the yard and dismounted, Lars strode out to meet him. "Has something happened to my son?" he demanded. "I told him that job was a bad idea. He should have listened. If he has been killed—" He loomed over Blake as if ready to strike him down.

"Alvar's all right," Blake said. "But there was an accident that gashed his leg. He'll recover and be fine, but my mother wanted to keep him at the house for a day or two to make sure he was healing all right."

"He belongs at home," Lars said. "Fool boy, I should not have let him go to that dangerous place. He doesn't know his own mind."

"Alvar isn't a boy, Papa." It was Hanna who stepped forward and spoke up. "He's a man. He made a choice to help our family in his own way. You should accept that choice, just as you accept the money he brings home."

"Hanna!" Inga's face had gone pale. "How dare you speak to your father in such a way?"

"Because it's the truth. Since Alvar isn't here to speak for himself, I will speak for him. He doesn't deserve to be called a foolish boy. He deserves your respect and your gratitude."

Blake had paid Hanna scant attention when he'd ridden in. Now, looking at her, he sensed that something had changed. Her air of childlike innocence had faded, to be replaced by a sharpness he'd never seen before. She was like a young hawk—fierce and defiant, as if a current of anger were flowing through her slender body.

"But you say that Alvar will be all right?" Inga had stepped in to defuse the tension between her daughter and her husband. "That's what is really important. Isn't it, Lars?"

Lars sighed. "Yes, I suppose it is. When will he be coming home?"

"I'd say late tomorrow or the next day. My mother has taken good care of him. But she wants to make sure there's no infection before he leaves."

"So when will he be able to work again?" Lars had changed his tune.

"He won't be strong enough to work at the mill until his wound is healed. But he should be able to do some light work around here." Blake paused, hoping Lars wouldn't resist what he was about to say. "Your house won't hold up to winter weather without some reinforcement. I'll be sending a load of spare lumber with Alvar when he goes home. You can use it to shore up the walls and roof and make a solid door. The snow and wind will blow right through that hide you've got nailed over the doorway. And you'll want to put a front on the shed to protect your animals."

"I hear there are wolves that come in the winter." The pitch of Inga's voice betrayed her fear. "Back in Sweden, wolves killed a boy from our village."

"That's been known to happen here in Montana. Mostly the wolves are afraid of people. But they'll take animals and any stored food they can get to. And if they're desperate enough . . ." Blake trailed the words off, letting the silence speak for itself. He wanted to make sure these people understood the importance of fortifying their home for the winter.

"I have a gun and I know how to use it," Lars said. "You can keep your wood. We'll buy what little we need. We don't accept charity."

Blake shook his head. "I had a feeling you'd say that, Lars. But think about your family. Which is worth more? Seeing them warm and safe, or nursing your blasted pride?"

Inga laid a hand on her husband's arm. "Please, Lars, take the wood. What we don't use, we can share with our friends."

The big man's chest rose and fell as he sighed. "I see I am outvoted here. Very well. But I won't be beholden to any man. Next week we'll be harvesting the wheat. When I get the money for my crop, I will pay you for every stick of that wood."

"We can talk about that when the time comes," Blake said. "For now, just take the wood."

Lars nodded in slow acquiescence. "Since you have come all this way, would you do us the honor of sharing our supper?"

Blake remembered the time Inga had apologized for not inviting him to lunch. Maybe it was up to her husband to extend an invitation. He hadn't planned on staying long, but Lars might take his refusal as an insult. "I'd be happy to join you," he said.

"It's almost ready." Inga, recovering from her surprise, began giving orders. "Axel, see to Mr. Dollarhide's horse. Britta, dip some fresh water in the basin by the barrel. Gerda, you come with me and help set the table. Hanna, I need you to tend the stove."

Blake and Lars were left alone.

"You have a fine family, Mr. Anderson," Blake said, making talk to fill the silence. "I've been impressed with Alvar. He's a smart young man. Given an education, he could go far. I'd even be willing to see that he gets some help with schooling."

"An education?" A note of anger had crept into the big man's voice. "Alvar is my son. When I am gone, he and his brother will work this land and raise their families here. That is my legacy, my dream for them. An education would only put wild ideas into Alvar's head. He's got too many of those already. Even working at your sawmill has made him restless. Maybe when he comes home, he should stay here and not go back."

"And what about your girls?"

He shrugged. "They will get married, of course, and go with their husbands. Their one duty to our family is to marry with honor."

Blake had been about to mention that his sister planned to become a doctor. He decided to hold his tongue.

"Hanna was going to marry Ulli Swenson," Lars continued. "He was well-off. He would have taken good care of her. But then, you know what happened."

"Yes, I know." The thought of that senseless tragedy still sickened Blake—as did knowing that the men who'd caused it were still free.

"At least Ulli didn't lose a son," Lars said. "A girl, that is sad enough, but a boy . . ." He shrugged, leaving Blake at a loss for words.

A call to supper broke the awkward moment. Blake followed his host into the house and joined the family at a table made of rough planks and covered with an embroidered linen cloth that must've been a family treasure.

A lantern on a hook above the table lent light to the dark space inside the tar paper home. Out of politeness, Blake avoided too much looking around, but he could see that every inch of space was put to use. Clothes and other items hung from nails driven into the supports. Chests and boxes lined the walls and served as extra seating. The place was remarkably neat and clean, the children well-groomed and well-mannered. His admiration grew for the work-worn woman who sat across the table, ladling a savory stew of carrots, potatoes, and some kind of meat onto his plate next to a thick slice of fresh bread.

After Axel's blessing on the food, they began to eat. There was a minimum of talk as was the custom. In the stillness,

Blake found his gaze lingering on Hanna. She sat with her eyes lowered as the lantern light gleamed on her pale gold hair, casting her face in shadow. She'd said nothing since her early outburst when her father had criticized Alvar's working. Maybe her mother had scolded her about it in the house.

But no, it had to be more than that. She'd changed since the last time he'd seen her in town, as if a shadow had been cast over her. She stared down at her plate, toying with the small amount of food she'd taken and never once glancing up to meet his eyes.

What's wrong, Hanna? Why won't you look at me? Is something the matter?

Maybe he should ask Alvar about her. But no, that would be out of line. Hanna's troubles, whatever they might be, were none of his business. She was a young girl from a traditional family. Any show of friendship or concern on his part might be misread as improper.

When the meal was finished, he thanked Lars and Inga for their hospitality and took his leave. As he mounted up and rode out of the gate, his anxious eyes scanned the yard for Hanna. She was nowhere to be seen.

But as he rode home through the deepening twilight with crickets singing in the prairie grass and a full moon rising over the mountains, her image lingered in his memory—from her fiery defense of her brother to her withdrawn silence over supper. He pictured her as he'd seen her tonight, sitting across from him like a wounded Madonna, the light making a halo of her golden hair. She was beautiful, defiant, and visibly unhappy—and there was nothing he could do for her.

But at least he could be relieved that she hadn't married Ulli Swenson.

By the time Blake arrived home, the house was dark except for a light in the upstairs window of the room where his mother had settled Alvar. Was everything all right? Could Alvar's condition have worsened?

After putting his horse away, he entered the quiet house

and ascended the familiar stairs in the dark. The door to his parents' bedroom was closed and there was no light from underneath. They were most likely asleep by now.

The door to Alvar's room stood ajar, casting a shaft of flickering light into the hallway. As he came closer, he heard the sound of chatting voices and laughter. He opened the door to see Kristin sitting on a chair next to Alvar's bed.

As Blake stepped into the room, his sister turned toward him with a guilty look, as if knowing she shouldn't be alone with a young man, in his room, at that late hour. But Blake couldn't help noticing how her eyes sparkled.

"We were just talking," she said. "Alvar was telling me about New York and what it was like to grow up there. He and his father worked on the docks, unloading cargo from all over the world. And there was a big library where he could read any book he wanted. Doesn't that sound wonderful? I'm going to ask Mother if he can borrow a few of her books. I know he'd take good care of them."

"It's late, Kristin. Time you were in bed," Blake said, playing the protective older brother.

"Oh, I know." Kristin stood. "I'll see you in the morning, Alvar. If you can't come down to the kitchen, I'll bring you some breakfast."

She floated out of the room, her eyes bright, her color high. Left alone with Alvar, Blake fixed him with a stern look that said more than words.

"I'm sorry, sir. We got talking and didn't realize how much time had passed. It won't happen again." The color rose in Alvar's face as he added, "Your sister's a nice girl, maybe the nicest girl I've ever met. But I would never presume to think I might be worthy of her."

Blake had to smile at the boy's formal speech, which probably came from some book he'd read. He took the chair next to the bed. "It's not that, Alvar. I'm guessing that Kristin told you she wants to become a doctor. She'll be leaving for school in a few months, as soon as the arrangements can be made, and she'll be gone for a long time, most likely for years. Once she finishes her training, she might never come back to Blue Moon."

"Yes, she told me. I think it's great that a woman can do such things. I only wish that Hanna—" Breaking off, he shook his head. "Never mind. Just know that I wish Kristin nothing but the best."

"Fine. But here's what you need to understand," Blake said. "I think I can speak for my parents when I say that you're welcome to be friends with Kristin. But if things were to go beyond friendship, you could both end up hurt. Do you understand?"

As he spoke, Blake couldn't help thinking of his own mother. If she hadn't fallen in love with Joe Dollarhide, who'd ridden off and unknowingly left her pregnant, she would be a doctor now. But the family she loved wouldn't exist.

Sarah had always claimed that she had no regrets. But she would never wish the same fate for her daughter. She was determined that nothing—including romance—be allowed to stand between Kristin and her dream.

"I do understand." Alvar's reply pulled his thoughts back to the present. "There's no need to worry. Kristin and I are friends. But we won't be seeing much of each other after I leave here and go home."

"That could happen as soon as tomorrow," Blake said. "Your family is anxious to have you back. I promised them some wood to shore up their house and shed for winter. Once my mother makes sure your leg is healing, I'll load up a wagon and send Garrity with you to drive it back here. You can take the mare along and keep it until you're ready to work again."

"I'll be back as soon as I can," Alvar said. "And thank you for being so kind to my family. I only wish we had a way to repay you."

"No need for that. But I had to talk your father into taking the wood. He's a proud man. And a stubborn man."

"Stubborn. Right. That's the word for him. He's determined to make me into a wheat farmer." Alvar shook his blond head. "I understand that it's been his dream to have his own land and pass it down to his sons. But spending my life on that farm would be like a prison sentence. Axel can have it all."

"I'd help you if I could," Blake said. "But it's not my place to go against your father's wishes."

"I know," Alvar said. "Any changes in my future will be up to me."

"What about your sisters?" As soon as he'd voiced the question, Blake knew that he was really asking about Hanna.

"It's even worse for them. Hanna's so bright and so hungry to learn. I know she'd like to go to school, maybe become a teacher. The same goes for Britta. And Gerda—she's a little firecracker. But all Papa wants to do is marry them off. He and Mama were devastated when Hanna didn't wed Ulli. It didn't matter that she didn't love him. It was all for the sake of the family. And now . . ." His words trailed off. A shadow seemed to pass across his face. "Never mind. You must be tired, and I'm keeping you awake."

Blake stood, stretching his legs. He'd had a long day and he was worn out. But tonight, the restlessness that flowed through his body threatened to keep him awake for hours. "Do you want me to put out the lamp?" he asked.

"No, leave it, thanks." Alvar picked up a thick book from the nightstand. "I've been asleep most of the day. And tonight Kristin brought me this book—*Huckleberry Finn*, by Mark Twain. I can't wait to start reading it."

"You'll enjoy the book. It's a great story. But get some sleep, too. You need to heal." Blake closed the door behind him, wandered back downstairs and out onto the broad front porch.

The full moon rode the peak of the sky, its golden disk drifting among scattered clouds that cast shadows over the grassland below. From where he stood at the rail, Blake could see beyond the Dollarhide spread to the railroad, and from there to the town, whose buildings lay like a scattering of pebbles on the horizon. Looking north, he could make out the wheat farms, edging on the borders of the Calder ranch.

Joe Dollarhide had chosen the site of his home and built this porch for the view it commanded. Standing here, gazing out over the slumbering countryside, it was easy enough to feel a sense of peace. But Blake knew that peace was only an illusion. The land was seething with conflict and change, with every day bringing new dangers and new challenges.

A raw wind swept in from the west carrying a chill, like a warning of the winter to come. Over the past few years Blake had felt like a rock in a river—the good son and brother, the responsible manager, the neutral friend, standing fast amid the forces that clashed around him. But a voice in the wind seemed to whisper that things were about to change—things he'd be powerless to prevent.

Clouds had drifted across the moon, casting the land in shadow. Standing in the darkness, hearing the distant wail of a coyote, Blake felt a strange premonition—a sense that the months ahead would try him as he'd never been tried in his life.

On Friday, two days after his accident, Alvar left for home. Sarah had replaced the dressing on his leg and declared that the wound was healing well. With a warning to keep it wrapped and clean, she saw him mounted and off down the road to the sawmill, from where he would take the wagonload of wood back to his family. With him, he carried a bundle that held extra wrappings for his wound, a small tin of salve, and the *Huckleberry Finn* volume he'd been allowed to borrow.

Riding alongside him, Blake couldn't help noticing how Alvar kept glancing back toward the house, where Kristin stood at the porch rail, holding him with her gaze until he rounded the bend and vanished from her sight. Any fool could see that the two young people had fallen in love, which didn't bode well any way it might be viewed. The difference in their stations, her school and career plans, his father's determination to keep him at home, and the enmity between ranchers and farmers combined into a sure recipe for disaster.

Blake knew better than to waste his breath offering more advice. He could only hope that some time apart would bring the two young people to their senses.

The earsplitting whine of steel cutting into wood grew louder as they neared the mill. The aroma of fresh sawdust drifted on the air. After the accident that had injured Alvar, Blake had sent the damaged blade to a blacksmith in town and installed a spare in its place so the work could go on.

After stacking a wagon with surplus boards and helping Garrity hitch up the team, he saw Alvar off, riding the bench next to the old man, with his borrowed mare tied alongside. After watching the wagon grow small with distance, he turned away and put his mind to other things.

The blacksmith had promised to have the blade repaired by this afternoon. Since Blake had other business in town and needed some items from the hardware store, he'd made plans to pick up the heavy blade and bring it back on the mill's two-wheeled flatbed cart. If things were going smoothly at the mill, he could go later today. Meanwhile, with Alvar gone, the crew was shorthanded. To get the current lumber orders out on time, he would need to roll up his sleeves and pitch in to help.

By midafternoon, the week's current orders were filled. Garrity had returned with the wagon, along with the bottle of cheap whiskey he'd bought on his way through town. With the next big log shipment not due until Monday, Blake paid his crew and sent them home. That done, he washed up at the pump and set out for Blue Moon.

As he followed the road to town, with a single horse pulling the flatbed cart, Blake's mind was on business. The past few months had been the most profitable ever for the Dollarhide Lumber Company. As long as Blue Moon continued to grow and prosper, the outlook for next spring would be even brighter. Those drylanders who reaped a crop this fall and survived the winter would be keen to build sturdy, comfortable homes, along with sheds for their farming equipment and barns for their animals. New businesses moving in would need lumber, too.

The sawmill was already running at capacity. To meet the demands of the growing community, Blake would need to install a second saw and hire a crew to run it—maybe add a couple more delivery wagons and another team of horses as well. A more reliable supply of prime logs would also be needed. It might be possible to lease the timber rights to a tract of land and hire his own crews to cut and haul the logs.

But he was letting his ambition get ahead of him now. Getting a second saw was a sound idea. He'd be smart to order it early, to have it ready for operation in the spring. But first he needed to slow down and make plans. Those plans would include talking everything over with his father.

The new saw, along with the boiler, the rails, and other hardware, as well as adding on to the work shed, wouldn't come cheap. He might want to talk to the bank about a loan. Dollarhide credit was golden. But the idea of asking Doyle Petit for money left a bad taste in Blake's mouth. Maybe if Mason were there things would be different. But Mason was little more than a front man for the bank. Blake had yet to catch his brother at work. He'd be better off dealing with the bank in Miles City.

Blake put his ideas on hold as he reached the bustling main street of Blue Moon and set about his errands. At the blacksmith's, he inspected the repair, paid for the work, and, with help, loaded the heavy circular blade onto the cart and lashed it into place. At the new hardware store, he bought some spare bolts for the saw and half a gallon of machine oil.

He was looking forward to wetting his dry throat in the

saloon when he remembered that his father had mentioned needing a couple of salt blocks for the south pasture. There should be some in the general store. If he didn't get them now, he'd be apt to forget later on.

Leaving his purchases on the cart outside the hardware store, he crossed the busy street, sidestepping buggies and wagons, and entered the general store. Inside, the place was crowded with shoppers, but he didn't plan to wait in line.

"Put a couple of salt blocks on our account and point me to them, Ollie," he told the proprietor. "I'll just carry them out."

"Back there in the far corner, Mr. Dollarhide. Two, you say?"

"That's right." Blake was already headed in that direction. He could see the blocks of pink rock salt stacked behind a row of shelves. They were solid and heavy. It would take two trips to carry them outside and load them on the cart.

He was bending to lift the first one when he heard a voice behind him—a familiar voice with an appealing note of shyness.

"Hello, Blake. What on earth are you doing back here?"

He straightened and turned around. Ruth Stanton, in a delicate lilac dress, was standing an arm's length away, smiling at him.

He groped for a clever reply and came up empty. "I'm buying rock salt for our cows. The question is what are *you* doing back here? I don't see anything in this corner that would interest a lady like yourself."

"Then you're not looking hard enough." Her smile broadened, showing small, pearl-like teeth set in shell-pink gums. "I saw you going back here and thought I'd take a chance. We haven't talked in a while."

"No, we haven't." As he recalled, the last time he'd seen her had been at the Calders' house, and she'd pretty much ignored him. But he wasn't about to bring that up. If Ruth wanted to be friendly, who was he to complain? "How've you been, Ruth?"

"About the same as usual. My father needed some things in town, so I asked to come along. When he's done with his errands, I'll be meeting him for dinner at the Roadhouse. Until then I'm just passing time. How's your sister?"

"Fine. I don't know if you heard that she wants to study medicine. She's mostly sending off applications for school and waiting to hear back."

"Medicine? My goodness, that's ambitious. But she always was a smart girl." She paused, her sky-blue eyes gazing up at him from beneath golden lashes. "Will you be at the big harvest celebration that's coming up? There'll be dancing."

"I hadn't thought about it, but if you'll promise to save me a dance, I'll do my best to be there." Blake studied her, wondering what was behind this friendliness that bordered on flirtation. Had she fallen out with Webb Calder—maybe lost patience with his attentions to a married woman? Or was she just using him to make Webb jealous? Whatever was going on in her pretty head, he wasn't above taking advantage.

She was Webb's girl. Everybody knew that, including Blake. But she deserved to be treated better. If she'd give him a chance, maybe he could convince her of that. At least he could try. After all, what did he have to lose?

CHAPTER 10

*A*LVAR HAD COME HOME ON FRIDAY. ON MONDAY, THREE McCormick-style reapers, a massive steam-powered thresher, and a crew of rough-looking men to run the machines arrived by rail to harvest the wheat.

Knowing what to expect, the local wheat farmers were waiting with teams of horses ready to tow the machinery out to the fields. They had signed together for a bank loan against this year's crop to pay for a job that only seasoned harvesters with machines could do efficiently.

In the week that followed, the whole farming community was flung into the harvest—the men and big boys driving the horses and loading the bundled sheaves onto wagons to be hauled to the thresher, which would separate the precious kernels from the chaff and funnel them into waiting burlap sacks.

The women and older girls were kept busy cooking an endless supply of food for the hungry men, some of it prepared in home kitchens and brought together for the huge meals. There were breads and biscuits, beans and potatoes, roasts, sandwiches, and stews, pies, cakes, and buckets of coffee—a feast for giants, eaten at long plank tables.

The pace of the work was exhausting, but it was a joyful time—a time to come together as a community, to share and to celebrate the fruits of a long season's backbreaking work.

Hanna moved among the women—their sure hands chopping, stirring, and slicing while they gossiped and chatted. As she carried dishes to the table, she felt isolated from the others, as if she were a stranger who'd wandered into this close-knit group by mistake. A few girls near her own age had formed a giggling cluster—probably talking about boys. They waved and beckoned, inviting Hanna to join them. She shook her head and went on working. There could be no more innocent girl talk for her. In her own mind, at least, her secret sin had set her apart.

Someone handed her a platter of fried pork sausage to carry to the table. The rich, greasy aroma triggered a roiling sensation in her stomach. The September sun was hot, the air hazy with yellow dust from the crushed chaff spat out by the threshing machine, whose deafening bellow could be heard a mile away. The noise, the dust, the heat, and the mélange of food smells were making her head swim. She needed a break, just to sit down and drink some cold water. But she knew her mother would scold her for slacking.

The men ate in shifts. Alvar was in the group just coming off the field, dusty, sweating, and hungry. Over his mother's protests and Hanna's, he had wrapped his injured leg and gone to work with the other men. Hanna was glad to have him nearby. But since he'd returned from his time with the Dollarhides, she sensed a change in him. He was distant and withdrawn, given to long silences in which his thoughts seemed far away.

At first Hanna had blamed herself and the searing confession she'd given him after he'd caught her coming home in the night. But no, the change in Alvar had come about later, after the two days he'd spent in the Dollarhide home. Perhaps seeing how privileged people lived had given him a clear view of his own family's poor circumstances—and sharpened his longing for a life beyond his reach. Whatever the reason, Hanna could sense the restlessness in him, and she was worried.

He'd taken his seat on the bench with the other men and boys. As she placed a pan of fried potatoes on the table, Hanna leaned close to him. "How's your leg?" she asked, making an excuse to speak to him.

"It's fine. No need to fuss over me, Hanna." He looked up at her. "You look tired. Are you all right?"

"I'm fine. Like you." She turned away and headed back toward the makeshift kitchen.

"Hanna!" A girl in the group of friends called to her. "We've been talking about the harvest festival. We're all planning to go. Will you be there, too?"

"Maybe. I might be busy." Hanna hurried on her way. She'd avoided thinking about the harvest celebration in town. Ordinarily she would have been excited to go with her family, show off her new dress, and twirl around the dance floor. But after what had happened with Mason, how could she show up and act as if nothing had changed?

Would Mason be there? If he were to speak to her, or ask her to dance, how would she respond? How could she even bear to look at him? But how would she feel if he ignored her? Would it be a relief, or would it be the crowning humiliation?

"Hanna!" It was her mother's voice. "Stop daydreaming and get this bread on the table!"

Shoving thoughts of Mason to the back of her mind, she murmured an apology and rushed to do her work.

Blake had ridden into Blue Moon to deposit the funds from last week's lumber sales into the business bank account. He'd also set aside some idle time to take the pulse of the town, walk around, get a drink, maybe hear a few rumors. As a businessman who needed to plan ahead, he'd found that it paid to know what folks were thinking.

He'd already noticed that there were few people on the street today. The reason was no mystery. The drylanders were harvesting their wheat. The threshing machine—so noisy that it could be heard even in town—was spewing out chaff, most of it as straw, which would be hauled away and put to use. But the finer particles rose in windblown clouds of yellow dust that spread over the landscape, irritating to the eyes, throats, and nostrils of man and beast alike.

Blake took refuge in the saloon. As he expected, the place was full of cowboys, and nobody was in a good mood. They were grumbling about the dust, the noise, and the drylanders in general. Squeezing into a vacant spot at the bar, he ordered a beer, paid, and stepped back to make room for other customers. The tables were all taken. He was drinking on his feet when he heard his name called.

"Blake Dollarhide. Come take a seat."

He turned. The speaker was Webb Calder. He was sitting at a small corner table with an empty chair tucked under the opposite side.

"Thanks. Don't mind if I do." Masking his surprise, Blake pulled out the chair and sat down. Webb, looking hot and dusty, was partway through a glass of whiskey. Blake sipped his beer and waited for the other man to start the conversation.

"My dad said you came to see him," Webb said.

"That's right. I wanted some help tracking down the bastards who dynamited that house and killed the little girl, before the drylanders caught up with them and started a war."

"And what did he tell you?"

"Pretty much the same as you told me when I asked for your help."

"And look how it all turned out. Nothing happened. The raiders are scattered to the four winds, and the honyockers are reaping their damned wheat." Webb was almost gloating. "So what did you learn from this, Blake?"

"Just this. The next time I need help seeing justice done, I won't bother asking a Calder."

Webb chuckled. "Mark my word, those sodbusters won't last the winter. Come spring, the ones who haven't starved or frozen will be pulling up stakes and selling out—not that their land will be good for much now that they've plowed up all the grass." His gaze narrowed. "Rumor has it you've hired one of them at the sawmill."

"That's right. He's a good worker. I could use another dozen like him."

Webb leaned closer across the table and lowered his voice. "Me, I don't give a damn who works for you. But there are folks who don't like your hiring honyockers—the idea being that if they can get jobs around here, they'll be more likely to stay."

"I can't see that it's anyone else's business," Blake said. "As long as they can do the work, I'll hire whomever I please."

"Blast it, man, this is for your own good. There's talk that you've gone over to their side."

"Thanks for the warning, but I'm not on anybody's side." Blake had heard enough. "As long as I'm here, do you mind if I change the subject? There's something I want to ask you."

Webb shrugged. "Go ahead."

"It's about Ruth."

"You want to know if she's my girl?"

"Yes. Do you have plans? Or is she free to see somebody else, like me?"

"Ruth is a great girl. And I know what my mother expects. But for me, marrying Ruth would feel like marrying my sister. So no, we don't have plans. And yes, she's free. So do your damnedest. Take her off my hands and make her happy. I'll dance at your wedding."

With that, Webb tossed down the rest of his whiskey, rose to his feet, and walked out of the saloon.

Taking his time, Blake finished his beer and did the same

at a more measured pace. By the time he stepped out into the yellow haze, Webb was nowhere in sight. Mounting his horse, Blake headed south, out of town.

If Webb hadn't been sitting right in front of him, Blake probably wouldn't have bothered to ask about Ruth. Anybody with eyes could guess where things stood between them. She was waiting patiently for Webb to come around. And he was burning with lust for another woman.

But maybe she was getting tired of waiting. Maybe her friendliness in the store was a signal that things were about to change.

Was he, himself, in love with her? He could be, Blake thought, if he were to let it happen. She was pretty and smart and gentle. What more could a man want in a woman?

Over the last few weeks he'd harbored a sense that change was coming—he'd assumed that any change would be for the worse, but what if he was wrong? Maybe the upcoming harvest festival would be a turning point, the beginning of something good.

Whatever was coming, all he could do was brace for it and be ready.

The wheat harvest was done—the threshing crew was gone with their machines, the sacks filled, hauled, and weighed at the grain office in Blue Moon. The long-awaited money had been paid to the farmers who'd opened accounts in the bank to keep their riches safe.

When Lars came home and showed his family the bank receipt, his wife gasped. "So much money, Lars! Now we can build a real house, with a floor and glass windows."

But Lars shook his head. "No house yet. This money is for next year's seed and a new plow, and more land if we can find some to buy. This is our family's future, Inga, right here in my hand."

Hanna saw the expression on her mother's face as she turned away. Inga had worked her fingers raw for her family's survival in a tumbledown shack that was barely fit for livestock. Now she would have to make do for another year, if not longer. And the most grueling season, the winter, lay just ahead. Children died in winter.

But Inga spoke no word of displeasure to her husband or showed him the desperate unhappiness in her face. Instead, she walked to the table, sat, and began peeling potatoes for supper. Without a word, Hanna took a seat, picked up a spare knife, and began helping her.

Only the younger girls were animated. "Now we can have the harvest festival!" Britta sang out, seizing Gerda's hands and dancing around the table. "There'll be food and games and music. And dancing—it'll be the best time ever!"

Mason brushed the grass off his trousers, wiped his mouth, and headed down the lane to his waiting buggy. When he had a hankering for a woman and there was no one else available, he could always count on Polly Mae Ferguson. She was a little past her prime but still not bad looking. And the fact that she was married to an old farmer who drank himself to sleep most nights made everything simple. All Polly Mae wanted was a good time, and Mason gave as good as he got.

The waning moon was descending the arc of the sky as he drove homeward. The night was quiet, the air crisp, reminding him that the next time he visited Polly Mae, they might need to take refuge in the hayloft. For now, he felt a pleasant buzz of sexual satisfaction. But Mason was a man who craved variety, and it had been a while since he'd been with sweet little Hanna Anderson.

Her first time hadn't gone as well as he'd hoped. Thinking back, he realized maybe he should've taken things slower. Next time, he'd show her what a skilled lover could do, and maybe teach her a few things she could do for a man. With luck he'd see her at the harvest festival and be able to arrange a rendezvous. He was already looking forward to it.

Whistling a tune, he drove through the ranch gate, stopped outside the stable, and roused the sleeping hired man to take care of his horse. In the house, he tiptoed past the closed door of his mother's room. No doubt Ralph Tomlinson, her foreman, would be in her bed. They'd had the same arrangement for more than twenty years, one that seemed to suit them both.

Ralph was all right. He was nice looking, competent, soft-spoken, and had no problem with taking orders from a woman. But they lived apart on the ranch; and Amelia would never marry him or any other man. Marriage would mean turning over her property and her independence to a husband, something she refused to do.

In his own room, Mason stripped down and fell into bed. He was so deliciously tired that he began to sink into sleep almost as soon as his head touched the pillow. As he drifted off, the last image that faded from his mind was of Hanna lying beneath him, the golden glory of her hair framing her face like the petals of a sunflower.

The harvest festival was held the following Saturday, a day bright with early autumn. On the hillsides, the oak brush and maples had turned a fiery crimson. Higher up, on the mountain slopes, aspen gold contrasted with the dark hues and velvety texture of pines. Ducks and geese, the last of the flocks flying south, strung their long V formations across a clear blue sky.

The celebration would begin in the early afternoon with a buffet, a talent show, and games for the children. A dance would end the day.

Hanna had made up her mind to stay home and avoid the shame of seeing Mason again. She'd pleaded a headache, but her family had overruled her. As she crowded onto the rear wagon seat with Axel and her sisters, all dressed in their best, she cherished one last hope—that the young ones would get tired and want to go home before the dance.

Only Alvar, never one for social gatherings, had gotten away clean. Muttering something about extra work at the lumber mill, he'd saddled his horse and left, no questions asked.

Except for Hanna, the family was in a festive mood. They laughed, joked, and sang the old Swedish nursery songs that Inga had taught them. Even Lars joined in with his big, booming voice. As they neared the town, they could hear accordion music playing a polka. A number of the immigrants were musical, and they'd all been invited to show off their talents.

Hanna scanned the crowd as her father drove down the main street to the area between the school and the bank that was cordoned off for the festival. People were already lining up at the buffet table. Most were farm families, along with a few towns-people, including Sheriff Potter, who was there to make sure there was no drinking or rowdiness. The cowboys and other ranch people would probably show up later for the dance.

There was no sign of Mason. When her eyes searched the crowd and failed to find him, Hanna began to breathe again. Maybe he wouldn't be coming at all. For now, at least, she could relax and try to have a good time. Taking the apple pies she and her mother had made, she carried them to the dessert section of the buffet table, then joined her family in the line.

Not far ahead of them, she could see Lillian and her husband filling their plates. She hadn't seen Lillian since the day of Ulli's daughter's funeral, and they hadn't really talked since the day when Hanna had asked her about being married. It would raise Hanna's spirits to be with her friend again.

But as she waited in line, Hanna couldn't help remembering what had happened during the last two celebrations in town—the fire that had burned the Gilberg place and the terrible explosion that had killed Ulli's little girl.

Were those men really gone? Or were they just out of

sight, waiting for an event like this one, when the farms were unguarded, so they could strike again?

But no one else seemed to be worried. The harvested wheat fields were nothing but stubble. The money from the crops was safe in the bank. It was time for a party.

Shaded by golden leaves that cast dappled shadows on their skin, Kristin and Alvar lay side by side on a blanket under overhanging willows. This small canyon had been Kristin's secret place since she was a little girl. She had never shared it with anyone—except Alvar, the man she loved.

When they were here together, it was all too easy to make the world go away and pretend that nothing mattered except the two of them. But they both knew better. Any chance they found to be together could be for the last time.

When they were kissing and holding each other, it was hard not to go all the way. It was usually Alvar who backed off. Kristin had told him her mother's story, and she knew he was thinking of her future. But she never stopped wishing that, just once, she could love him as her body and her heart yearned to.

She curled toward him, pressing her face against his chest. "I wish we could just run away," she whispered.

"Where would we go?" He nuzzled her dark hair.

"I don't care. Anyplace where we can be together."

"You're going to be a doctor," he said. "If I were to keep that from happening, I'd never forgive myself."

"But what about you?"

"If my father has his way, I'm going to be a Montana wheat farmer. But I'd wait for you. I'd wait forever if I thought there was a chance you'd come back. But I can't ask you to promise that, Kristin."

"No more than I could expect your promise to wait. All we have is now. Just hold me."

His arms tightened around her. As she pressed into him,

trying to memorize the scent and feel of him and the sound of his heart, an autumn breeze swept down the canyon, wrapping them in its chill. "We need to go," Alvar said, releasing her.

Kristin sat up and arranged her rumpled clothes. "I love you," she said, meeting his eyes.

"And I love you. That will have to last us until next time."

They walked to where they'd left their horses. After a last lingering handclasp, they mounted up; he turned away and headed down the canyon. She watched him until he vanished from sight, then swung her horse toward home.

As Blake rode into town, the day was fading into autumn twilight. From the festival up the street his ears caught the sound of music—a pair of fiddles and a banjo playing an old-time toe-tapper. A smile tugged at his lips. He was arriving later than he'd planned. But with luck, Ruth would be at the dance and he'd get to spend some time with her.

Dismounting, he tied his horse to the rail outside the general store and set out from there on foot. He'd come alone. His father had strained his injured leg training an unruly horse and was in some pain. Sarah had elected to stay with him. Kristin had declared she wasn't interested in dancing and vanished into her room.

Blake wouldn't have minded having his family along. But at least if he got a chance to pursue pretty Ruth, he wouldn't have to put up with their questions afterward. He knew that his parents wanted to see him married, and Ruth would be a good choice. But even thinking, let alone talking about her in that way would be jumping the gun—especially if she was still in love with Webb.

Lanterns had been hung from the wagons around the dance floor. The glow lent a softness to the twilight. Stepping into the circle of onlookers, Blake cast his gaze over the dancers and the people standing around the edges of the floor, searching for one special, pretty face. His spirits sank as he realized that Ruth wasn't here. Nor were any of the Calders, including Webb. She would have come with them. Maybe they'd left the party early—Benteen's frail appearance would justify that. Or maybe they hadn't come at all.

Blake had passed Mason's buggy on the way in, so he knew that his brother was here. At first, Blake didn't see him. Then, as the music paused and changed from a two-step to a gentle waltz, he spotted his brother among the dancers. Only as Mason turned to one side did Blake get a full view of his partner. It was Hanna Anderson, and she didn't look happy.

"I've been missing you like crazy, Hanna. My, but you look beautiful in that dress. It matches your blue eyes." Mason smiled down at her, showing his perfect white teeth. His hand clasped the small of her back, pulling her body close—too close—against him.

Hanna had enjoyed dancing with the cowboys, who knew enough to behave like gentlemen. But when Mason had walked in, come straight to her, and asked for a dance with the cockiness of a man used to getting his way, Hanna had gone cold. Any words she'd been prepared to say had dried up in her mouth. A flat, metallic taste had welled in her throat as he took her hand, giving her no chance to refuse without making a scene.

But then, as the music began, she recovered her wits and her voice—and she knew what she had to say to him.

"We need another date," he murmured, his lips almost brushing her ear. "I promise to make it more enjoyable for you than the last time."

"No." She kept her voice low, not wanting to be overheard by people around them. "You took advantage of me once. It's not going to happen again."

He looked startled. Then his mouth twisted in an ugly way. "*I* took advantage of *you*? As I recall, you came to me of your own free will. You encouraged me every step of the way. I thought you wanted me, Hanna. I thought you wanted what we did."

"I was too innocent to understand what you wanted. Now I know better. When I think about how I let you use me, all I feel is shame." She pushed back, resisting his firm clasp. "Now walk me off this floor and leave me. I never want to see your face again."

His grip tightened on the small of her back. "Let's not make a scene for these nice people to watch. Finish this waltz with me. If I can't change your mind, then I'll be a gentleman and do as you ask." He pulled her in hard against him. "You can feel how much I want you, Hanna." His voice was a velvety rasp in her ear. "Come outside and I'll show you how much."

"Let . . . me . . . go!" she muttered, doing her best not to draw attention. "Let me go before I—"

Surprise cut off her words as a tall form loomed behind Mason. A hand settled on his shoulder. A deep, familiar voice spoke. "If you don't mind, brother, I believe it's my turn to dance with the lady."

Mason released his intimate hold on Hanna. "The devil it is. I claimed her for this dance, and I have the right to enjoy all of it."

"I've been watching you. I'd say you lost your right when you crossed the line." Blake kept his tone low, his manner easy. "But this shouldn't be up to you and me. What do you say we let the lady decide?"

He stepped away and held out his hand. With barely a beat of hesitation, Hanna took it and moved to his side.

"So that's how it's to be." Mason was seething. "Fine. Dance with her, Blake. When you're finished, we'll settle this outside." He turned, pushed through the crowd, and stalked away.

Trembling, Hanna gazed up at her rescuer. She'd known Blake Dollarhide as a friend of her family and as Alvar's boss, but this was different. This time she was seeing him as a man—powerful and surprisingly gentle. "We don't have to finish the dance," she said.

"Sure, we do." Blake caught her waist with his free hand and swung her into the swirl of waltzing dancers. He held her as if she were a porcelain doll that might break if he clasped her too tightly. But she didn't have to be close to him to follow his sure, easy steps.

He didn't know she'd been with Mason, Hanna reminded herself. He probably believed her to be as pure and innocent as the day they'd met. He'd called her a lady. What would he call her if he were to learn the truth?

"Thank you for coming to my rescue," she said. "Not that I mean to speak ill of your brother, but I suspect he's accustomed to getting his own way."

"That's the least of it. I'm sorry I didn't warn you about Mason. He can be charming, but he's earned a bad reputation with the ladies. You'd be smart to avoid him in the future."

Good advice, but given too late. She'd learned her lesson about Mason and men like him, but she couldn't undo the past. Never again would she be the girl that Blake believed he was seeing.

"Is your family here?" he asked.

"They've gone home. Axel and Gerda were tired and Papa didn't want Britta at the dance. I'd have gone with them, but my friend Lillian wanted me to stay and keep her company. I'll be riding home with her and her husband. I don't expect they'll be staying much longer."

"Good. I don't like the idea of your wandering around here alone. Some cowboy might get the wrong idea."

She forced herself to smile up at him. He was taller and leaner than Mason, his palms calloused where Mason's were smooth and soft. "You always seem to be protecting me," she said. "Don't you get tired of that?"

"Some things are worth protecting."

Hanna swallowed the lump in her throat. She had no

words for an honest reply. Instead she tried to focus on the tender music of the waltz and the footwork of the dance. But a tingle of awareness grew from where his hand rested against her corseted waist. The subtle scent of his skin stole through her senses. She felt safe in his arms—so safe that she found herself wishing the music would go on all night. But it was already drawing to an end.

The musicians finished the tune and put down their instruments for a break. As the dance floor cleared, Blake gave her his arm and led her toward the spot where Lillian and Stefan waited. "Will you be all right?" he asked, and she knew he was thinking about Mason coming back.

"Yes. My friends should be ready to leave soon." She looked up at him. "Thank you. I owe you a longer dance."

"Another time. Be careful, Hanna. I mean it."

He turned and walked away.

Lingering among the crowd, Blake watched as Hanna left with the Reisners. She looked so grown-up tonight, he thought, and so beautiful with that deep blue dress and her hair tied up with a matching ribbon. Of course, he hadn't told her so. A compliment might have given her the wrong impression. When he'd strode onto the dance floor, he'd been set on rescuing the girl, not courting her. He hoped his manner had made that clear.

But his business wouldn't be finished until he'd confronted Mason.

He waited until Hanna had gone. Then he left the circle of wagons and walked out to where he'd noticed Mason's buggy. He could see Mason's cigarette tip glowing in the shadows. The dressing-down he planned to give his brother was bound to be ill received. But it needed to be done.

As Blake approached, Mason tossed the cigarette to the ground and crushed it under his boot heel. "You were out of line, brother," he said.

Blake stepped closer, keeping his voice low, his instincts alert. Mason had a hair-trigger temper. When it exploded, anything could happen. "You were the one out of line, Mason," he said. "Manhandling that girl on the dance floor, holding her against you like that."

"Hell, she was enjoying it. Believe me, I could tell."

"I saw her face. She was scared. All she wanted was to get away."

"So you rode to her rescue like a knight on a damned white horse." Mason guffawed. "Blake Dollarhide, defender of purity!"

"This isn't funny, Mason. You can't treat an innocent young girl like Hanna the way you might treat one of those dance-hall floozies in Miles City."

"Innocent?" Mason's impudent grin broadened to a smirk. "If that's what you think, I've got news for you, brother. As far as sweet little Hanna is concerned, that ship has already left the dock."

Blake stared at him, feeling as if he'd been kicked in the gut.

"She was all over me," Mason said. "Just begging for it, grinding her hips, grabbing at my crotch. I tell you, man, I couldn't get it into her fast enough."

Blake only punched him once—but it was almost hard enough to break his fist.

CHAPTER 1 1

*T*HE SUN-MELLOWED DAYS OF OCTOBER HAD FLED. NOW A colorless November sky hung over fields of frost-silvered brown stubble.

Above snow-dusted foothills, the peaks were blanketed in white.

Cattle on the ranches clustered for warmth and protection. Horses grew shaggy coats as the days shortened and the cold weather closed in.

Thanks to the wood from the lumber mill, the Anderson shack was as well fortified as the family could make it. A sturdy plank door with a sliding bolt had replaced the cowhide that had hung over the opening. Timbers had been added to the roof to keep it from collapsing under the weight of snow. The single window had a hinged wooden shutter, and a thick layer of straw covered the floor. More straw had been stuffed into every possible crack and opening. On the windward side of the house, an extra layer of tar paper had been added to the inner wall.

But even with a fire in the small iron stove, and layers of

clothing on her body, the warmth was barely enough to keep Hanna's teeth from chattering as she crawled out from under the quilts, leaving the younger children asleep. It was her job to help her mother make breakfast for the family—hot oatmeal porridge with a little milk that Lars had bought from a neighbor who had a cow.

It was still dark outside. Lars and Alvar had gone out to break the ice on the water barrel, feed, water, and hitch up the horses, and bring in wood for the stove. After breakfast they'd both be gone for the rest of the day, Lars to help a neighbor with his house and Alvar to work the closing shift at the lumber mill ahead of the coming snow. Hanna would spend time teaching the younger children their reading, writing, and arithmetic. Maybe next year they'd be able to attend school in Blue Moon. But this winter there would be no way to get there.

Standing by the stove, savoring its warmth, Hanna stirred the porridge with a big wooden spoon. The sight of the gooey, gray mass turned her stomach. Even the pasty smell made her want to gag. She didn't want to eat. All she really wanted to do was crawl back under the quilt and sleep. She'd been so tired the past few weeks, as if the energy had been sucked out of her body. And no amount of rest seemed to make any difference.

The men came inside, pulling off their worn woolen gloves, their faces reddened with cold. They added milk to their bowls, spooned the warm oatmeal into their mouths, and washed it down with steaming black coffee. As was usual, they didn't do much talking, but Alvar's gaze, concerned and questioning, met Hanna's across the table, as if he'd already guessed what she only suspected. She turned away, unable to keep looking at him.

Breakfast done, they went out again. Hanna listened as the sounds of their leaving faded away. Her body felt an urgent need for the privy, but she had waited to excuse herself until the men were gone.

Wrapping herself in a knitted shawl, she spoke a word to her mother and slipped out the door, closing it swiftly to keep the precious heat from escaping. A wall of icy wind struck her, stinging her face, whipping her hair and skirts. She staggered backward, then pushed ahead, around the house to where the outhouse stood, set back about twenty paces.

If the trek was a struggle now, what would it be like in the snow—with wolves on the prowl? Hanna shuddered as she latched the door from the inside and sat in darkness, on the frigid seat. The rank odors flooded her senses, making her stomach roil. She'd finished and stepped out when the nausea hit her, doubling her over as her stomach heaved.

As her head cleared, she made her way as far as the barrel, where she dipped water to splash her face and hands. By the time she reached the door and stepped into the house, her damp skin felt frozen. She pulled a chair close to the stove and sank onto it, exhausted.

The younger children were still asleep. Inga was setting the table for their breakfast. Hanna forced herself to stand. "I can do that, Mama," she said. "Let me help you."

"No, sit down. Get warm first. You look pale." Inga studied her daughter with narrowed eyes. She glanced at the sleeping children. Then, setting the bowls on the table, she walked close to Hanna and spoke in a low voice. "When did you last bleed, *kära?*"

Hanna gazed down at her clenched hands. She shook her head.

"You're sure?"

"I'm sure," Hanna said, fighting tears. "I was sick this morning, just like you used to be."

Inga drew a sharp breath. Then she gathered her daughter into her arms. "My poor girl," she murmured. "My poor, foolish girl. This will kill your father."

* * *

It was dark outside when Lars arrived home. Hanna heard the jingle of harness and the creak of the wagon wheels as he drove up. She glanced at her mother. "Do we have to tell him now?" she whispered. "Can't we at least wait until he's eaten? Or maybe until Alvar comes home?"

Inga shook her head. "I know him. If we wait, he'll be even angrier. I'll go outside and talk to him. That way he won't be getting the news in front of the children."

She wrapped herself in her shawl and hurried outside. Hanna waited by the door, listening. She'd told her mother that Mason had fathered her baby, that he'd taken advantage of her, and that she didn't love him. She hadn't mentioned the part about sneaking out in the night. But she trusted Alvar not to talk.

With her ear close to the door, she couldn't make out words, but she could hear her father shouting and her mother trying to calm him. Moments later, the door burst open and Lars strode in. Hanna had expected more shouting, but when he spoke, his voice was flat and cold.

"Get your shawl and a blanket to keep you warm, Hanna. We're leaving. Now. And you don't have to ask me where we're going."

"It's getting late, and there's a storm blowing in," Hanna pleaded. "Please, Papa, can't we wait till morning?"

"No. And not another word from you, miss. I don't even want to hear your voice."

Fighting tears, Hanna wrapped the shawl around her head and shoulders and bundled up in the thick feather-filled quilt her mother gave her. Britta, Axel, and Gerda watched wide-eyed as she followed her father out to the wagon. It would be Inga's painful task to explain to her younger children what they'd seen and heard.

Outside, the sky was clear overhead, the air warmer than it had been earlier in the day. But a low cloud bank shadowed the western horizon. A storm front was moving in, pushing the warmth ahead of snow and cold. By slow-moving wagon, the Hollister Ranch, where Hanna assumed they were going, was almost two hours away. And the wagon had no cover.

But she knew that trying to explain this to her father would be a waste of breath. Lars had forbidden her to talk. And even if she were to speak up, he would be too angry to listen. Her behavior had dishonored her family. Whatever happened now was no worse than she deserved.

As the wagon pulled out of the gate, Hanna huddled into the quilt and prepared herself for the most miserable, humiliating night of her life.

A loud pounding on the front door woke Amelia Hollister Dollarhide from a sound sleep. She swore an unladylike oath and sat up. Beside her, Ralph Tomlinson lay undisturbed and snoring. The man could sleep through the damned Spanish-American war.

As the pounding continued, she was tempted to rouse him. But why take the time? It was most likely Mason, back from tomcatting and missing his key. It wouldn't be the first time he'd lost it in some hayloft or some widow's bed.

Except that, as far as she knew, Mason hadn't gone out tonight. He'd mentioned something about a storm and gone to his room early.

Slipping out of bed, she donned a warm wrapper over her silk nightgown and, as an afterthought, opened the drawer of the nightstand and took out the loaded Colt .45 revolver she kept there. If the late-night visitor wasn't friendly, the heavy pistol was capable of blowing a man to kingdom come.

With one hand on the banister and the other gripping the gun, Amelia made her way down the stairs. By the faint light that fell through the front parlor window, she could see her way across the entry. She cocked the pistol, then turned the latch and opened the front door.

The man whose size filled the doorway was a stranger,

but his clothes, beard, and heavy work boots marked him as one of the immigrant wheat farmers. His coat and knitted cap were covered with the snow that was falling beyond the sheltered porch.

Amelia raised the pistol, angling it toward his chest. "Take one step and I'll pull this trigger. What are you doing here at this hour?"

"I'm here to see Mason Dollarhide." The voice, slightly accented, matched his size.

It didn't take much intuition to warn her that Mason was in trouble. What had he done this time? Slept with the man's wife?

"I'm Mr. Dollarhide's mother," she said. "What business do you have with my son?"

The man's voice deepened to a growl. "Your son has got my innocent girl in a family way. I'm here to see that he owns up like a man and marries her."

Damn!

Looking beyond the man, Amelia could make out a forlorn figure bundled in a patchwork quilt, sheltering at the edge of the porch. A farm wagon, drawn by a team of drooping horses, waited at the foot of the walk. She lowered the pistol. "What makes you so sure the baby is my son's?" she demanded.

"My Hanna was a good girl before he got his hands on her. She says he was the only one. I believe her. Now go and get your son."

Amelia thought fast. "My son is out of town on business. When he comes home, I'll tell him about your daughter. But even if she slept with him, nothing's going to happen without proof. From what I've heard, you nesters breed like rabbits. That baby could be anybody's."

The big man drew a quick, hard breath. "This baby is your grandchild. That should mean something to you."

Your grandchild. The words struck Amelia like a slap. *No!* Even if the baby was Mason's, she wasn't ready to be some little brat's grandmother. And the last thing she wanted was to see her son married to a penniless, dirt-grubbing honyocker girl!

"We're finished here," she said. "Your daughter wouldn't be the first girl who's used a baby to trick a rich man into marriage. I won't have her taking advantage of my son." She paused in thought. "But since you've taken the trouble to come here, I'm prepared to be generous. I'll give you a hundred dollars cash to walk away and forget this ever happened. That should be enough to get the baby off to a good start."

The big man drew himself up. Amelia could almost feel the heat of his anger. "We're not beggars. We don't want your money. All we want is for your son to do the right thing for this poor girl and his child."

"Then, as I said, we're finished here." Amelia slammed the door in his face, locked it, and released the hammer on the Colt. There was no more pounding. The man and his daughter were driving away. She could hear them leaving. But something told her she hadn't seen the last of them.

Turning, she raced up the stairs and down the hallway to Mason's room, where she found him asleep in his bed. Anger mounting with each breath, she seized a corner of the bedclothes and yanked them onto the floor.

Mason jerked, groaned, and opened his eyes. "Mother, what the devil . . . ?" he muttered.

"Get up, you fool!" She flung the words at him. "You've got some little honyocker girl in trouble. Her giant of a father was just here demanding that you marry her."

"Hanna?" He blinked, as if trying to clear his head. "Oh, hell."

"So the baby's yours?"

"I guess so. She was a virgin and the timing's about right. Now what do I do?"

Amelia reined back the impulse to slap his face. "Get dressed and pack your bags while I get you some cash out of the safe. Ralph can drive you to the train station in Miles City. You're getting out of here on the next train—whenever it comes and wherever it goes. And you're not to come back until you're suitably married and ready to do a man's work on this ranch."

He stared at her.

"You heard me!" she snapped. "Get moving."

"But it's snowing. And it's supposed to get worse."

"That's your problem. Ralph can spend the night at the hotel and come home in the morning. But you'll be in the station house, waiting for the next train."

Mason raked a curl back from his face. "You raised me to run this ranch. What am I supposed to do somewhere else?"

Amelia glared at him, wondering how she could have brought up such a spoiled, entitled man-child. She was probably doing that wretched girl a favor. With Mason gone, she could marry some buck-toothed dirt farmer who'd at least be a faithful husband.

"Do what most people do," she said. "Figure it out."

Snow was swirling out of the black night sky. Wet flakes spattered the road and coated the backs of the plodding horses. Hanna's quilt was already damp. She shivered beneath it, aware that complaining would be a waste of breath. Hunched over the reins, her father hadn't spoken a word to her. But there was no need for him to tell her what had happened at the ranch house. She had heard everything.

Not that she'd ever wanted Mason to marry her. She could imagine the kind of husband he would be, not to mention his harridan of a mother. But to Lars, this was a matter of honor. His daughter had smeared the family's reputation. Only marriage could wipe away the stain.

Earlier, another vehicle had come up behind them on the road—a black buggy with its top up, the two-horse team moving fast to get ahead of the lumbering farm wagon. Lars had given way, and the driver had sped past without a wave or a word of thanks. Watching the buggy disappear into the storm, Hanna had wondered where its passengers might be going in such a rush. But then the snowfall had thickened, the wind had sprung up, and all she could think about was how cold she was and how far from home they must be.

Lars must be cold, too, although he would never complain, let alone admit that setting out with a storm coming had been a mistake. Even the poor horses must be suffering, with their breath forming clouds and moisture freezing on their coats.

Hanna had lost track of how far they'd come, but since they hadn't yet passed through Blue Moon, they must have a long way to go. Maybe they could stop in town and find shelter somewhere. But at this hour, especially in this weather, all the businesses would be closed.

She'd heard of people freezing to death on the road in storms like this. It could happen to her and her father tonight—and if she were to die, her baby would die, too.

The awareness struck her like a shaft of light. She wrapped her arms around her body, as if to warm the tiny life inside her. Until now she'd thought of her condition in terms of the disgrace, the sickness, the uncertainty. But she'd been thinking only of herself. This was about a precious child, innocent of its parents' sin. This was her baby to nurture, protect, and love.

Tears welled in her eyes and spilled down her cheeks. She was brushing them away with the back of her hand when she caught sight of something through the swirling snow. It was a speck of light, moving, coming closer.

The light became a man on horseback with a lantern. As he came within sight of the wagon, the rider spurred the horse to a trot.

"Thank God!" The voice was Alvar's.

Wearing a black slicker, he reined in alongside the wagon, keeping pace with its crawling progress.

"When Mama told me you went out with a storm coming, I got worried," he said. "I knew I needed to find you."

"Well, now that you've found us, you can take Hanna home on your horse. I'll drive the rest of the way by myself." The cold and strain had taken its toll on Lars's voice.

"You'd never make it, Papa," Alvar said. "You're not even halfway to Blue Moon, and everything's closed up there. I'm not even sure that Hanna and I could make it home on the horse. But I've got another plan. The turnoff to the Dollarhide Ranch is just a quarter mile down the road. They're good people, and they know me. They'll take us in for the night."

Hanna half expected her father to argue. But all he said was, "Lead the way."

They found the snow-coated wagon road that led across the pastures and followed it past the closed lumber mill to the foot of the hill, where it climbed in a series of switchbacks to the Dollarhide house. Lars studied the steep ascent through the falling snow, frowning. "I can make it with the team, but we'll have to take it slow, especially around those turns."

"Let me take Hanna up on the mare and leave her at the house," Alvar said. "Then I'll come back down to guide you."

Chilled and exhausted, Hanna left the quilt on the wagon and let Alvar pull her up behind him with the back of the slicker covering her like a tent. She wrapped her arms around him and held on tight as the sure-footed mare made its way up the road.

"Mama tells me I'm to be an uncle," Alvar said. "I'm prepared to be a good one." He paused, giving her a chance to reply. When she didn't speak, he continued. "I take it the bastard refused to marry you."

Hanna found her voice. "His mother did the refusing for him. She was awful. I'd rather raise my baby alone than be part of that family. But poor Papa. I've disgraced our family and it's killing him."

"Give him time. He'll come around."

"Won't Mama be worried if we don't come home?"

"I told her we might have to find shelter someplace. She'll understand."

They rounded the last turn and came up on the level of the house. Reflected light on snow revealed a rambling structure of logs with a broad, covered front porch and outbuildings behind. It was a grand place, almost frighteningly so. This was where Alvar had spent time after he'd injured his leg. This was where Blake Dollarhide lived.

What would Blake say when he heard about his brother's baby?

Suddenly the last thing Hanna wanted to do was step inside that big house and face him.

Alvar stopped the horse below the porch, helped her dismount, and led her up to the massive front door. The house was dark. Everyone inside would be asleep. How would they react to being awakened in the middle of the night?

She held her breath as Alvar raised the heavy brass knocker.

The rap on the door echoed through the silent house. Blake, who was having a restless night, sat up at once and swung his feet to the floor. Flinging on a warm flannel robe, he reached for the pistol he kept near his bed. He didn't know who might be at the door, but nothing good happened at this hour of the night.

The house was chilly, the coals barely glowing in the big stone fireplace. As he made his way through the shadows to the door, he could see snow falling beyond the front windows. Whoever was outside couldn't have had an easy time getting here.

Cocking the pistol as a precaution, he slid back the bolt and opened the door a few inches. Standing on the threshold was Alvar, his slicker covered in snow. A small figure, damp and shivering, stood beside him. Blake's pulse skipped as he recognized Hanna.

"I'm sorry—" Alvar began, but Blake cut him off.

"For God's sake, man, come in. I'll light the fire, and then you can tell me what you two are doing here."

"I can't wait for the fire," Alvar said. "My father and sister were caught in the storm. This was the closest place I could bring them for shelter. My father is coming up with the wagon. I need to go right back down in case he needs help. But I thought it best to bring Hanna up first." He cleared his throat. "I know this is an imposition, but—"

"It's nothing of the sort, Alvar. Bring your father up. You can put the horses in the barn. There should be feed and water for them there. I'll take care of your sister."

"Thank you." Alvar was out the door again, closing it behind him, leaving Blake alone with Hanna.

Wrapped in a damp shawl, she was shivering, her hair hanging in strings around her face. Not once had she looked up at him. Was she aware of what Mason had told him?

He couldn't let himself think about that now.

"We need to get you warm," he said. "I'll take that shawl." When she didn't respond, he lifted it away and laid a warm knitted afghan over her shoulders. Leaving her, he added some shavings and kindling sticks to the coals in the fireplace. Within minutes he had a small blaze going.

He was adding more wood when he glanced around to see that she had seated herself on a nearby footstool, close to the heat, with the afghan wrapped around her body.

"Better?" he asked.

She nodded. A beat of silence passed before she spoke. "You don't have to do anything for me, Blake. I don't deserve it."

"It's not a question of deserving. It's a question of needing," he said. "I know about you and Mason. He told me."

"I thought he might have. It wouldn't be like Mason to keep it to himself."

Blake remembered Mason bragging about how eager she'd been, how she'd yanked at his belt and spread her legs. Knowing Mason, he suspected that might not have been entirely true. But he would never know.

"Did you love him?" Blake could have bitten his tongue off for asking.

"No. It was exciting to be wanted by a man like Mason. But I was a silly little fool. I should have known he was only using me." She rearranged her skirt, exposing more of its wet folds to the heat. "But there's something else. Better you hear it from me than from my father."

Even before she spoke, Blake knew what she was going to say. But he was still unprepared to hear it.

She stared into the fire, then met his gaze. "I'm going to have a baby—Mason's baby."

Blake struggled to hide his dismay. He knew he should say something, but what? *I'm sorry* didn't quite seem fitting. He could imagine what might have happened tonight, a desperate father hauling his daughter to the man who'd ruined her, demanding that he do the responsible thing—and being turned away in a snowstorm. Mason deserved to be tarred and feathered for this.

"So I take it he's refused to marry you," he said. "Otherwise you wouldn't have ended up here."

"His mother refused for him. She said Mason was out of town, but I'm sure his answer would have been the same. And even if he'd agreed to marry me, I'm not at all sure I'd have him." She lowered her gaze to her hands. When she looked up at him again, Blake saw the glimmer of tears in her eyes. "But we didn't come here asking you to get involved. This isn't your problem, Blake. You're not responsible for your brother's actions, and certainly not for mine."

"So what are you going to do?" he asked her.

A single tear spilled over and flowed down her cheek. "I don't have much choice. And I don't deserve the right to ask for help, even from my family. All I can do is have this baby and try to be a good mother, even if I have to raise the poor little thing by myself."

"That's where you're wrong, young lady." The deep, gravelly voice startled them both. Joe Dollarhide, clad in his robe and slippers, stood in the opening to the hallway. Sarah stood just behind him. From the looks on their faces, Blake guessed that they'd heard most of the conversation.

"Your baby is a Dollarhide," Joe said. "No grandchild of mine is going to be an outcast from this family. Whatever you choose to do, know that Mason's child will want for nothing."

Hanna had risen to her feet. Proud but trembling, she faced Blake's powerful father. "Thank you for your kind offer, Mr. Dollarhide," she said in a polite voice. "I know you mean well. But I'm not a charity case. I won't use my baby as a reason to get help from you."

The older man looked startled. Then his steely gaze swung toward Blake. "We need to talk," he said. "In my study. Now."

As they headed out of the room, Sarah took charge. "Stay by the fire and wait for the others, Hanna," she said. "I'll go to the kitchen, light a lamp, and make us something hot to drink. Then I'll have my daughter find you some dry clothes."

There was no need for light in the study. Moonlight reflecting on snow outside the window cast Joe Dollarhide's features into craggy relief as he sat behind his desk. Blake settled in a side chair, tense and vaguely uneasy as he waited to hear what his father had in mind.

Joe stirred and spoke. "So do you think we can press Mason to marry the poor girl? According to what I heard, he didn't actually refuse. It was Amelia who spoke for him."

"Amelia said that Mason was out of town. I saw him in Blue Moon yesterday afternoon. He didn't appear to be going anywhere."

"So Amelia lied."

"Whether she lied or not, can you imagine the life Hanna would have, with Mason as a husband and Amelia as an unwilling mother-in-law? Can you imagine your grandchild growing up unwanted?"

"I can imagine it. That's why I'm not going to force Mason to marry the girl. Mason's not a bad man, but his mother's spoiled him. He has a lot of growing up to do." Joe sighed. "So we need to find some other answer. We can't just abandon the young woman who's carrying my grandchild."

"Hanna's family is poor," Blake said. "At least they appear to love each other, but their house isn't much better than a chicken coop."

"After hearing what Hanna said to me, I get the impression that if we offered them money to help, they wouldn't accept it."

Blake nodded. "They're as proud as they are poor."

Joe swiveled his chair to gaze out the window at the falling snow. After what seemed like a long silence he spoke. "Then, as I see it, there's only one solution. But it has to come from you."

Blake didn't have to ask what his father meant. But the idea shook him to the core. Hanna was beautiful, spirited, and intelligent. But she was so young. And his relationship with her had been like that of a protective older brother—certainly not romantic in any way. More disturbing was the fact that she'd given herself to Mason and was carrying his child. How could he even look at her without remembering that?

And then there was Ruth Stanton—an ideal wife in his eyes. But having Ruth was no more than a fantasy based on faint hope. She would never love any man but Webb Calder.

Blake had been almost five years old when his parents had finally married. He remembered his mother's loneliness in her years as a single mother, how she'd struggled to survive, alone and almost friendless, abandoned by the society that judged her.

He would never wish the same fate for Hanna. But if he were to walk away from her now, that would be her lot—one more mouth to feed in a wretched shack that was already bursting at the seams; people who would gossip behind her back and turn away when she passed them on the street; the stain of dishonor that her family would carry for years to come—and the horrible epithet of *bastard* that would be hurled at her innocent child.

As Blake's father had said, there was only one solution.

CHAPTER 12

*H*ANNA HUDDLED BY THE FIRE, CRADLING A MUG OF HOT coffee between her hands. By now, Alvar and her father had come in, stomping the snow off their boots and shaking it off their coats before they entered the house.

A pretty, dark-haired girl, who would be Blake's sister, Kristin, had come running to greet Alvar. As they stood together in the lamplight, not quite touching, Hanna understood the change in her brother. Seeing how the two of them looked at each other made whatever she might have felt for Mason seem cheap and tawdry.

Lars mumbled his thanks as Sarah introduced herself and gave him coffee. He held the steaming china mug as if fearing his big, rough hands would break it, taking careful sips as his eyes surveyed the room with its high, beamed ceiling and huge fireplace. When Sarah offered him a chair, he shook his head and gestured toward his wet clothes. In this setting, he seemed almost shy.

Hanna could imagine how her father must feel. She felt much the same. Such a grand house and such warm, gracious people—she was overwhelmed, especially after the hostile reception Mason's mother had given them.

Alvar had disappeared into the kitchen with Blake's sister. Sarah was collecting the empty coffee mugs when Blake and his father walked back into the room.

Joe Dollarhide reached out to his wife and laid a hand behind her waist. She gave him a questioning glance. He returned a nod. His arm tightened around her before he spoke.

"Mr. Anderson, Blake and I have discussed your daughter's situation. Now my son has a question to ask you."

Blake stepped forward. From where she sat, Hanna couldn't see his face, but she sensed something momentous hanging in the balance.

"Mr. Anderson," he said in a formal voice that didn't sound at all like him. "For the good of all concerned—my family and yours—I am asking your consent to make Hanna my wife."

Thunderstruck, Hanna froze. Her hands clenched in her lap, bunching a fold of her skirt. Blake didn't love her. Her baby wasn't his. Why was he doing this?

Lars appeared startled for a moment. Then he arranged his features into a semblance of dignity and nodded. "You have my consent, Mr. Dollarhide. But only if Hanna agrees. For that, you'll have to ask her."

"I intend to. But not here." He strode across the room to where Hanna sat and held out his hand. "Come with me, Hanna, and we'll talk."

She took his hand, her fingers trembling against his palm as he pulled her to her feet and led her down the hall to an open doorway. "My father's study," he said, ushering her inside. "Take this chair. I'll light a lamp."

Hanna sank onto the edge of an upholstered leather chair, perching like a bird about to fly as Blake lit the lamp on the desk. The soft light revealed a cozy but very masculine room, simply but richly furnished with a massive desk, several chairs, and a bookshelf that filled an entire wall. So many books.

The curtainless window behind the desk had given her a glimpse of snow and darkness. Now that Blake had lit the lamp, it became a mirror. From where she sat, Hanna could see her reflection—huddled on the chair, her clothes patched and faded, strands of hair plastered around her colorless face. She looked pathetic.

"How could you do this, Blake?" The words burst out of her. "How can you even stand to look at me, knowing what you know?"

He pulled up another chair and sat facing her. Lamplight softened the rugged planes of his face.

"What I told your father was true," he said. "This is the best choice for my family, your family, the baby, and you."

"But not for you. Did your father force you to do this?"

"No. It was my decision. Listen to me, Hanna. Your baby is a Dollarhide. If you were to agree to the marriage, he—or she—would have a legal father and a legal name. And you could raise your child here, in this house. Your family could visit you. You could visit them. And between us, we could find ways to make their lives better."

"And if you were to find someone else, a woman you could really love?" Hanna asked.

"We'd deal with that if or when the time came—the same as we would for you."

Hanna gazed down at her hands, looked up to meet his eyes, and forced herself to ask the one unspoken question that had been hanging between them since they walked into the room. "I don't suppose you'd expect me to be a true wife to you."

His mouth tightened. He cleared his throat. "No, of course not. I'd never lay an improper hand on you—not unless you wanted me to. This marriage would be a legal arrangement for the sake of the baby. Nothing more."

He fell silent, as if waiting for her to speak. Hanna had more questions, but they were better left unasked. Blake was a man with a man's needs. Were there other women in his life? If she married him, would he be getting his satisfaction elsewhere?

But why should it matter? Marrying Blake would guarantee her baby a secure future in a powerful family. Whatever the cost to her pride, she'd be a fool to turn down his offer.

"I know that marrying me will be a sacrifice for you, Blake," she said. "Surely you must've had other plans. But I owe my baby the best possible life. So my answer is yes. I will wed you on your terms."

He rose from his chair and took her hand. It was a gracious gesture, but Hanna couldn't help wondering if he'd wanted her to turn him down. For all she knew, he could be feeling trapped. But she was doing this for her baby. She couldn't back down now.

"Come on, then," he said, urging her to her feet. "Let's go back and tell the family. They'll probably be waiting to celebrate."

Celebrate? Hanna was not so sure, but she let him sweep her back down the hall toward the warmth of the big room. She thought of Sarah, who hadn't even been consulted about her husband's decision. She'd be taking in an unsuitable daughter-in-law, carrying the grandchild of a woman she had every reason to dislike. Blake's mother impressed Hanna as a fine person. But what she was being asked to accept would try the kindest heart. Hanna would do well to remember that in the days ahead.

As she emerged from the hallway on Blake's arm, all faces turned in their direction. "She said yes," Blake answered their expectant looks.

"Well, this calls for a toast!" his father said. "I've got a bottle of champagne I've been saving for a special occasion like this. What do you say we break it out?"

Blake spoke into the awkward silence that followed. "Let's save the champagne for the wedding, Dad. Our guests are cold and tired. What they need now is rest. There's a guest room with two beds made up at the end of the hall. If that will do for you and Alvar, Mr. Anderson, I'll show you the way. And you'll be welcome to stay for breakfast in the morning."

"You can sleep in the room next to mine." Kristin took Hanna's arm and led her toward the stairs. "I'll lend you a warm nightgown. We're going to have such good times together. I've never had a sister."

Hanna blinked back tears as they climbed the stairs together. So much kindness to a stranger whose mistake had upended all their lives. She'd earned the contempt of this good family. Instead she'd been met with nothing but friendship and acceptance.

Only Sarah had remained silent.

The next morning, Hanna had insisted on going home with the wagon to see her family and share the news of her coming marriage. She planned on staying two days. On the third day, weather permitting, Blake would come for her in the buggy and drive her to Miles City, where they would be married in a private ceremony by a justice of the peace. The two of them had agreed that this was no time for a family celebration.

The storm had moved on, leaving a sky bright with sunlight. Early that morning, the Dollarhide ranch hands had driven a sleigh down the road to clear the snow. Warm and well fed, Lars and Hanna had left on the wagon, with Alvar leading on the horse.

Blake stood at the porch rail, his gaze following the wagon until it had rounded the first bend. Last night the course of his life had changed with a knock on the door. Days from now, Hanna would be his legal wife, her unborn baby his child.

Where was Mason in all this? Blake wondered. He'd be wise to find his brother before the wedding and make sure he wanted to make no claim on Hanna or her baby. Mason's mother was a schemer, capable of turning Hanna and her father away without telling her son. Not that Mason would be itching to settle down. He was about as faithful as a prowling tomcat, and a shotgun marriage wasn't likely to change him.

Mason's description of Hanna's behavior rose in his memory. It would be like Mason to exaggerate, but unless Blake could block the images those words conjured up, the two of them together, Hanna eager and wanton, they would haunt his marriage. If he sought Mason out today, he would likely get more of the same. But that was a risk he would have to take.

"What are you thinking, son?" Sarah had come to stand beside him, dressed for the day in her classic dark blue dress with her hair brushed back and coiled in a knot at the nape of her elegant neck. Against the cold, she wore a soft, gray shawl she'd knitted herself.

"I'm thinking I need to go and find my brother," Blake said. "This marriage can only happen if I'm square with him."

"Of course." Sarah stood silent for a moment. "You know this isn't what I planned for you. I always hoped to see you married to a woman with some education and a degree of refinement. Someone like Ruth."

"I know. I had the same idea. But you, of all people, know how plans can change. Hanna's poor, but she's good and kind. And she's strong. She's had to work hard and go without all her life. You can't fault her for that."

"No. But she's so young. And she's carrying your brother's child. How can you accept her pregnancy, knowing what she did?"

"That's the hard part. But the baby is innocent. And Dad wants his Dollarhide grandchild."

"This would be easier if the baby were my grandchild, too, and not Amelia's. I've always tried to love Mason like he was my own. But the truth is, he was never my own. And you were always cleaning up after him when he made a mess. Now he's made the biggest mess of all. That poor, foolish girl. What was she thinking?"

"You know Mason. An innocent young girl wouldn't have a chance against all that charm. I hope you won't turn your back on Hanna. She'll be scared and uncertain. She's bound to make mistakes. But I can imagine how much she'll want you to like her, and how hard she'll try to please you."

"I'll do my best." Sarah pulled her shawl tight against a stray breeze. She cleared her throat. "I hesitate to ask, but I need to know what the sleeping arrangements will be so I can have things ready when you bring your bride home."

"Sleeping arrangements?" Blake raised an eyebrow. "That's a delicate way of putting it. Separate beds, at least. Separate rooms might be even better for now. I don't want Hanna to feel uncomfortable. But we can talk about it after I've paid a visit to Mason."

Sarah turned to go back inside, then paused. "Give my regards to Amelia. I take it she isn't exactly overjoyed about being a grandma."

"I'll give her your best." Mason headed for the stables to saddle his horse.

Half an hour later, Blake was on his way down to the main road. The air was crisp and clear, the blazing ball of the sun already melting the surface of the snow. A flock of crows rose from a white field, swept low, then rose against the blue sky in a single cloud.

The Hollister Ranch lay south of town on six hundred acres of prime, hilly land with a good water supply. Loren Hollister, Amelia's father, had settled it soon after Benteen Calder's arrival and built a handsome frame home at the end of a long driveway.

In the years when Joe Dollarhide's two sons were growing up, Mason had spent a good share of time on his father's ranch. But Blake had never felt welcome in the home of Blake's mother. Even now, knocking on the door, he felt ill at ease, especially given the nature of his errand.

An older man, dressed in a white shirt, black vest, and

bow tie, in imitation of a butler, answered the knock. Amelia had always been one to put on airs.

"May I help you, sir?" He sounded as if he'd been coached.

"I'm here to see Mason Dollarhide. He's my brother."

"I'm sorry, sir, but Mr. Dollarhide is out of town at present."

"Then I need to speak with Mrs. Amelia Dollarhide. It's important."

"I'll see if she's receiving visitors." The man had just turned away when Amelia walked into the room.

"Oh—Blake!" She sounded surprised but had probably been listening just out of sight. Chic and glamorous as always, she was dressed in a white shirtwaist with a skirt of rust-colored wool that matched the brooch at her throat and the color of her hair.

"It's all right, Sidney," she said. "Mr. Dollarhide is family—of sorts. Please come in and have a seat, Blake. I'm sorry Mason isn't here. He's . . . away and will be for some time."

Blake settled beside her on the settee. "Since I spoke with Mason in town, and he said nothing about taking a trip, I'm guessing he left in a hurry."

"Yes, his departure was quite unexpected." Amelia's voice had taken on an edgy tone.

"Then I take it you know why I've come."

"Is it that little slut who claims Mason got her pregnant?" Amelia's hands clenched into fists. "Don't tell me she and her father went to you, too! I offered them money and the wretched man turned me down. Maybe he was looking for a higher bid to leave the Dollarhides in peace."

Blake checked his temper. "I know her family, and she's no slut. She was an innocent girl when Mason took advantage of her—as he told me himself."

"Well!" Amelia huffed. "If you think you can force Mason to marry her, you can forget it. He has no intention of doing anything of the kind, especially since that baby could be anybody's! He left rather than face a shotgun marriage, and I don't blame him. I told him not to come back until he found a wife more suitable to his station."

"And the baby? Your grandchild?"

The color rose in Amelia's flawless face. "That girl's bastard is no grandchild of mine. In any case, I'm not ready to be anybody's grandmother. I'm much too young."

This would have been the time for Blake to tell Amelia that he was going to marry Hanna and raise her baby as a Dollarhide. But after hearing Amelia's vehement words, he decided against it. He had the answer he'd come for. Mason and his mother wanted nothing to do with the baby. That was all he needed to know.

He took his leave with one less burden, although he had his own worries about a future with Hanna and his brother's child. *One thing at a time,* he told himself.

As he walked down the front steps to his horse, he saw Ralph Tomlinson coming out a side door of the house. A tall man, still handsome in middle age, he gave Blake a nod. "Good to see you," he muttered.

"You, too." Blake returned the greeting as Ralph turned away and strode toward the stables. The two men had known each other for more than twenty years but had never been more than casual acquaintances. Blake had sometimes wondered how Ralph viewed his lot—under the thumb of a domineering woman who took him into her bed but had no intention of marrying him or giving him any power except that involved in the day-to-day running of the ranch. He lived in a cabin on ranch property, had few friends, and appeared to own little more than his clothes and his gear. Yet he seemed almost slavishly devoted to Amelia. How could a man who was any man at all be satisfied with so little?

Putting the question aside, Blake mounted up and headed out the gate, his thoughts on the preparations for his coming marriage.

* * *

After a sleepless night, Hanna was up early on the morning of her wedding day. In a dark corner of the shack, with her family still asleep, she used a cloth and a bucket to wash as best she could and put on the clothes she'd laid out the night before. Her clean underthings were shabby at best, but they would have to do, as would her worn Sunday shoes and the blue calico dress she'd made for the harvest festival. It wasn't as if she'd be walking down the aisle of a church in a white veil. This marriage to Blake would be little more than a business arrangement.

As she began brushing her hair for her mother to braid later, Hanna could feel her heart pounding. What would it be like, being Mrs. Blake Dollarhide? How would her old neighbors and the people in town treat her? How would Blake and his family treat her? After all, why would any man want to marry a poor, uneducated girl carrying another man's child?

What if Blake had thought things over and changed his mind?

What if he wasn't coming?

If Blake failed to show up, she would die of humiliation. But she wouldn't blame him.

At least the weather wouldn't be a problem. A glance out the window showed a clear sky fading to dawn.

After breakfast, her father and Alvar left to work on the neighbor's barn they were helping to finish. The neighbor, who had a couple of cows, would be paying them in milk and in the promise to shelter the Anderson horses in any winter blizzard.

On his way out the door, Lars planted an awkward kiss on Hanna's cheek. Things had been strained between them since the news of her pregnancy, but she knew he wished her well. Alvar hugged her and promised to visit. With Kristin as his sweetheart, Hanna knew he would be as good as his word.

While the rest of the family went about their morning chores, Hanna helped her mother wash and dry the dishes—both of them fighting tears because it would probably be the last time. Inga had braided her daughter's hair and arranged it into a golden crown atop her head. "Now you will look like a queen," she'd said. "The queen of your new family. Oh, how I wish I could be there to see you married!"

The sun was warming the frozen earth by the time Blake arrived in the buggy. As he climbed to the ground, Hanna's knees weakened at the sight of him, so handsome in a gray suit with a black bowler hat. Beside him, she would look as shabby as a biddy hen next to an eagle.

Inga, weeping openly, embraced Blake. "You're a good man, Blake Dollarhide, to do this for my girl and her little one. May the Lord bless your marriage."

Hanna hugged Axel, Gerda, and Britta, who would take over the schoolwork for herself and the younger ones. One final embrace for her mother and she turned to Blake, ready to go. He helped her into the buggy and tucked a warm lap robe around her. Then they were off to whatever new life awaited them.

By the time they reached Miles City, the sun had melted the last of the snow and thawed the frozen mud in the streets. Rust-colored goo clung to the wheels of buggies and wagons and coated the hooves of the horses. Here and there, planks had been laid out over the mud. Blake halted the buggy next to the boardwalk and came around to lift Hanna to a clean landing.

"I have some arrangements to make before the ceremony," he told her. "To keep you busy in the meantime, I'll be taking you to a ladies' shop down the street. My family has an account there. They'll outfit you with a proper dress and everything to go with it."

"Oh!" Hanna protested, thinking of the cost. "I don't need all that—"

"You'll be Mrs. Blake Dollarhide, Hanna. It's time you started looking the part, especially for your wedding. Take all the time you need. When you're finished at the shop, the hotel is two doors down the street. I'll meet you in the lobby."

Offering her his arm, he escorted her to the shop, which was several doors down along the boardwalk. Even the window displays were so elegant that Hanna wanted to turn around and flee. She didn't belong in a place like this. The people inside would laugh behind their hands at her home-made clothes and country ways.

Blake, however, walked her firmly inside, where they were greeted by a plump woman with silver hair, rosy cheeks, and dimples that deepened when she smiled.

"Hello, Mr. Dollarhide," she greeted him. "How are your mother and sister? Did they come with you for some shopping today?"

"Not today, Mildred." He nudged Hanna forward. "This young lady is Miss Anderson. She's to become a bride this afternoon, and she's arrived empty-handed. I'm trusting you to outfit her with a dress and everything else she'll need for a simple wedding. No limits. She's to leave here ready for the ceremony."

Hanna noticed that he left out any mention of the groom. Was he ashamed of her, or simply being discreet? Maybe the latter. Mildred struck her as the sort of woman who'd enjoy passing on a bit of juicy gossip.

Mildred looked Hanna up and down with a practiced eye. "Of course! It will be my pleasure. I'm thinking of something in a soft color to highlight that lovely hair and complexion. Come on back, dear, and we'll get started."

Hanna lost track of the time she spent getting in and out of clothes, turning this way and that before a three-way mirror, being measured and studied like a mare at an auction. Mildred clucked and shook her head when she saw Hanna's underthings, so they had to be replaced, too, with silky garments that felt like rose petals against her skin. Her new satin corset was laced so tightly that she could scarcely breathe, but it made her look as wasp-waisted as the fashionable ladies she'd seen in New York. At least her pregnancy wasn't showing yet. That would have been embarrassing to explain. But then, she suspected that Mildred had probably seen every situation there was to see.

When she'd chosen everything and put it on, down to silk stockings and new high-topped shoes, Mildred stepped back to survey the whole effect.

"Almost perfect," she said. "But I wish you'd let me fix your hair. It would be so lovely, curling loose around your face."

Hanna shook her head. "My mother did my hair this way for my wedding. I wouldn't think of changing it."

"Then you're ready to go, my dear. Here are some bags with your extra things and your old clothes and shoes—unless you just want me to throw them out."

Hanna hesitated—but no, her old clothes were a reminder of who she was and where she'd come from. And if things didn't work out with the Dollarhides, she would need something to wear when she left. "I'll take everything," she said.

Blake had made an appointment with the justice of the peace to perform the ceremony later that afternoon with the man's wife as a witness. He'd bought a ring—a simple gold band, sized to fit Hanna's small finger. At the hotel, he'd booked a suite with a couch in the miniature parlor, where he planned to spend the night.

Now he took a seat in the lobby and picked up a worn copy of *Life* magazine to pass the time. Hanna hadn't been here when he arrived, but she'd had plenty of time to spend at the shop. He shouldn't have long to wait.

Unless she'd gotten cold feet.

He was doing the best he could for her, the baby, and his family, Blake told himself. The marriage was anything but a romantic love match, but today he'd wanted to make her feel like a real bride—someone special, someone who was cared for. He would soon find out whether his good intentions had succeeded.

He was leafing through the magazine when she walked in. The magazine dropped from his hands and fluttered unheeded to the floor.

She was wearing a long-sleeved dress of rose-colored silk patterned with tiny diamonds in a deeper shade. A matching quilted cape with pearl buttons covered her to the waist, its high collar framing her face. Simple pearls adorned her ears.

Mildred had gone all out to enhance Hanna's beauty, adding a touch of rouge to her cheeks and lips. Even the strange hairstyle she'd probably refused to change looked as regal as a crown.

Hanna held her breath as Blake rose and walked toward her. Did she look all right? Was the gown too extravagant? Would he make fun of her or complain about the exorbitant sum her visit to Mildred's shop must have cost?

As he stood before her, she arranged her features into a bright, if somewhat artificial smile.

"You look like a princess," he said.

Oh, no, the dress is too much. I look like someone from a stage drama.

"Thank you," she said. "I feel like Cinderella at the ball, waiting for the clock to strike twelve. I know this gown must've cost a small fortune, but I thought I might give it to Kristin when we get home. She's about my size, and she'd look lovely in it."

"Nonsense, Hanna. The gown is yours to keep," he said, then changed the subject. "We don't have to show up at the justice's house for more than an hour. Are you hungry? We've got time for a light lunch in the dining room before we go."

She shook her head. "I couldn't eat a bite. And what if I

were to spill on this beautiful dress? Thank you, by the way.
I know you're trying to make this a special day, but this is far
more than I deserve."

"It isn't a question of deserving, Hanna. In every way but
one, you'll be my wife. That's how I intend to treat you.
Now, since you're not hungry, why don't we take those spare
bags from the shop up to the room?"

"The room? We're staying here?"

Blake looked mildly exasperated. "By the time we finish
dinner, it will be getting dark and cold outside. We can drive
home in the morning." He took the two bags from her hand.
"Come on. Our room's on the second floor. You can rest if
you're tired."

Hanna could feel her heart pounding as they climbed the
stairs to the second floor of the hotel. Had Blake lied about
not wanting her in his bed?

But she was being silly. If there was one thing she already
knew about Blake Dollarhide, it was that he kept his word.

"I'm aware that we have an arrangement, Hanna," he said,
as if reading her thoughts. "But there's the matter of appear-
ances. As far as the outside world is concerned, you'll be my
wife in every respect. The rest is nobody's business but
ours."

To Hanna's eyes, the room was as luxurious as a palace,
with the biggest bed she'd ever seen. In the small sitting area
was an armchair, a low table, and an overstuffed couch. "I'll
be sleeping there." Blake indicated the couch. "Don't worry,
I've had worse nights. The bed is yours."

The couch appeared far too short for Blake's long frame.
His feet would hang over the end. But Hanna knew better
than to argue. Any comment that might be taken as an invitation for him to join her in the bed would only make them
both uncomfortable.

She took the shopping bags from him and laid them on
the bed. One bag held her old clothes and shoes. The other
contained the purchases from Mildred's shop—a nightgown, extra stockings and underthings, and a simple gray

wool dress for traveling. The total cost, along with her gown, had almost made her ill, but Mildred had assured her that Mr. Dollarhide was a generous man who could well afford to pay.

She was wondering whether to unpack the new items when she noticed a door standing ajar on the far side of the room. "What's in there?" she asked, thinking it might be a closet.

"Open it and find out," Blake said.

Hanna crossed the room and opened the door. "Oh!" she gasped.

Beyond the door was a fully equipped bathroom. The basin had taps for hot and cold water. The flush toilet was similar to the one she'd seen and marveled at in the Dollarhide home. But the crowning touch was the immense porcelain bathtub with claw-shaped feet like the paws of a lion. "Oh!" she said again. "Oh my goodness!"

Blake was chuckling. "Haven't you ever seen a bathtub before?"

"Not like this one. At home we took sponge baths using a bucket. Oh, I know what I'm going to do tonight!"

"Enjoy yourself. We have a tub at home, but it's only about half this size, and the water to fill it needs to be heated. Just so you'll know, that purple jar next to the tub contains bath salts. You pour in a little as the tub fills. Then watch what happens."

"You sound as if you've tried it." Hanna stifled a yawn.

"I have, but I'll pass this time." He studied her with a slight frown. "You look worn out. Did you get any sleep last night?"

"Did you?"

Shaking his head, he smiled. "Why don't I step out and let you take a nap before the ceremony? Unless you want to be a yawning bride."

"That's not a bad idea. But my dress—I'll wrinkle it."

"Not if you're careful. Go ahead. I'll just be downstairs. When it's time to leave, I'll wake you."

As he stepped out and closed the door behind him, Hanna surveyed the bed. The coverlet looked divinely soft, and she really was tired.

Arranging her skirt to lie flat beneath her, she eased herself down and closed her eyes. The bed was even softer than it had looked, like resting on a cloud.

As Hanna sank into sleep, the last thought to fade from her mind was that maybe all this was a dream. Maybe she would wake up at home, next to her sisters, with no gown, no wedding, no Blake Dollarhide, and maybe even no baby.

CHAPTER 13

B LAKE HAD BEEN TEMPTED BY A GLASS OF LIQUID courage in the hotel bar but had settled for coffee. After finishing his cup, he spent some idle time watching passers-by through the lobby window. It would take time for Hanna to adjust to his presence. For now, he would give her the time and privacy to get some rest.

He was about to check the hour on his pocket watch when a tall, familiar figure passed the window outside on the boardwalk. It was Ralph Tomlinson, moving fast, probably on some errand for Amelia.

Drawn by idle curiosity and boredom, Blake stepped outside after Ralph passed. From the hotel's recessed doorway, he saw Amelia's foreman turn into the building that housed the bank and the land office. Blake knew that Amelia had moved her accounts, or most of them, to the Blue Moon bank in which Mason was a partner with Doyle Petit. So Ralph's business was more likely with the land office. Did that mean Amelia was buying up more land? The intriguing question would have to be saved for another time. Right now, Blake had other things on his mind.

After checking his watch, he steeled his resolve and climbed the stairs to the second floor. It was time to wake Hanna for the wedding.

He was doing the right thing, Blake told himself. Hanna's baby—Mason's baby—needed a proper name and family. With Mason out of the picture and Amelia having closed her door, this was the only way to see it done. So why did he feel so nervous about the coming marriage?

Never mind the questions. It was too late to back out now.

When his light tap on the door went unanswered, he used his key, opened the door, and entered the room.

Hanna lay on the quilted satin coverlet, her skirt carefully placed beneath and around her. Her eyes were closed, the lashes thick and golden against her cheeks. Her beauty took his breath away. She looked like the sleeping princess in the fairy-tale book his mother had read to him as a boy. Only her hands—reddened and callused, the nails worn to the quick from a lifetime of hard work—spoke of where she'd come from and who she'd been. Somehow the sight of those hands gave him reassurance. Hanna was a good girl, an honest girl, who'd been led astray by an unprincipled man.

In less than an hour, she would be his wife.

Her petal-soft lips were parted. As he stood next to the bed, the urge to bend and kiss her awake was almost overpowering. But no, after the promise he'd made, taking liberties was out of the question.

"Hanna, it's time to wake up," he said softly.

He waited a moment. When she didn't respond, he bent closer and ran a light finger down her cheek. She stirred as if dreaming. Her eyelids fluttered. Then her eyes opened with a startled look.

"It's time to go," he said, offering a hand to pull her up. She took it, still looking dazed. "I must've been tired," she said. "I was dreaming that I was home."

Looking into her wide eyes, Blake realized how scared she must be. "Don't worry, Hanna. Everything will be fine," he said, doing his best to reassure her. "Before long, your new place will be home to you."

They were married late that afternoon, in the cozy parlor of the elderly justice's home. His wife, still in her apron, with a dab of flour on her plump cheek, stood by as a witness.

The words of the traditional ceremony weighed on Hanna with unexpected gravity.

. . . *To have and to hold . . . to love and to cherish . . .*

Blake uttered the vows in an emotionless voice, as if executing a business contract. Hanna spoke them in a shaky whisper, knowing they were a lie. Blake didn't love her. She didn't love him. They were making sacred promises that they didn't intend to keep.

. . . *For better or for worse . . . in sickness and in health . . .*

Hanna willed herself to repeat the words like a student reciting in class. She managed to keep her composure through the *I do's* and the moment the weight of a ring slid onto her finger. Then the justice intoned the words: "I now pronounce you man and wife. You may kiss the bride."

For an awkward moment she gazed up at him, her knees going limp beneath her. Blake's expression was unreadable as he caught her waist with one hand and bent toward her. "Maybe we should have practiced this ahead of time," he muttered.

His lips were firm and cool. The kiss was gentle, but the contact ignited a curl of heat low in her body. Her pulse slammed as his mouth lingered on hers for an instant. When he released her, he left behind a strange hungering for more.

He stepped back, a polite smile on his face, as if their kiss hadn't affected him in the least. After a pause, he spoke. "Well, Mrs. Dollarhide, shall we be on our way?"

It took Hanna the space of a breath to realize he was speaking to her. *Mrs. Dollarhide.* That was her name now.

Her baby had a legal name and a legal father. She had a handsome, generous husband and a home finer than anything beyond her wildest dreams.

In light of all that, only a fool would ask for love in the
bargain.

Dinner that evening was a feast of prime beefsteak and
delicacies that Hanna had never heard of, let alone tasted—
although the bread wasn't as light and crusty as her mother's.
Dark red wine was ceremoniously poured into stemmed
glasses that looked as if they might shatter at a touch. The
wine tasted like sour grape juice. She put the glass down
after a few sips.

When Blake had seated her, Hanna had let him lift her
quilted cape off her shoulders and hang it on the back of the
chair. Underneath, the bodice was cut low and wide, to display her shoulders and skim the tops of her breasts.

Now she noticed that a few men in the room had swiveled
their heads to look at her. Their admiring gazes made her uneasy—like the dreams she'd had of being naked in public.
She felt her cheeks flushing. "Maybe—" she began, meaning to ask for her cape to cover her shoulders.

"There's no need to hide yourself, Hanna," Blake said.
"You look beautiful. Right now every man in the room is en-
vious of me."

If only they knew, she thought. But she knew better than
to speak of the arrangement they'd made.

As the waiter brought more food, she surveyed the com-
plicated table setting. "All those forks and spoons," she murmured. "What would happen if I were to use the wrong
one?"

"Nothing." Blake gave her a smile. "But at home, my mother
is a stickler for table manners. There, if you don't know what to
do, just follow me or Kristin. We'll set you right."

"Speaking of Kristin, I've been meaning to ask," she said.

"What do your parents think of Alvar spending time with her?"

"Alvar's a fine young man, and Kristen is old enough to have a beau. But she has her heart set on becoming a doctor, and she'll be leaving for school, probably this coming spring. She says that Alvar supports her ambition, even knowing that when she goes it may be for good. So with that understanding in place, my parents are fine with her seeing Alvar."

Of course, things would be different if they wanted to marry, Hanna thought. A man could marry beneath his station. A woman, never.

"And what about me?" she dared to ask. "How can I expect your family to treat me?"

"Kristin is delighted to have you, especially since you're Alvar's sister. She'll be your friend from the first day. My dad started his life as a farm boy, so he'll understand where you came from. And he's happy about his coming grandchild. You'll have no trouble winning him over."

"And your mother?"

"My mother may take some time. But she's kind and fair, and she's had her own struggles. Just be patient yourself. She'll come around."

Blake put down his wineglass and leaned toward her. His gaze held hers. "I'll be on your side, too, Hanna. I want my family to love you. And I want us to be friends. You can come to me for anything you want to talk about or to ask for whatever you need."

She lowered her gaze. "Thank you. You're a good man, Blake. I knew that the first time I met you, when you rescued me at the dance." She'd almost mentioned Mason's name but checked herself. Mason was out of their lives now.

"We've both come a long way since then," he said.

Yes, she thought, *and we have a very long way to go.*

* * *

They took their time finishing the meal, eating more than talking, perhaps each of them putting off the moment when it would be time to go up to their room.

Blake had already planned what he would do—find an excuse to leave and give her privacy until she'd had time to go to sleep.

"Hanna, I know you'll want to take advantage of the bathtub before bedtime," he said as they stepped into the room. "The saloon up the street usually has a good late-night poker game going. I brought some spare cash, and I've got a hankering to try my luck. That should give you plenty of private time before I come back. Does that plan suit you?"

"My mother always said gambling was evil, but who am I to judge? Go and have yourself a good, wicked time."

She had made him smile. A real smile, not the one he'd pasted on his face most of the day. "Don't wait up for me," he said. "The game tends to run late. Enjoy the tub."

He was about to leave when she called him back. He turned. She was standing in the middle of the floor, a helpless expression on her face.

"Oh, no—Blake, please don't go yet. I need help. Mildred got me into this dress, and the buttons go all the way up the back. I can't reach to unfasten them."

"What's a husband for?" His joke had an edge to it. "Turn around and hold still."

The fragile silk gown must've had at least twenty miniscule, fabric-covered buttons, each one passing through a matching loop. The seamstress who'd made the gown must've gone half-blind by the time she finished. Hanna was right. There was no way she could get out of this dress by herself.

He started at the top, his big hands fumbling with the devilish little fastenings. He could hear Hanna breathing as he struggled to ignore the nape of her lovely neck, laid bare by her upswept hairstyle. Her skin was the color of rich cream, lightly golden and as soft as satin. If this had been an ordinary wedding night, he would have kissed his way down her back as he undressed her, then swept her into the bed. As it was, all he could do was fight the temptation to press his lips to her bare skin and lose himself in the taste, feel, and scent of her.

He reached the top of her corset and kept working his way downward. Still slim as a willow, she was warm and desirable—and she was his wife. Blake could feel the pressure of his body responding to her nearness.

He forced himself to think of Mason—having her, loving her, planting his seed in her eager young body. It was something he'd sworn in his mind not to do when he'd made Hanna his bride. But the mental image was helping. By the time he reached the last button, his lust had ebbed—but at a price.

"Can you manage the rest?" he asked.

"Yes, thank you." She turned around, holding the top of the gown against her chest. "If you hadn't been here, I'd have been trapped in this dress. Now go out and have fun."

"Enjoy your bath." He left, taking his key and his warm coat with him.

Two doors past the bank was a saloon known for attracting high-stakes players to its poker tables. It was also known for discreet goings-on with the pretty girls in the upstairs rooms. Blake had been an occasional client in the past but that wasn't part of his plan now. He wanted to present an honest face to his bride—and to himself—in the morning. Tonight, he was here to play poker.

Standing in the doorway, Blake could see a couple of men he'd played with before, along with a gambler from out of town. The game was just starting. He ordered a beer, asked to join, took a seat, and laid a few bills on the table.

Blake enjoyed gambling for the challenge, the suspense, and the drama. The money mattered less because he never wagered more than he could afford to lose. For him, it was only a game, to be played for fun.

He had played a few hands and was breaking about even when he realized that he'd left his spare cash in his valise at the hotel. Distracted by the task of unbuttoning Hanna's gown, he'd walked out and forgotten it. If he wanted to stay in the game, he was going to need it.

Excusing himself, he put on his coat, strode back to the hotel, and climbed the stairs. When his knock went unanswered, he opened the door.

The room was empty, the lights turned off except for the bedside lamp. A thin ribbon of light glowed from under the closed bathroom door.

Blake's valise was in the wardrobe, around the corner from the bathroom door. As he walked toward it, he could hear the sound of happy splashing, then what sounded like a lively children's song, in a soft, musical voice. It took a moment for him to realize that the words were in Swedish, sung with such simple joy that Blake had to smile. The fragrance of lavender wafted under the door and into the room. He could imagine Hanna's delight when the bath salts turned into foaming bubbles under the water taps.

If this had been a real wedding night, he might have opened the door, soaped her back, and moved on from there, slicking all the sweet, intimate parts of her, then scooping her up in a towel and carrying her, damp and fragrant, to the waiting bed, where . . .

Damn!

He had married Hanna for the sake of her baby and his family. When he'd promised not to touch her, he'd believed that her youth and her circumstances would make that promise easy to keep. Now, mere hours after the wedding, he was panting after her like a blasted bull elk in rut. If he didn't get out of here now, he could lose control, bust into that bathroom, and probably scare her half to death.

This time, even thinking about Mason didn't help. Steeling his resolve, he found his valise in the wardrobe, took out the envelope of bills, stuffed it into his waistcoat, and left the room. With luck, the poker game would last until the wee hours, and he would return too tired to do anything but collapse on the sofa and sleep.

* * *

A sudden attack of morning sickness woke Hanna at dawn. She scrambled out of the soft, warm bed and stumbled to the bathroom, where she heaved over the toilet. The baby was making its presence known this morning.

Through the window, the sky outside had just begun to pale with first light. It was early, but Hanna knew she wouldn't go back to sleep.

A glance into the shadows of the sitting room revealed Blake sprawled on the couch in his clothes, his feet hanging over the upholstered end, one arm dangling to the floor. His hair was mussed, his cheeks and jaw dark with stubble.

She'd awakened after midnight to find him still gone. She knew what kind of businesses thrived in a cow town like Miles City. It was easy to imagine where he'd been and what he'd been doing—something she didn't want to name, let alone think about.

Letting him sleep, she dressed quietly in her old under-clothes and shoes and her prim, gray traveling dress. Her magical day as Cinderella was over. The rest of her married life had begun, and this was how it was to be.

But even this, Hanna reminded herself, was better than she deserved.

One month later

Hanna stood by the parlor window, watching the flying snow through the glass. Behind her, a fire crackled in the stone fireplace. Her knitting lay abandoned, for the moment, on the ottoman.

The December days were getting shorter, the storms more frequent; but so far they'd been little more than flurries, as this one would likely be as well. But the big storms would be coming soon. They always did. Everyone said so.

These days she saw little of Blake. He spent most of his days on the range with the three hired cowhands, mending fences, checking on the cattle, clearing their water sources, and making sure they had access to graze and salt licks. Most days he came back to the house at dusk, hungry and so tired that he usually fell asleep right after supper.

Sometimes Alvar came to help, mostly as an excuse to see Kristin. He brought Hanna news of the family and took home cash from Blake to buy food and other supplies for them in town.

Hanna missed her family every day. Blake had promised to take her on a visit, but it had yet to happen, and with the weather growing more uncertain, the chances of seeing them dimmed.

The guest room on the main floor at the end of the hall had been converted for Hanna and Blake to share. It was spacious and private with its own bathroom and two separate beds. Blake had hung a blanket down the middle, between the beds, to give Hanna some privacy—not that they spent much time there except to sleep. He was kind but distant, willing to listen to her needs but not to open himself to her in any way. The lines had been drawn and were holding firm.

Hanna returned to the chair and took up her knitting—a colorful cap for her father's Christmas gift. When she sat, she could see the round bulge of her growing belly rising beneath her skirt. Her morning sickness had ebbed, and she'd begun to feel the slightest little flutters. Were they just gas, or had the tiny life inside her begun to make itself known?

This afternoon she was alone, as she often was. Blake was out on the range. Kristin was studying in her room. And Sarah was checking on a neighboring ranch wife who was due to give birth soon.

For all Hanna's efforts, her mother-in-law remained polite and kind but still distant. When Blake had first brought her home, Hanna had offered her help around the house cooking, washing, and cleaning. Only then had she discovered that the Dollarhides employed a surly retired cowhand named Shep, who lived in his own cabin on the property. He cooked the meals for the family and the hired cowboys, kept the house tidy, and hauled the weekly laundry to a widow in town who took in washing. And he didn't socialize with the family.

Later, Hanna had let slip that she'd helped deliver her youngest sister when her mother went into labor, and that she'd be happy to lend Sarah a hand if it was ever needed. Sarah had ignored her offer, leaving Hanna, who'd never known an idle day, with empty hours to fill.

It was Kristin who'd come to her rescue. When Hanna had mentioned that she liked to knit, Blake's sister had brought her a big basket of colorful yarns with a selection of knitting needles, left over from a long-ago project of Sarah's. Hanna had come up with the idea of making Christmas presents. She started with her own family—a scarf for her mother and warm hats for the rest, in rainbow hues from different combinations of yarn. Hanna was still lonely, but at least her restless hands had something to do. If she didn't get a chance to visit her family for the holiday, she could send the small gifts with Alvar. Then, if she had time, she could try making something for the Dollarhides—in the hope that they wouldn't look down their noses at her poor offering. Surely, if she were to ask, Blake would give her an allowance for her needs—like fabric and new yarn, and maybe the ingredients for special Christmas treats the next time she could get to town.

Now, working to the end of a row, she realized she'd almost run out of the yarn she'd brought from the basket she kept in the bedroom. Putting aside the partly finished hat, she rose and set off down the hall to get another skein of yarn.

The door to the study stood open. As Hanna hurried past, a familiar deep voice called to her.

"Hanna, do you have a minute?"

Turning, she walked back to the open door and entered the study. Joe Dollarhide was sitting behind a desk cluttered with paperwork. Hanna had spoken with him in passing and at meals, but never privately, and she was still a bit in awe of the man. He looked like an older version of Blake, handsome and distinguished, his body still lean, his hair streaked with silver.

Like Benteen Calder, he was among the earliest settlers of this area; and like Benteen, he was something of a legend.

So why had he called her in now? Had she done something wrong?

"Have a seat," he said, gesturing toward the chair that faced him across the desk.

"Is everything all right, Mr. Dollarhide?" she asked.

He raised an eyebrow, a gesture that reminded her of Blake. "Everything's fine, except for the fact that after all these weeks, you're still calling me Mr. Dollarhide. I'm not expecting you to call me Dad, mind you. But my name is Joe. Please use it."

"Thank you. I will . . . Joe." The name still had a strange feel on her tongue. "Why did you want to talk to me?"

"Because it's too damned quiet in this place. I need to hear the sound of a friendly voice." He paused. "How is that son of mine treating you? Any complaints?"

"No. Blake is kind and considerate—what little I see of him. I only wish—" She hesitated, then, overcome by the offer of a sympathetic ear, she began to open up. "I just wish I felt less like a guest and more like part of the family. Nobody needs my help. They're all busy with their own pursuits. I've worked hard all my life." She shrugged. "I need something to do."

"You're growing my grandchild. I take it that's not enough."

"It's just that I feel so useless, as if I had nothing to offer. Your family—they're so smart, so well spoken. And I'm just a poor farm girl. I know I'm not the kind of woman your wife wanted Blake to marry. But I want to become that woman—polished and cultivated, always knowing how to act and what to say, a woman your family can be proud of. But I don't even know where to begin."

Joe didn't reply at first. Had she said too much? Hanna's gaze roamed to the bookshelves on the side wall. So many books. A whole world of them.

"I see you're looking at my books. Do you like to read, Hanna?"

"I can read well enough, but growing up, I never had the chance. Alvar was allowed to read as much as he wanted, as long as he got his work done. But our father always said that girls were meant to be wives and mothers, and that reading would only put foolish ideas into our heads."

"As you can imagine, my wife and daughter would send me packing if I were to say that. I don't consider myself well educated, but . . . ." He trailed off, thinking. "Do you have time to listen to a story?"

"I have all the time you need to tell it."

"All right. I hope you'll be entertained—and maybe even inspired." He leaned back in his chair, gazing past her as if drifting through time.

"Like you, I was a farm kid. I was younger than you are now when I signed up as a wrangler's helper on Benteen Calder's cattle drive. My mother was a God-fearing woman. She'd taught me to read her Bible, but that, and the church hymnal, were the only books I'd ever opened.

"I'll skip over the details, but after I got separated from the cattle drive in a stampede, I ended up with some pretty rough characters. I stayed with them because they'd threatened my life if I tried to leave. But when a band of vigilantes showed up, I lit out and ran—no horse, no food, no water, nothing. I would've died in the badlands, but I was rescued by the finest old man I'll ever know. He took me in, taught me how to catch and break wild horses—and he had a whole shelf full of books in his cabin. By the time I left, I'd read them all, some of them two or three times."

A shadow seemed to drift across Joe's face. "In the end, I let him down. We parted on bad terms, and I never saw him again. As it turned out, I had more lessons to learn the hard way. But those books stayed with me in my head. Their words and their wisdom have made all the difference for me."

He sat up in his chair again. "You're welcome to borrow any of these books. Browse through the shelves, take anything that strikes your fancy. And Hanna . . ." His gaze met and held hers. "Know that I'm your friend."

CHAPTER 14

WITH CHRISTMAS LESS THAN A WEEK AWAY, THE BIG SEAsonal storms had yet to arrive. Between flurries that were more wind than snow, the frozen ground was bare. Some ranchers and settlers had begun to hope that this winter would be a mild one. But Blake, who'd lived through more than twenty Montana winters, knew better. The snows would come, burying fields and roads and stranding hungry livestock in the pastures.

Still, he understood how much Hanna missed her family, especially at Christmastime. As his wife, she'd kept mostly to herself, knitting and reading books from his father's study. She'd asked little of him in the way of time or attention. But the sadness that crept into her face at unguarded moments hadn't escaped his notice.

When he'd suggested a two-day visit with her family, Hanna's face had lit with joy. They would leave in the morning, take the wagon loaded with firewood, spare blankets, food, including a frozen side of beef, and other supplies. Hanna would bring the little gifts she'd made. He would leave her with her family until the morning of the third day—Christmas Eve. Then he would bring her home to share Christmas with his family.

They left at full sunup, the morning clear but so cold that the breath of the huge draft horses froze on their eyelashes and whiskered noses. Hanna sat primly beside Blake, wrapped in her shawl, a warm buffalo robe tucked around her lower body.

Even bundled as she was, Blake was aware of her rounding belly, which had seemed to blossom in recent days. Her baby was growing. Hers and Mason's. Blake cursed the thought. Why couldn't he think of the baby as his? Lord knew, he'd tried. But when he looked at her, Mason's mocking words still echoed in his memory.

They'd taken a shortcut across the frozen grassland and arrived at the Anderson homestead by midmorning. Lars and Alvar were nowhere in sight—probably working or hunting—but Inga and the younger children came running out to meet the wagon. Hanna jumped to the ground and opened her arms. Her mother and the girls ran into them, Inga exclaiming over the size of her growing belly. The young boy, Axel, held back out of manly restraint. But he was clearly glad to see his sister.

Blake began to unload the supplies he'd brought, giving the firewood to Axel to carry into the shed, and hanging the side of beef from a rafter. Inga shook her head in amazement at the bounty.

"Thank you, Blake, but you've been too generous this time!" she exclaimed. "I hope you won't mind if we share these things with our neighbors. They need help, too."

"How could I mind?" Blake responded. "These things are yours. What you do with them is up to you."

After the unloading and a brief visit, Blake was ready to leave. On the way home he planned to go through town and pick up more supplies for the house and ranch.

"I'll be back to pick you up the day after tomorrow in the morning," he told her. "Meanwhile, enjoy your family."

Her face shone as she looked up at him. "Thank you, Blake," she said. "This means the world to me."

Blake had never seen her look happier. Maybe if he made an effort to please her at home, he would see that look more often.

In town, at the feed and hardware store, he bought several gallons of kerosene, six bags of oats for the horses, several boxes of ammunition in different calibers, and plenty of shotgun shells, to replace the supply he'd left with the Andersons. He'd brought along one list from his mother and another from Garrity, who was holed up in his cabin with his dog, so he would also need to stop by the general store.

Blake crossed the street, entered the store, and gave both lists to Ollie Ellis. He was walking to the back of the store to look at some boots when a voice from behind stopped him in his tracks.

"Hello, Blake. Where've you been keeping yourself? I haven't seen you in a couple of months."

Ruth Stanton stood next to a display of sewing notions, looking as pretty as ever in a blue hooded cape edged with fur.

"I've been . . . busy, Ruth." Blake groped for a suitable reply. Had word gotten around that he was married? Did she know?

"I've been hoping to see you and maybe invite you over for Sunday dinner with me and my father," she said, smiling. "I cook a mean pot roast."

So she hadn't heard. He needed to let her know before the situation got even more awkward than it already was. But how much should he tell her? As little as possible, he decided.

There was no easy way to say it, except to blurt it out. "Ruth, I'm married," he said. "I was married last month."

Ruth's face paled with shock. "Oh, I'm sorry," she stammered. "You must think me a fool, but I really didn't know." With visible effort, she forced a smile. "Congratulations. Who's the lucky girl?"

"You might say that I'm the lucky one. Her name is—was—Hanna Anderson. Her father's a wheat farmer, one of the homesteaders."

"You mean . . ." Ruth's face again reflected shock. "You mean you married one of *them?* I hesitate to say this, Blake, but you're going to lose some friends over this, choosing *their* side over the people you've known all your life."

"You know I've never been one to choose sides. And Hanna's a fine girl, from an honest family."

"But—wait! I know who she is. That pretty little blond girl. I heard some rumor about you befriending her family, but I never thought you'd marry their daughter. Why, she's barely more than a child."

"It was a sudden decision. But I haven't regretted it." That much was true, Blake realized. He couldn't fault Hanna in any way.

"I remember now." A note of bitterness had crept into Ruth's voice. "She's a friend of that red-haired woman who's married to the old farmer. I've seen them together."

"Yes, I suppose she is." Blake was growing more uncomfortable by the minute. "Nice seeing you again, Ruth. I wish you the best."

"The same to you." Her expression had frozen. "I thought you and I had a lot in common, Blake. I guess I was wrong."

She walked away, her proud head held high. Only then did Blake see the gray-haired matron, a notorious busybody, standing on the other side of the display, close enough to have heard every word.

Lars and Alvar returned home in time for supper. Another neighbor had hired them to do some carpentry, and they were grateful for the little money it brought in.

Both of them were surprised to see Hanna. Alvar, who'd visited her a few times, squeezed her shoulder and went back outside to put away the horses. Lars hugged her as if she were made of blown glass. "Is your husband treating you well?" he asked with a worried look. "You haven't left him, have you?"

"No, Papa. I'm just here for a visit. Blake has treated me fine. His whole family has been kind. Let Mama show you the presents they sent with me."

"Yes, come and see, Lars." Inga led him outside to the shed, leaving Hanna alone with the younger children.

"Come here, Britta." While Axel and Gerda were setting the table, Hanna motioned her sister aside. "I brought you something special," she said, opening her satchel. "Blake's sister gave it to me, and she said I could pass it on to you when I was finished with it." She reached into the satchel, slipped out a leather-covered book, and handed it to Britta.

"*Little Women*." Britta gazed at the title on the cover. "You brought this for me?"

"It's a wonderful story, Britta, about a family of sisters. One of them, Jo, reminded me a lot of you. I know you can read well enough to enjoy it."

"But Papa—" Britta protested. "You know how he is. I'll have to hide it from him, and maybe from Mama, too, or she might tell him."

"Not if I have anything to say about it. I'm going to talk to him. Now that I'm a married woman, maybe he'll listen. Besides, I know that Alvar will back me up."

Britta hugged the book to her chest. Her eyes shone. "Can I really keep it?"

"Of course, you can. Maybe you can pass it on to Gerda when she's older. Or maybe you could even read it to Mama. I'll bet she would love it."

Growing up as a poor Swedish farm girl, Inga had married and become a mother at fifteen. Neither her parents nor her husband had cared about her learning to read. At least, to her credit, she'd allowed her daughters to attend school in the city and encouraged them to continue their lessons at home.

Britta was still admiring the book when the door opened. Hanna's parents came in, followed by Alvar.

Lars was grumbling as usual. "Do I have to remind you that we're not a charity case? It's all too much. You should have told him to take half of it back, Inga. We can do for ourselves."

"Blake is family now," Inga said. "And with winter coming, we can't eat your fool pride or burn it in the stove or use it to keep our children warm at night. If he's given us too much, we can share with the neighbors."

"And what if they think we're showing off?" His words broke off as he saw the book in Britta's hands. "Where did that come from?"

Hanna stepped between them before he could snatch the book away. "I brought it for her to read, Papa. It's a good book. She'll enjoy it."

He made a *harrumph* of annoyance. "Well, take it back where it came from. It'll just waste her time when she should be learning to keep a house and be a wife. You know my feelings about the duties of a woman. Just because you're married, that doesn't mean you can come in here and start changing things."

Hanna stood her ground. "Some things need to be changed, Papa. This is the twentieth century. Women are becoming educated. They're going to college, having careers—and reading books."

"She's right, Papa," Alvar said. "Blake's mother was a teacher, and she knows a lot about doctoring. Blake's sister is going to become a real doctor. Even women who stay home need to learn about the world. They need to read."

"Then maybe I was born too late!" Lars declared. "Look at your mother. She's never read a book in her life. But you wouldn't find a finer woman or a better wife and mother. And she's happy as she is, aren't you, Inga?"

"For heaven's sake, supper's ready." Inga hung up her shawl. "Stop fighting and sit down. Hanna's with us. We have a warm home and enough to eat—and nobody's sick. Let's count our blessings."

Hanna took her old seat at the table and lowered her head for the blessing on the food. She was happy to be here, but until she'd arrived, she hadn't realized how much being Blake's wife and living with his family had changed her.

Months ago, she would have meekly resigned herself to marrying Ulli Swenson. As a dutiful wife and daughter she'd assumed that she had no choice in the matter. Now the thought that her sisters might face a similar fate steeled her determination to change things for them—and maybe even for her mother.

She would be here all day tomorrow and through tomorrow night. Somehow she had to make a difference for them, even if it meant going toe-to-toe with the most stubborn, intractable man she had ever known—her father.

Blake stood on the porch, watching a bank of clouds darken the western horizon. The morning breeze carried the crisp, biting scent of snow.

Would the approaching storm be another flurry like the last few had been, or would this one be the roaring blizzard that, sure as winter cold, was bound to arrive?

Maybe leaving Hanna with her family for two days had been a mistake. If a big storm struck, she could be stranded there, and possibly in danger. The prudent course of action would be to hitch up the buggy and go get her now.

But based on what he knew of Hanna, she might refuse to go home with him until the promised time was up. If he were to persuade her, or even force her to go, and the storm turned out to be no more than a few flakes, she would be justifiably bitter. Time with her family was precious. She wouldn't choose to be deprived of a single minute.

He would watch the sky and wait, Blake decided. If the weather showed signs of worsening, he would take the buggy at a fast clip and bring his wife home.

My wife. He was just beginning to think of her that way. Last night had felt unnatural, lying awake without the whispery sound of her sleeping in the next bed. He remembered yesterday's conversation with Ruth, and the old biddy who'd probably eavesdropped on every word. By now, word of his sudden marriage would be all over Blue Moon. At least he hadn't mentioned that Hanna was pregnant—although there was bound to be some speculation about that. But with Mason gone and Amelia in denial, the real secret should be safe enough. Still, he knew how vicious small-town gossip could be. He would do whatever it took to protect the girl he'd married.

By midday the wind had picked up. The cloud bank was rolling closer, dark and angry, like an army of goblins. Blake was watching the sky, thinking that if he meant to retrieve Hanna, he would need to leave soon; then Chuck, one of the three hired cowhands, came riding up to the house at full gallop.

He reined in below the porch, jerking the horse to a halt. "Boss, we got trouble! Fence down in the east pasture and two cows tangled in the barbed wire. If we can't get 'em free, we'll have to shoot 'em."

Blake swore silently. This kind of trouble was the last thing he needed now. The cows in the east pasture were prime breeding stock, all of them pregnant. Losing even one would be a blow to the future, as well as the finances, of the ranch. "Have you got wire cutters?"

"Ferg's got a pair, but we need somethin' better. And them cows is fightin' like crazy. Charley is off somewhere, so we're gonna need an extra pair of hands."

"Get the big cutters out of the shed and go. I'll saddle up and be right there." Going after Hanna would have to wait.

Blake could only hope the storm would be a fast mover, gone in a few hours. But a look at the darkening sky told him otherwise.

He grabbed his heavy canvas coat and thick leather gloves, along with a high-powered rifle to use in case the worst were to happen. If an animal couldn't be saved, the decision to destroy it would be made and carried out by the boss. That was ranch policy, but he dreaded the thought of having to shoot those beautiful cows.

By the time Blake reached the pasture, the storm front was in full fury. Wind howled in his ears. The first snowflakes, blown sideways, stung his face like buckshot.

Through the blur of whiteness, he could see the imperiled cows, one standing, one lying on its side. Both animals were thrashing and kicking. Their terrified bawling rose above the wail of the wind.

Blake's heart sank when he saw how badly entangled the two cows were. Their struggles had wound the wire around their legs and bodies and driven the ugly barbs into their hides. If they weren't freed soon, they would be too badly injured to save.

Dismounting, he dropped the reins and raised his voice above the wind and the bawling cows. "Give me the cutter. We'll do the one that's standing first. Both of you, hold her steady. Don't let her kick."

While the two men braced the cow, Blake crouched low and began to work, snipping through each strand of wire and peeling it carefully away to free the barbs from the cow's flesh. With snow flying in his face, blurring his vision, the job seemed to take forever. But little by little, all the wire was removed, and the cow was standing on its own. "Put a rope on her so she won't run off," Blake said. "Then we'll do the other one."

The second cow, the one lying down, was even harder to free than the first one. As the minutes crawled past, Blake began to fear that he'd have to shoot her. But finally the last strand of wire was cut, the last barbs worked out of her hide. Freed, she staggered upright, but she was weak. From the looks of her, she might not last the day. But Blake wasn't about to leave her out here for the wolves, coyotes, and ravens.

Exhausted and half-frozen, Blake pushed to his feet. Snow was flying around him, getting heavier by the minute. "Ferg, get on your horse and herd these two cows into the lower shed, along with any others you can find. Take a look at those cuts. The bad ones might need some salve. Chuck, you and I need to get the fence back up before the snow gets deep. Go get that coil of wire and the tools from the line shack. By the time you're back, I should have this mess cleaned up. After all the cutting we've done, there won't be much to salvage here."

After the men had mounted up and vanished into the swirling snow, Blake bent to the task of gathering up the cut wire and sorting the pieces into two piles—reusable and too small for anything but scrap. There could be no leaving the mess for the snow to cover. Hidden, the sharp pieces could be deadly to an unsuspecting animal.

Standing to rest a moment, he gazed into the blurred whiteness of falling snow. Going to get Hanna now would be out of the question. Even if he could make it through the storm to the Anderson place, there was no way he could get her safely back home. For now, she'd be better off with her family. But he would be restless with worry until she was home with him again.

The posts for the broken fence lay at a low angle that would have allowed the sharp barbed wire to catch and trap any cow that tried to pass between them. What could have brought them down to that position? They looked as if they'd been pushed partway over, or roped and dragged.

No cow, or even a bull, would push them over and leave them like that. And this spot, on private land, was too far out of anyone's way to have been accidentally knocked over. He remembered how Webb Calder had warned him that people would resent his hiring homesteaders. And only yesterday, when Ruth had learned about his marriage, she'd told him that he would lose friends because of it.

Things were beginning to make sense, but he didn't like what he was thinking. Was someone trying to send him a message?

Hanna sneezed and wiped her nose with a handkerchief. If she'd known she was coming down with a cold, she would probably have put off her visit. Now, all she could do was try to keep a safe distance from her family.

Through the single window, she could see the swirling snowflakes, falling thick and fast. She'd experienced snow in New York—the kind of snow that turned the streets to dirty, frozen slush. But she had never seen a storm like this one. Wind and flying snow battered the tar paper shanty, whistling through the thinnest crack and threatening to lift the roof off its supports. Without the additions they'd made that fall, it would surely have blown the house to pieces.

The storm had moved in earlier that day, after Lars and Alvar had gone to work. There was no chance they could make it safely home in this murderous weather. They would have to shelter wherever they were.

As for Blake, who had planned to come for her tomorrow morning, there was little to no chance he would get here. For his own safety, she could only hope he wouldn't try.

The men had taken the wagon and the two big Belgian horses. But the docile mare that Alvar had borrowed from the Dollarhides was still here in its stall. At least her father had built a stout front and a gate on the shed, so the horse would be safe; but someone would need to feed and water it in the morning.

"I'm scared, Hanna." Eight-year-old Gerda had joined

her sister on the bench, close to the warm stove. She huddled against Hanna's side. "What if the wind blows the house down? What if the wolves come?"

"I'm not scared," Axel bragged. "If the wolves come, I'll shoot them all with Papa's gun."

"You'll do no such thing, Axel," his mother scolded. "You're only ten years old. You're not big enough to handle a gun." She pointed to the loaded shotgun mounted on hooks above the door, out of his reach.

"But I'm the man of the house when Papa and Alvar aren't here. That's what Papa told me. And you girls have to do what I say."

"Ha!" Britta looked up from the book she was reading. She'd been lost in it since Hanna had given it to her yesterday. "Just try telling me what to do, you little weed."

"You may be the man of the house," Inga said, "but that doesn't mean you can shoot a gun. Britta, what's wrong with you, girl? You've been buried in that book all morning. I need you to peel these potatoes for the beef stew I'm making. While it's cooking, if everyone's good, we'll make a batch of pepparkakor."

That lightened the mood. The whole family loved the ginger-flavored cookies that would make the house smell like Christmas.

"Mama, when's Christmas?" Gerda asked.

"In two more days. Tomorrow will be Christmas Eve." A wistful sadness flickered across Inga's face. Even with the gifts and supplies they'd brought, Hanna knew this wouldn't be much of a Christmas for her family, especially the younger children. In New York, poor as they'd been, they'd at least managed to have a scraggly Christmas tree, with treats for friends who came by and caroling up and down the halls of their tenement building. This year, even those small pleasures would be out of reach. But at least there would be enough to eat and a few little presents to open on Christmas morning.

"What if Santa can't find us in the storm?" Gerda asked. The traditional Swedish Santa was a sour little gnome called Tomte. The children had readily adopted the more cheerful American Santa Claus.

"Then we'll just have to make our own Christmas, won't we?" Inga turned toward her second daughter, who was still immersed in her book, a rapt expression on her freckled face. "Britta, put that book down. I need your help."

Britta closed the book but left her finger between the pages to mark her place. "Please, Mama, it's such a good story."

"None of that, Britta. There's work to be done."

"Wait, Mama," Hanna said. "I have an idea. While I help you with the stew, maybe Britta can read the story out loud to us. Then afterward, we can make pepparkakor. Think how wonderful it will smell. What do you say?"

Inga gave the idea a moment's thought. "Well, all right, if Britta will do her part. I wouldn't mind hearing a good story."

"Britta?" Hanna gave her sister a questioning look.

"If I read it to you, I'll have to start over . . ." She sighed. "All right. But if people start interrupting me, I'll stop." She opened the book to the first page of the story and began to read.

" 'Christmas won't be Christmas without any presents,' grumbled Jo, lying on the rug . . ."

By nightfall, the snow was almost knee deep and blowing in drifts around the house. Earlier in the day, declining Hanna's offer to help, Inga had shoveled a narrow path to the privy. But now even that was covered.

Lars and Alvar had yet to arrive home. Hanna could tell her mother was worried. But, as always, Inga kept a cheerful face for the sake of her children. Now that Hanna was about to become a mother, she found herself watching Inga—this tough, illiterate farm girl from Sweden who had somehow managed to become everything a wife and mother should be. Hanna was learning from everything Inga said and did.

Supper had been a feast of savory beef stew, fresh bread, and the promised pepparkakor for dessert. The meal had been meant to be shared by the entire family. But the sight of two empty places at the table had dampened the pleasure of it. Everyone was worried, even Gerda.

After supper, Inga and the younger children had talked Britta into reading more of *Little Women*. Not only had they become enthralled by the classic story, but they also needed a distraction from the keening wind outside and the worry about Lars and Alvar.

Lighting a lamp, they listened until Britta's voice grew scratchy and Gerda began to nod. Then they said their nightly prayers, blew out the lamp, and went to bed.

As she lay awake in the bed her mother had fashioned for her by folding layers of quilts, Hanna's thoughts returned to Blake. He had planned to come for her tomorrow. But with the storm still raging outside and the snow so deep, the way could be blocked for days. She would likely be here for Christmas, maybe longer. But at least she would be with her family.

Would Blake miss her? Or would he be too preoccupied with the cattle and the weather to give her a moment's thought? But how could she fault him for that? Blake was a man with a man's responsibilities. And it wasn't as if he'd married her for love.

As the hours passed, she drifted in and out of restless sleep. Outside, the wind whistled around the corners of the house. As Hanna lay awake, her hand gently resting on her rounded belly, another sound reached her ears—a low-throated howl, answered by another, then another, close around the house. Hanna's blood ran cold. She'd heard the high-pitched cries of coyotes at night, but these deeper sounds came from animals far more powerful and dangerous. She was hearing wolves, and they were right outside.

She sat up, still huddled in her quilt. Her mother, a sound sleeper, hadn't stirred—otherwise she would have been terrified.

Hanna was frightened, too. Could the wolves break in? What would she do if the house wasn't strong enough to keep them out?

As she sat trembling in the chilly room, another sound struck to the very root of her soul. Alvar's mare—she was screaming in terror. The animal was in the shed, but the gate to the shed was constructed of cross-braces, with spaces in between. Could a wolf get through? Or could Britta and Axel have left the gate unlatched that morning when they'd finished doing chores?

The wolves might have been attracted by the side of beef that was hanging at the far end of the shed, but Nellie, Alvar's mare, would be prey, as well.

Without stopping to think, she jammed her bare feet into her boots and grabbed the shotgun from its place above the door. Gripping the heavy weapon with one hand, she closed the door with the other hand to keep out the cold and the danger.

Outside, the snowfall had lessened but the wind was still strong. It whipped her flannel nightgown around her body. Hanna cocked the heavy, double-barreled shotgun as she staggered forward. The snowdrifts around the house were so deep she could barely walk. The cold was bone-chilling. But nothing mattered now except saving the precious mare.

Pale shapes, barely a stone's throw away, seemed to float in the darkness. The wolves had probably backed off when she came outside. But if they decided she wasn't a threat, they could close in and attack her. She needed to do something now.

Her finger found the double triggers and locked on the trigger in front. She'd never had good aim, and there were too many wolves to take out with two shots. Her only chance was to fire into the pack and hope to scare them away with the noise and a peppering of lead.

The gun was so heavy that she could barely hold it level, but she braced it against her shoulder and pulled the trigger. The blast was deafening, the recoil so powerful that it knocked her backward. The wolves yelped and fled into the black night. Hanna was tempted to shoot again, but she had only one shot left, and she couldn't afford to waste it. Right now, what mattered was making sure the mare was safe.

Keeping the gun at the ready, she pushed ahead through the wind and snow to where the outline of the shed rose against the darkness. A few more steps and she was there. Around her, the snow was trampled by pawprints where the wolves had tried to get to the horse. But Hanna found the gate sound and securely latched. Alvar's mare was wild-eyed, stamping and snorting, but safe enough for now.

Only as she began to breathe deeply again, gulping the icy air into her lungs, did she realize the danger she was in. She could no longer see or hear the wolves, but she was so cold and weak from fighting her way through the snow that she could barely move. She had to get back to the house before she froze.

She pushed through the swirl of blowing snow. Beneath her nightgown and underthings her body had gone numb. Her feet were like ice clumps in the boots she hadn't taken time to lace. The shotgun felt as heavy as an anvil. Her arms ached from its weight, but she mustn't drop it in the snow, even to rest. It was all the protection her family had.

The wind had picked up again. Driven by its force, the blowing snow was like a wall of white around her. She could see nothing in any direction, not even the house, which couldn't be far. She'd heard stories of people dying ten feet from their doorsteps in weather like this. The same thing could happen to her—not just to her, but to her baby.

And what if the wolves were to come back?

She had lost all sense of direction. Any step she took could carry her away from the house, not toward it. She was as good as trapped. Her only hope was the gun she carried. She had one shot left. She could only pray that someone would hear it.

Aiming the barrels upward, Hanna checked the hammer, found the second trigger, and pulled it.

CHAPTER 15

*H*ANNA BECAME AWARE OF LIGHT, WARMTH, AND PAIN. With effort, she opened her eyes. She was looking up at the timbers that supported the roof of the family shack. Sunlight poured through the east-facing window.

She listened for the sound of the wind, but all she heard was a far-off scraping, like someone clearing a path through snow.

As she struggled into wakefulness, like a swimmer breaking the surface of water, she realized that she was lying in her parents' bed, covered by layers of quilts. But something wasn't right. Every joint and muscle in her body ached. And how could it be that she was shivering at the same time she felt burning hot?

"Mama! Papa! Hanna's awake!" Gerda's small face appeared above her for an instant before she wheeled and raced outside.

Outside. The storm must be over. How long had she been like this?

Closing her eyes again, Hanna struggled to collect her thoughts. She remembered the howling wolves, the screaming mare, and the ear-shattering explosion of the shotgun. And she remembered being lost in blinding, freezing whiteness. Had she fired the gun again?

But what was it Gerda had said? Had Papa and Alvar come home?

Hanna tried to sit up, but she was seized by a spell of dizziness that sent her crashing back onto the pillow. Her mouth felt as dry as cotton, her skin hot but chilling.

The baby! Was her baby all right?

She laid a hand on her belly. It was as round and firm as ever. But something could still be wrong. Heaven save her, what if her foray into the storm had hurt her little one?

"Hanna, how do you feel?" Britta was leaning over her, an anxious expression on her freckled face.

"I'm . . . not sure." He throat felt as if it had been raked with steel claws. "How did I get here? I can't remember."

"Mama heard the gunshot. She tied herself to the door with a long rope so she wouldn't get lost and went out looking for you. When she finally got you back inside, you were so cold you couldn't even talk. We got you into a dry nightgown and put you in her bed. Then she and I lay down next to you to get you warm. You don't remember?"

Hanna shook her head. Tears welled in her eyes as she imagined her mother, unarmed, braving not only the storm but the creatures that struck terror into her very soul—the wolves—to rescue her child. That was love in its strongest, purest form, the kind of love she was just beginning to feel for her unborn baby.

Dear Lord, please let my baby be all right, she prayed silently.

"Papa and Alvar came home this morning," Britta said. "They're outside digging paths through the snow. They said they heard wolves, too, at the neighbors'. But Nellie was all right. Can I bring you some hot coffee?"

"Not yet. Right now I just want to be here and sleep." Hanna closed her eyes and began to drift.

The morning passed in a blur of sleep, pain, and a vague

memory of faces bending over her—her worried father, and her mother, laying a cool hand against her forehead, and the words ". . . She's burning up, Lars. Back in Sweden we used to make a tea of willow bark for fevers. But there are no willows here, and I don't know what to do. I'm worried for her and the baby. Alvar says that Blake's mother is like a doctor. Maybe he'll get here and take her home. He said he would."

"But Blake doesn't even know Hanna is sick. With all this snow, he may not try. I would take her home myself, but the wagon could barely make it here from the neighbor's. Two times we got stuck, and Alvar had to jump down and free the wheels. All that time with Hanna out in the cold—no, she's better off here."

Her father's voice faded as Hanna sank back into a fevered half sleep. It appeared that Blake probably wouldn't be coming after all. That was her last thought before the fog closed over her mind.

She surfaced again, sometime later, to the aroma of her mother's soup simmering on the stove, and a low voice close to her ear.

"Hanna, wake up. I've come to take you home."

Was the voice really Blake's, or was she dreaming?

She forced her eyes to open. He was there, a worried half smile on his tired face. His eyes were weary, his jaw dark with stubble. She tried to speak, but her throat hurt, and it was all she could do to breathe. She should have known that he would come. Blake was, if nothing else, a man of his word.

Bending, he raised her upright with a hand to her back and stuffed her pillow behind her. "Let's get some good, hot soup in you," he said. "After that, we'll bundle you up and take you home, where my mother can take care of you."

She stifled a cough with her hand to her mouth. "But the snow—how—?"

"He's got a sleigh! Just like Santa Claus!" Gerda warbled. "And the horses have boots on."

"That's right, Gerda," Blake said. "The boots are to protect the horses' feet, just like your boots do. Here's your mother with some soup, Hanna. Eat all you can. It'll help keep you warm. But we've got to leave soon. There are more clouds coming in, and the weather could change anytime."

Blake looked on while Inga spooned the steaming soup into Hanna's mouth. She swallowed it with effort. He'd looked forward to bringing her home in time to celebrate Christmas Eve with his family. Instead, he'd be racing against time to save her and her baby.

Inga had told him about her foray into the storm last night. The bad chill she'd taken must have driven congestion to her lungs. If he didn't get her to his mother in time, he could lose her—a thought that opened a dark hole inside him. Little by little, whether he'd willed it to happen or not, she'd become a part of his life.

But all that mattered now was keeping her warm and getting her home fast.

He'd brought two buffalo robes in the sleigh and now hung them by the stove to warm them. When Hanna had finished the soup, he helped her mother put socks and boots on her feet and a shawl over her head. Then they bundled her in quilts. Blake carried her outside, set her on the sleigh bench where she'd be close to him, and covered her with the warm buffalo robes.

"Send word when you can." Inga stood with clasped hands beside Lars and the children as Blake climbed into the driver's place and, with a nod and a wave, clucked to the horses and drove the sleigh out of the yard.

The powerful draft horses had had a strenuous push getting through the knee-deep snow, but they'd be going home on the trail they'd already broken, so the going should be easier and faster. It would have to be.

Slapping the reins on the horses' backs, he urged the team to a brisk trot—the fastest he dared take them with the sleigh. The runners hissed through the snow. Hanna huddled beside him, her head resting lightly against his shoulder. The cold, fresh air seemed to revive her spirits a little, but she still coughed every few minutes, and her breathing was still shallow.

"How did you come to have this sleigh?" she asked, speaking with effort.

"My father ordered it made after he built our house. We've used it every winter, for years. Ask him about the time he saved Benteen Calder's life in this sleigh. It's quite a story, and he enjoys telling it."

"I like your father."

"I know. And he likes you. You've made a conquest."

She said little else as they followed the trail along a fence line. Cattle in the field were standing up to their bellies in snow, bawling with hunger. These animals wore the brand of the Snake M, the ranch Hobie Evans worked for. Was Hobie still there? he wondered. Or had he fled with his cohorts after the dynamiting of the house and the death of Ulli Swenson's daughter?

One of the cows tangled in the barbed wire had died in the night—a blow to the Dollarhide Ranch. The snowstorm had wiped out any tracks or other evidence of foul play. But Blake knew better than to believe the downed fence had been an accident. Somebody out there was still making trouble, and now they'd made him a target, probably because he appeared to have sided with the homesteaders.

Now that his marriage to Hanna had become common knowledge, the list of suspects had grown. Ruth would have told the Calders about the marriage. But pulling down fences wasn't their style. The Calders were fiercely ambitious but never petty or underhanded. His money was still on Hobie. But without proof, there was little he could do. And he still had no idea who was bankrolling the deviltry.

Hanna had fallen silent. Her head sagged toward his shoulder. Controlling the reins with one hand, he slipped his arm around her shoulders and pulled her close to his side. She settled against him with a sigh.

"Don't worry, girl," he said, his lips brushing her hot forehead. "I'll get you home. I wouldn't let anything happen to you or your baby for the world."

She didn't reply—maybe because he'd said *your* baby instead of *our* baby. He was trying. But he still hadn't come all the way to accepting the child that was really Mason's.

"Hanna," he said, changing the subject, "what the devil were you thinking, going out in the middle of the night to fight a pack of wolves in a blizzard? Hell, you could have died. You and the baby."

"I know." Her strained voice was barely above a whisper. "But the mare—I heard her screaming. I couldn't let her be torn to pieces by those wolves."

"But she was safe in the shed, wasn't he?"

"Yes. She was just scared."

"Damn it, I get scared, too, just thinking about what you did. We could have lost you."

I could still lose her, Blake thought. *All for a damn fool horse that I gave to Alvar because it was too old and slow to work cattle.*

Blake drove the sleigh into the yard, tossed the reins to a stable hand, and lifted Hanna in his arms to carry her into the house. Her eyes opened—their expression scared, questioning, and vaguely lost.

"Don't worry, Hanna," he murmured. "You're safely home now. You're going to be all right." If only he felt as confident as he'd tried to sound.

As he went up the steps, his mother and sister came rushing out onto the porch. "What's wrong?" Sarah demanded. "What's happened to her?"

"Pneumonia, I think." Blake strode past her, hurried through the front door, and laid Hanna, still bundled in blankets, onto the couch. "Her mother said she had a cold. Then last night she got a bad chill. Now she's burning up with fever."

Hanna had closed her eyes again. Sarah laid a hand on her forehead, frowned, and nodded. "I think you're right. Kristin, get my medical bag. Then make some tea—you know what kind and how to do it. Hurry!"

Hanna opened her eyes again, clutching at Sarah's hand. "My baby!" Her voice was a raw whisper. "Is my baby all right? Do you know how to tell?"

"Let's find out." Sarah laid back the quilts to expose Hanna's nightgown. Reaching into the black leather medical bag that Kristin had brought her, she lifted out her stethoscope and inserted the earpieces. "Lie still, Hanna. Hold your breath if you can. That makes it a little easier." She placed the opening of the bell on Hanna's belly, moving it here and there as she listened. After a moment, she nodded. "Your baby appears to be fine. The heartbeat's strong and regular, just as it should be."

"Oh, thank heaven!" Hanna breathed the words.

"When you're feeling better, I'll let you listen—you, too, if you want, Blake."

"It can wait until Hanna's out of danger." Blake felt a prickle of discomfort. Was he still hesitant to accept Hanna's baby as his own? But that question could wait. For now, nothing mattered except saving both their lives.

"Now I need to listen to your lungs, Hanna," Sarah said. "Can you sit up?"

"I'll . . . try." She struggled but she was too weak. Blake lifted her, holding her upright as his mother placed the bell of the stethoscope on her back.

"Deep breaths if you can—no, never mind, I can tell it hurts." Sarah listened, moving the bell from the left side to the right. She shook her head. "We're going to have to steam her."

Kristin had brought the tea and set the cup on the coffee table. Sarah nodded toward it as she put her stethoscope back in the bag. "Blake, you get some tea down her, as much as she'll take, while Kirstin and I set up in the kitchen."

The tea, Sarah's own remedy, was made from willow bark, honey, and lemon. Having been dosed with it in his growing-up years, Blake knew that, although the flavor was odd, it was good for reducing fever.

Hanna's head lolled like a broken doll's, but he had to get the tea down her. Cradling her in a sitting position with one arm around her shoulders, he lifted the cup to her lips. But she made no effort to drink it. Desperation surged in him. She had to help herself. If not, he was going to lose her.

"Blast it, Hanna, if you won't drink this for yourself, then do it for your baby. He's all right now. But he won't be if you don't help him."

Something flickered in her eyes—determination, maybe, or at least understanding. She took a sip of the tea, grimaced, then took more until most of it was gone. Then he held her and waited.

"Bring her in here. We're ready," Sarah's voice called from the kitchen. Leaving the blankets on the couch, he lifted Hanna in his arms. She whimpered as he carried her through the swinging door. Tendrils of golden hair clung to her face. Her hair was damp, but her skin was hot and dry from fever.

His mother and sister had fashioned a makeshift tent by laying some blankets and a canvas tarpaulin over a framework of high-backed kitchen chairs. Pots of water were steaming on the stove. Blake knew what had to be done. As a boy, he'd gone with his mother to treat patients who were suffering from fever and congestion. The improvised tent would be filled with steam from boiling hot water. The patient would stay inside, breathing the moist vapor, until the fever broke and the congestion cleared, a process that could take hours, or even overnight.

If the patient was a child, or too weak to sit in the tent alone, someone else, usually a parent or spouse, would have to sit with them.

Blake didn't wait to be asked. "I'll hold her," he said. "You two can keep the steam coming."

* * *

Shirtless, his skin beaded with sweat, Blake sat on the low stool that had been placed under the makeshift tent. Hanna rested sideways across his knees, her damp head resting in the hollow of his throat. On the floor around them, pans of boiling hot water filled the cramped space with steam.

Outside the tent, in the kitchen, Sarah and Kristin rotated the pans, reheating the water and passing it under the quilts.

Where his hands supported her, Blake could feel Hanna's heart beating. He could hear the congestion in her lungs when she breathed and coughed. Steaming like this, to loosen the phlegm, was a last-resort measure. More often than not, it saved lives. But Blake could remember times with his mother when it hadn't. He didn't want to think about those times now.

Hanna's nightgown was soaked from the steam. Her wet hair clung to her scalp, but her skin was still dry and feverish. If she were to start sweating, that would be the best of signs. It would mean the fever had broken. Blake had given her more tea that his mother had passed to him. But so far, nothing had helped.

He had long since lost track of how much time had elapsed. More than once, he'd heard his father come into the kitchen and ask, "How is she doing?" Blake hadn't heard his mother's reply, but he could picture her shaking her head.

Even Shep, the crotchety part-time cook and housekeeper, had stopped by to ask after her. In her time here, Hanna had managed to charm the old curmudgeon—something no one else in the family had succeeded in doing.

Sitting here in the steamy darkness, his mind knotted with worry, it was all too easy to forget that tonight was Christmas Eve. In the parlor, the fresh-cut pine tree, decorated with tinsel and handmade ornaments, wafted its fragrance through the house. Wrapped presents were piled beneath it, including little toys and garments for the baby.

Pies, breads, and cookies, baked earlier in the day, sat on the counter, ready for tomorrow's feast.

Blake had looked forward to bringing Hanna home to celebrate with his family and letting her open the presents they'd chosen for her and the baby, some of them ordered from the Sears catalog and shipped by train. He knew she'd felt out of place here, but maybe the gifts would help bring her a sense of belonging.

But now she was battling for her life and her baby's. If she lost that battle, there would be no keeping Christmas. Instead, they would be planning a funeral.

And my life would be empty, with a hole in my heart that would never heal.

"I'm sorry, Blake." Her raw voice, straining with every word, startled him. "I didn't mean to cause you so much trouble. But Alvar loves that old mare . . . I couldn't let the wolves get to her."

"Hush." Blake kissed her burning forehead. "Just get well. That's all that matters now."

"No, listen . . . I need to say this." She pushed away and sat upright to face him. In the dim light, the shadows below her eyes were dark pools. "If I don't make it, I want to thank you. You saved me and my family from dishonor. You gave me a beautiful wedding and a fine home." She paused, coughing. The sound of her ravaged throat and lungs tore at Blake's heart. Moments passed before she was able to speak again. "I can't fault you for not loving me. It makes what you did even more of a kindness. . . ." Her voice faded.

"Blast it, Hanna, you mustn't talk like that." Blake reined back the impulse to shake her. "You're strong. You can fight this."

"I want to believe you . . . but I'm so tired." She settled back against him with a sigh. "Talk to me. Give me something to listen to—a story."

He waited while Kristin's hands pushed a pan of steaming water under the edge of the quilt. "What kind of story would you like?"

She nestled her head beneath his chin. "Tell me about your family," she said.

So he told her the story as he'd heard it growing up—how young Joe Dollarhide, working as a wrangler for Benteen Calder's cattle drive, had met a pretty girl in Dodge City and promised to see her again; how he'd narrowly escaped death in a stampede, joined the outlaws who'd saved him; and how a bullet and the kindness of old friends had brought him back to Sarah; then how he'd left her again, not knowing she was pregnant with his child.

Hanna lay against him, her eyes closed, the sound of her labored breath growing fainter. Was she giving up? Was he about to lose her?

"Hanna?" His heart slammed. "Are you all right? Say something."

She stirred with a faint murmur. Her hand found his and lifted it to her face. Her skin was cool and damp with perspiration. The fever had broken.

Two months later

After a frigid winter, the land was experiencing its first mid-season thaw. Nobody doubted that the storms would return, but the sound of water dripping from the eaves was as sweet as music to the ear.

People who'd been shut in since Christmas hitched up their buggies and headed to town or to visit friends. Flocks of blackbirds fed on the newly exposed fields of wheat stubble. Coyotes and buzzards fed on the carcasses of the cattle that had perished in the snow. Ranchers rode out to check on their herds and count their losses.

Hanna stood at the parlor window, gazing out at the melting snow. She was alone in the room. Blake was with the cattle. Kristin was upstairs. Sarah and Joe had taken the buggy to town. Hanna would have enjoyed a trip to town herself, but nowadays, that was out of the question. Now that her pregnancy was showing, there were too many prying eyes and wagging tongues.

Hanna's recovery had been long and slow, her congested lungs taking weeks to clear. But as Blake had said, she was strong. Once the fever had broken, she had been eager to return to life and look ahead to the birth of her baby.

By now, she could sense the little one turning and kicking inside her. Once she had invited Blake to feel the baby kicking. He had looked uncomfortable, made a hasty excuse, and left the room. Hanna hadn't asked again. Blake had been kind to her, even tender in her illness. But she could tell that her appearance was a constant reminder that the baby had been sired by another man.

When he was home with her in the daytime, which was seldom, she caught her gaze following him, tracing the breadth of his shoulders, the shape of his hands, and the way his Levi's denims fit snugly around his hips. Listening to the deep cadence of his breathing at night, she found herself wanting more from her marriage than a name and a home. But when he went out at night and returned late, she knew better than to ask where he'd been or whether there was some woman who took what he held back from his lawful wife. If there were parts of his life that he declined to share with her, that was his right. All she could do was try to be content with what she had.

At least Sarah had warmed toward her, greeting her with a genuine smile and talking with her about the baby. Sarah was still somewhat distant, but Hanna had learned that what she'd mistaken for her mother-in-law's coldness was in fact natural reserve. It was just Sarah's way.

Hanna was about to sit down and take up the baby sweater she'd been knitting when she heard a knock at the front door. She opened it to find Alvar standing on the threshold. She flung her arms around his neck and hugged him tight.

After a moment he eased her away and studied her at arm's length. "Good heavens, you look like you've swallowed a pumpkin!" he teased.

"And I just keep getting bigger. How's the family?"

"All right. Papa cut his leg splitting kindling, but he's on the mend. Axel's shot up a couple of inches since you last saw him. And you'll be proud. Britta is teaching Mama to read and write."

"That's wonderful! It's about time."

"Oh—and here's a bit of gossip. Stefan Reisner came home and caught his wife with Webb Calder. Stefan shot him. Webb will live but it was a pretty serious wound. He'll be laid up for a while."

"Oh, no!" Hanna thought of her beautiful friend and how happy she'd looked dancing with Webb. Lillian would stay with her husband—that was the way of their people. But she would pay a bitter price for giving in to her secret desire.

"Alvar!" Kristin rushed down the stairs and hurled herself into his arms. Another doomed love, Hanna thought, knowing what her brother was about to hear.

"I've got some news." Kristin took a deep breath, as if aware of how her news would affect the young man she loved. Then the words spilled out of her in a torrent. "I've been accepted at a new women's preparatory college in Kansas City. My mother's aunt, who lives there, has invited me to stay with her. I won't be starting school until next fall. But Aunt Elvira, who's a widow, wants to spend the summer on a grand tour of Europe. She needs a strong young traveling companion, so she's asked me to go along. I'll be joining her. Can you imagine—London, Paris, Vienna . . . ?" She gazed up at him, as if noticing his devastated expression for the first time. "Oh, Alvar!"

"It's all right," he said. "We both knew something like this was bound to happen. Celebrate your wonderful news."

She took his hand. "Come on. Let's go upstairs and talk."

Hanna could almost feel her brother's heart breaking as he followed Kristin up the stairs. In time, Alvar would find another sweetheart. But he would never forget his first love.

With a sigh, she settled back into the rocking chair and took up knitting the tiny sweater again. She was lucky, she reminded herself. She had a secure home for herself and her baby. She had a husband who was kind, generous, and handsome enough to make any woman's heart flutter. And she had no illusions about the state of her marriage. Surely, in the balance, that was enough.

But she'd seen how luck could change in a heartbeat. It had changed for Ulli Swenson. It had changed for Lillian and Webb Calder. And she had just seen it change for Alvar.

Luck could change for her, or for Blake, for her family, or even for her baby. All she could do was hold on to all that was precious, all that she loved, and hope to avoid the unseen calamities that hung over them all.

CHAPTER 16

SPRING TOOK ITS TIME ARRIVING ON THE MONTANA PRAIRIE. March had passed before the deep snow melted to patches of white. April was well along before the pastures greened and the ground was soft enough for plowing and planting. By then the ducks and geese had flown home to their wetland nesting grounds, and the meadowlarks had staked out territory with their songs. Even then, the season was too early for the wildflowers that would paint the land with color.

Blake had started up the lumber mill as soon as the first wagonloads of logs arrived. To him, the shriek of saw blades biting through wood was a welcome sound, the scent of fresh-cut pine sweeter than perfume. With new homes and businesses going up, the demand for lumber should be high, the profits better than ever. Alvar was back at work, and Blake had hired two more husky farmers' sons to handle the heavy logs.

On the ranges, the spring roundup was underway. Joe Dollarhide had hired extra hands to help with the calving and the branding, and the task of moving the herd to greener pastures. The market for beef was still depressed, but rumor had it that cattle prices had bottomed out and were set to improve in the months ahead.

Blake understood the value of rumors. Profits could turn on a dropped word or a line in a news article. Keeping his eyes and ears open was part of his business strategy, and like any good poker player, he'd learned to keep his cards close to his vest. While he listened, he said as little as possible.

Today, he'd come into Blue Moon for supplies. But he'd allowed himself time to take the pulse of the town. He would start with the bank.

Doyle Petit had never been a friend. He'd always reminded Blake of a slick weasel, smart but shifty and not to be trusted. But after selling off the ranch he'd inherited, he'd become a powerful businessman with fingers in a surprising number of pies. Whatever Doyle had to say would be worth hearing, even if it might not be true.

Blake paid him a call on the pretext of financing a lease on timber rights. As usual, the banker was in a mood to talk. "Draw up a list of what you need, Blake," he said. "When I've got it in hand, I'll see what we can do. You know your credit with us is solid gold."

"Thanks. Right now it's just an idea." Not that Blake would ever borrow money from Doyle. If he needed a loan he would get it from his bank in Miles City.

"Of course, we're always happy to help out the Dollarhides," Doyle said. "After all, Mason is still a partner in this bank. I don't suppose you've heard from him, have you?"

Blake shook his head—though the mention of his brother caused his stomach to clench. Busy as he was, he'd wondered what he might do if Mason were to come back and demand a role in the life of his unborn child—the child he'd abandoned along with its young mother. His first impulse would be to threaten Mason with his life if he came near her. But that choice, he realized, wouldn't be up to him. It would have to be up to Hanna.

"If you hear from Mason," Doyle said, "you might pass on the word that I'd like to buy out his share of the bank."

"You might talk to his mother about that. Amelia should be able to help you. But if you're in a position to buy Mason's share, it sounds like your businesses must be doing fine."

Doyle beamed. "Fine? Hell, I've made ten times what I'd have earned if I'd kept Dad's ranch. Just this week I've bought parcels from three drylanders who are giving up on Montana life. Bought them out for pennies on the dollar. Next week, there'll be more. And then I'll resell the land at a profit."

"Is that legal?"

"Sure, it is. If you want to buy in, I could even cut you a share of the action." His gaze narrowed. "Of course, with your wife being from a sodbuster family, you might have a different view of the situation."

"Well, you never know." Blake shrugged. "I do have a question. The wheat harvest was good last fall, and wheat prices are still sky-high. The farmers made money. Why do so many of them want to leave?"

"Why don't you ask your in-laws that question?"

"I'm asking you."

"All right." Doyle hesitated, his lower lip jutting, before he spoke. "It's because they aren't welcome here, and people are letting them know it. Now, don't look at me. Their money's as good as anybody else's. I welcome their business. But after what happened last summer with that little girl dying in the dynamite blast, they're worried that their families will be next. And I can't say I blame them. All I can do is help them out by buying their property."

"I see." Blake rose from the chair he'd taken, preparing to leave.

"Let me be straight with you." Doyle stood and offered his hand. "You can count on me to be your friend. But some folks aren't happy with you cozying up to those honyockers. If I were you, I'd watch my back."

"Thanks for the warning." Blake accepted the handshake and left the bank. Could Doyle be talking out of both sides of his mouth? True, the homesteaders had given the banker plenty of business. But he appeared to do even better reselling their property to ranchers, speculators, and more immigrants who wanted land they could farm.

With so many drylanders pulling up stakes after a good season, something had to be going on. Had the raiders returned? And if they had, which seemed likely, who was paying them? Was it Doyle? He had the cash and the motivation. So did the Calders and several other ranchers in the area, including Amelia.

But these people were all prominent citizens, well-known in the community and with a great deal to lose. To communicate with the raiders and transfer the cash payments, a go-between would be needed, a silent partner, trusted and discreet, someone beneath notice.

But he was speculating now. Maybe the raiders were just people who hated the sodbusters. Or maybe the raids weren't even happening. With a muttered curse, he strode down the boardwalk in the direction of the saloon.

From across the street, he noticed a wagon loaded with cut boards pulling up alongside Doyle's lumber store. He recognized it as belonging to the sawmill outside Miles City. Only then did Blake recall how he'd refused to give Doyle a discount on his lumber and the use of his wagons. So Doyle had taken his business elsewhere, as was his right. Not that it bothered Blake much. He had plenty of other customers. And with the demand for lumber so high, there was room for competition.

In the saloon, he ordered a beer and drank it alone at the bar. A couple of ranchers he knew were sitting at a corner table with an empty chair. A few months ago they might have asked him to join them. Today they barely glanced in his direction. Clearly, he wasn't the most popular man in town. After talking to Doyle, he knew why. He could only hope his connection to the homesteaders wouldn't affect his business—and that Hanna's family wouldn't become a target.

His attention veered as he caught snatches of conversation from the table behind him. He'd noticed the four cowboys sitting there when he came in. Blake remembered seeing them around town, but he didn't know their names or where they worked. He hadn't given them much thought until his ears caught a well-remembered name.

"Talk to Hobie Evans," one cowboy was saying. "He says there's good money in it. Better'n chasin' those damned cows. And you won't have to hurt nobody, just scare 'em good. Maybe burn a few barns or pull down a few fences and scatter the stock. Give them honyockers a reason to pack up and leave. Then this country will be like it was before."

"So where do I find this Hobie?"

"He works for the Snake M. Ed Mace is the boss, but he gives Hobie plenty of leeway. He usually comes in here on a Saturday night. Big feller. You can't miss him. Him and the boys are plannin' a little fun over the next couple of weeks, so if you want to make some money, you'll want to sign up afore then."

So the harassment was already underway. And people were already leaving. Doyle probably had a hand in it, but who else? And how could the trouble be stopped before people like the Andersons started dying?

The cowboys finished their drinks and left. Blake was about to leave, as well, when the door swung open again and Webb Calder walked in.

Alvar had told Blake about Stefan Reisner shooting Webb. Still Blake was unprepared for Webb's appearance. He'd lost so much weight that his face was hollow-cheeked, his eyes sunk into shadows. His plaid flannel shirt hung loose on his once-powerful body, and he carried one shoulder slightly higher than the other.

Blake greeted him. "Can I buy you a drink, Webb?"

"Why not? Thanks." Webb took a seat at the table the cowboys had vacated. "I'll have a whiskey."

Blake ordered two whiskeys and carried them to the table. "Glad to see you're on the mend, Webb," he said.

Webb raised the glass to his lips, taking time to let the mellow burn linger in his mouth. "I guess you know what happened," he said.

"It's not exactly a secret. I'm just glad Reisner didn't kill you."

"If he had, I'd have deserved it. But the worst thing is knowing I can't ever be with Lili again." He took another sip of whiskey. "Ruth tells me you married that little blond girl my boys were raving about. Yellow Braids, they called her."

Blake chose to ignore the subtle jab. He wasn't here to quarrel with the Calder heir. "That's right. It was a quiet wedding, but it seems that word's gotten around."

"Well, at least nobody shot you." Clearly Webb didn't know the truth. Maybe the secret reason for the wedding would stay safe.

"Hanna's a fine girl. I could've done worse." Blake studied the man he'd never called his friend. He remembered their earlier conversation, when Webb had turned his back on the idea of helping stop the violence between ranchers and homesteaders. Now that it seemed about to happen again, he could still use Webb's help. It was possible that Webb's involvement with the Reisners had left him even more embittered than before. But Blake would have to take that chance.

"I'm concerned about my wife's family," he said. "There's talk of more raids starting up. Some of the farmers are already leaving."

Webb's expression hardened. "Then let them leave. Good riddance."

"Somebody's paying the raiders for their dirty work. And no, I don't believe it's your family. I never really did. But the settlers who aren't leaving are digging in. They'll be ready to fight. If this isn't stopped, people will die—maybe people you and I care about."

Webb drained his glass and set it on the table with a click. "I know what you're asking. But look at me, Blake. I damn near died from that gunshot, and I'm as broken inside as I am on the outside. Dad's slowing down, and he's looking to me to take over running the ranch. Don't ask me to get involved in this mess, especially since I'd be dealing with the man who shot me. And you've already talked to Dad. Nothing has changed since then except that now he hates the drylanders even more than he did before."

"I understand," Blake said, and he did. He couldn't count on the Calders for any kind of help. He would have to find another way. He thought of Hanna's family, good people who deserved to live safely and prosper. The loss of any one of them would break Hanna's heart.

On his way home he stopped at the sawmill. After unloading the supplies he'd bought, he drew Alvar out into the yard where they could talk and told him what he'd heard in town.

"If you know about the raids, Alvar, you need to tell me everything," he said. "Is someone just floating rumors, or are they really happening?"

Alvar hesitated, frowning, before he spoke. "They're happening—like you say, a few burned outhouses, fences down, horses and cows let loose. Nothing that can't be fixed. But people are remembering what happened to Ulli Swenson's house and his little girl, and they're taking the mischief as a warning. The folks who are scared are selling out. The rest, the ones who are determined to stay, are getting ready to fight."

"And your family?"

"Do you need to ask? I might've said something sooner, but my folks didn't want to alarm Hanna with her baby almost due." Alvar brushed the sawdust off his trousers. "I guess you're wondering why we haven't told you. It's because we remember what you said after those men assaulted Hanna—about not starting a fight. We took your advice, and after that, Ulli's house got dynamited. We're not going to let anything like that happen again. If we catch any of those men, they're going to pay."

"Can't I talk to your parents and neighbors, to at least find out what they're planning?"

"They won't listen to you. And I'm under orders not to tell you any more than I already have. Please don't make me choose between you and my people."

"Fine," Blake said. "But promise me one thing. If things get dangerous, send your mother and the young ones to my house. They'll be safe there, and they'll be welcome."

Alvar shook his head. "We talked about that because we knew you might offer. But my mother says that as long as the neighbor families have to fight to protect themselves, we'll do the same. We don't want any special treatment. It's about pride—and about all of us standing together."

Blake sent Alvar back to work. It stung that Alvar would keep secrets from his brother-in-law, mentor, and friend. But Blake couldn't fault a boy whose first loyalty was to his family.

Acting alone, there appeared to be just one way he could stop the raids and reprisals—find and expose the person, or persons, paying out money to the raiders. Then what? Sheriff Potter's jurisdiction only encompassed Blue Moon. But there was a U.S. Marshal's office in Miles City. When he'd gathered enough evidence, he would take it there and hope for the best.

Or, if there was no other way, he would deal with the situation himself.

The day was getting on. After talking with Garrity and making sure everything at the mill was running smoothly, Blake mounted his buckskin horse and rode up the hill to the house.

As he walked in the front door, he could smell baked beans and biscuits cooking in the kitchen. But the place was quiet. His father was probably still checking the new calves. Sarah and Kristin had gone to Miles City to choose a wardrobe for Kristin's upcoming European tour.

In the parlor, he found Hanna asleep on the couch, her head on a cushion, her slippered feet tucked under her skirt, and her arms cradling her round belly. With the baby most likely due in the next two weeks, she spent much of her time resting. But everything appeared to be ready for the little one to arrive.

Kristin's former baby bassinet was set up in the bedroom, supplies of diapers and baby clothes, along with sheets and towels for the birth, laid inside. Now, for Hanna and the family, there was little to do except wait.

A well-worn copy of *Great Expectations* lay next to her on the coffee table, opened facedown to mark the place she'd reached when sleep overtook her. She devoured books the way he had when he was younger. It was just one of the things he liked about her.

Now, as he gazed down at her sleeping face, a surge of protective tenderness almost made him moan out loud. Her fierce courage when roused by danger or a sense of right, her gracious acceptance of her place in his family, and her sweet trust in him moved Blake in a way he'd never known before.

She was his wife, to have and to hold, to love and to cherish . . .

Those wedding vows had been lies when he'd spoken them. They were lies no longer. He wanted her—all of her. And sometime after the baby was born, when Hanna was ready, he would make her his.

Maybe then, the memory of Mason's cruel laughter, the memory he'd grown to hate, would leave him forever. And maybe then, he would even forget that the baby he'd legally claimed was his brother's child.

He was turning to go when she opened her eyes. "Blake, you look troubled," she said. "Is everything all right?"

"Everything's fine," he lied, wanting to protect her from the things he'd learned today, cspccially about the danger to her family. "How's your book?" He nodded toward the copy on the table.

"I love it. I understand how Pip must feel, dropped into a comfortable world he's done nothing to deserve." Her gaze darted to the windows, where low sunlight slanted through the glass. "It must be getting late. Where is everybody?"

"No one's home except us and Shep in the kitchen. They should all be here by suppertime. If you're hungry, I could get you something."

"Heavens, I'm not an invalid. I can do for myself." She stirred and tried to get up, struggling to offset the bulk of her belly. With a little chuckle, she sank back onto the pillow.

"But maybe you could give me a hand."

She took the hand he offered, keeping hold as she swung her feet to the floor and sat up. "Almost there. One more good pull."

Laughing, she tightened her grip and let him pull her to her feet. Once she regained her balance, she released him. "That's better, thanks. Now, if I can just—oh!" Her eyes rounded. "Oh, no!" She looked down at her skirt, which was soaked in spots, with water trickling down over her ankles and onto her slippers. "No! This can't be happening! It's too soon!"

"The baby." It wasn't a question. Blake's pulse broke into a gallop.

"Yes—it's coming early. What if—oh!" Her body curled with pain, her tight lips holding back a cry.

Blake sprang into action, trying to keep a level head.

"Let's put you to bed and hope my mother gets here soon. Don't worry, you'll be fine." He scooped her into his arms and strode down the hall toward their room at the end. He'd delivered calves and foals and done all right. But he wasn't qualified to deliver a baby. He wasn't usually a praying man, but he prayed now that Sarah would walk in the door before time ran out.

Hanna lay in her bed, with a flannel sheet and a blanket to keep her warm and clean towels under her body. Blake had taken down the blanket between their beds to create more room. By the time he'd gotten her out of her wet clothes and into a clean nightgown, the question of modesty was little more than a joke. He was her husband, and she was about to have a baby. Right now, nothing else mattered.

Blake had pulled up a chair next to the bed. Hanna had never seen him look more worried. But surely his mother, calm, sensible Sarah, who'd probably delivered a hundred babies in her lifetime, would show up and take over before the baby came. If not, the delivery would be up to Blake. If the birth was normal, catching a newborn baby wouldn't be that difficult—Hanna had done it herself when Gerda was born. But what if something were to go wrong?

A contraction gripped her body—not so hard that she couldn't stand it, but hard enough. She tried to smile, to show Blake that she wasn't hurting, but the smile became a grimace as the pain crested and passed. Taking a deep breath, she willed herself to relax.

"Are you all right?" Blake asked her.

"Fine. Just a little scared maybe."

"And I thought I was scared enough for both of us. I'm just hoping my mother gets here before the baby does."

"I'm just hoping he'll be all right. I wasn't expecting him for another two weeks. He could be underweight, or even have breathing problems. That's what I read in one of your mother's books."

"Now you're scaring me. But you said *him*. How do you know it's a boy?"

"I don't really. Just a feeling. I—oh!"

Her fists tightened as another pain stuck, this one deeper and longer than the last.

Blake reached for her hand. "Whichever he or she is . . ." The words trailed off as if he couldn't finish the thought. If she'd pushed him, would he have said, *Whichever he or she is, this baby will be ours*?

Maybe that was too much to ask of him. Maybe she would have to love her child enough for them both.

More time and more contractions. As Blake gripped his wife's hands, he could tell her pains were getting more intense; and there was still no sign of his mother. Hanna's face was pale, her skin beaded with sweat. But after each contraction passed, she would give him a tired smile as if to say, *Everything's fine*. He loved her for that, and for so many other things. A woman could die in childbirth. Many of them had. What would he do if he were to lose her?

Where was Sarah when they needed her so desperately?

Finally, after a hard contraction had passed, Blake stood and told her, "I'm going out onto the porch and look down the road. If the buggy is coming, maybe I can wave and hurry them. Don't worry, I'll be right back."

He strode toward the door and would have gone out, but she called to him.

"Blake! Don't go! The baby—it's coming now!"

He raced back to the bed, flung aside the blanket that covered her, and raised the hem of her nightgown.

Mere seconds later, a tiny, perfect little dark-haired boy slid into the world and right into his hands. Small as he was, he was screaming his healthy little lungs out.

Blake's heart melted at the sight of him.

Moments later, Sarah rushed into the room to take the baby, cut the umbilical cord, and wrap him in a flannel receiving blanket before placing him in Hanna's arms. Hanna was weeping with joyous exhaustion.

Minutes behind her mother, Kristin burst through the door and saw the baby. "Heavens to Betsy," she gasped, out of breath. "I'm an auntie!"

Blake sank onto the chair next to the bed, his eyes on Hanna and the child he'd just helped bring into the family.

"And I'm . . ." *What? An uncle? No!*

"I'm a father," he said.

CHAPTER 17

Two weeks later

BLAKE OPENED THE BEDROOM DOOR TO FIND HANNA ON
her bed nursing their baby. His breath caught at the sight of
them—the beautiful boy with his thatch of dark Dollarhide
hair, his tiny face buried against the satiny breast of a ravish-
ing woman—his wife.

The quilt that divided the space between their two beds
had been rehung. Blake had done it without asking, assum-
ing she would want privacy. But looking at her now, he made
a silent vow that it wouldn't remain in place forever.

Young Joseph Lars Dollarhide, named for his grand-
fathers and known as Little Joe, was changing every day.
Thanks to a ravenous appetite, he was gaining weight, filling
out, already growing plump and rosy. And he already had
the members of his family wrapped around his tiny finger.
Sarah and Joe doted on him and on their new role as grand-
parents. Kristin adored him. And even crusty old Shep
cracked a smile when the baby was carried into the kitchen.

A few days earlier, Alvar had brought Inga to see her grandchild. Sarah had received her graciously; but Inga, though she loved the baby, had been visibly overwhelmed by the size of the house. She'd seemed relieved when Alvar told her it was time to go.

As for Blake, he'd once thought that he'd be doing well to accept Hanna's child as his legal son. Now, when he held the boy, he imagined watching him grow up, teaching him to ride, fish, and hunt, and taking him on roundup. In every way that mattered he was Little Joe's proud father.

And then there was the baby's mother.

Hanna had blossomed with motherhood, her delicate beauty becoming softer, rounder, and warmer. Seeing her now, with the baby at her breast, Blake felt the familiar tug of arousal. But it was too soon for what he ached to have. She was still healing, and when the time came, he would need her to want him, too. For now, all he could do was control his hunger and bide his time.

Sensing his presence, she looked up and smiled. "I didn't expect you home so early," she said.

"I'm not here to stay. I needed some paperwork from Dad's study—an invoice. Then I'll be going. I just wanted to see you and make sure you were all right."

"I'm all right, but with the raids getting worse, I'm worried about my family."

"So am I, and they're my family, too. Your mother's insisting that they have to stand with their neighbors. To run away to our place would show weakness."

"She's as proud and stubborn as Papa is."

"Anybody who touches them or their property will be dealing with me. The raiders should know that."

"But it might not be enough to protect them."

He walked over to the bed and brushed a kiss on her forehead. "I've got to go. There's a delivery wagon waiting at the mill. I should be home by suppertime."

Blake mounted his waiting horse and rode back down to the lumber mill. Becoming a father had sharpened his awareness of the need to protect his wife and child, and to protect Hanna's family. Now that the fields were green with sprouting wheat, the raiders were growing bolder. Drawn by the money offered, their number was increasing.

So far, the raids amounted to little more than mischief—pulling down fences, sending range cattle stampeding over the growing wheat, burning a few sheds and outhouses. But the settlers who hadn't sold out and left were digging in, determined to stay and fight if they had to—and men like Stefan Reisner's friend, Franz Kreuger, were stirring them up, urging them to take reprisals. Meanwhile, big ranchers like the Calders were turning a blind eye.

Blake knew that it wouldn't take much to blow the lid off the powder keg. He'd been keeping his eyes open and his ear to the ground but had learned nothing new about the people with the money.

Doyle Petit had to be in this up to his ears, but he was smart enough not to get his hands dirty. Beyond buying up the vacated property, which was legal, there was nothing to tie him to the raids and no evidence of who his go-between could be.

It was time he dug deeper, Blake told himself. And there was one person who might be able to shed light on what was happening—if he could trust her to tell the truth.

The next day he left the mill to pay a call. He hadn't spoken with Amelia since their encounter before the wedding, when she'd assured him that she wanted nothing to do with Hanna or her baby. He knew better than to think she might change her mind. All the same, as he tied his horse to the hitching rail and walked up to the front porch, he couldn't deny a mixed sense of trepidation and distaste. He had never liked Blake's mother. And he liked her even less now.

He didn't plan to tell her she was a grandmother because she neither wanted nor deserved the title. And he wouldn't ask her about Mason because he didn't give a damn about his half brother. He would keep his visit short and to the point.

It was Amelia herself who answered his knock, dressed in a tailored white shirtwaist and narrow skirt which seemed to be the latest fashion. "Blake." Her smile was friendly, but her eyes like green ice. "What a surprise. Won't you come in?" She stepped aside for him to enter. "Have a seat. Can I get you a drink?"

"I'll take the seat, but no drink, thanks. I won't be staying long." He took the chair she indicated. She faced him, perched on the edge of the settee.

"What can I do for you? I take it your family is well."

"They're fine. I'll give them your best."

She cleared her throat with a ladylike cough. "If you've come to ask about Mason, I haven't heard from him in some time. I can only assume he's enjoying his independence."

"This isn't about him. Actually I've come to ask you about Doyle Petit. I know the two of you had some business ties—including part ownership of his bank."

"Which I turned over to Mason. Not that he showed me much gratitude for it."

"I'm aware of that. But a few weeks ago, Doyle told me that he'd like to buy out Mason's share in the bank. I told him to speak to you. Have you heard from him?"

"I have not." She made a little huffing sound. "Not that it's any of your business."

"Doyle also told me how he's been buying out the settlers who are leaving and holding the property for resale at a higher price. Was your family involved in that part of his business?"

"Certainly not!" Her gaze was level and unflinching. "I don't like the drylander riffraff, but as long as they keep their distance from my property, I'm willing to live and let live."

"But there are folks who don't feel that way," Blake said. "Somebody's paying a gang of thugs to harass them into leaving. Then Doyle buys them out for pennies on the dollar."

"Somebody's paying the raiders, you say? So you've

come to ask if it's me? I can assure you it isn't. Why on earth would I do such a thing?"

"Two reasons. Land and money."

"And since I have plenty of both, why should I stoop to paying a bunch of hoodlums to break the law? Whoever's doing this, Blake, it isn't me. I swear it on my father's grave." She rose, brushing the creases out of her skirt. "And now, if you don't mind, I think we've wasted enough of each other's time. You can show yourself out."

For Blake, it was a relief to mount his horse and ride away. Amelia's heart was about as warm as a snake's. But strangely enough, he was inclined to believe her. The Hollister Ranch was south of Blue Moon, well away from the homesteads. Her land, while perfect for cattle, was too hilly for wheat farming. There was little chance of settlers encroaching on her property.

And, as she'd said, she was rich in both land and money. It was a messy business, driving homesteaders off their land; and if there was anything Amelia disliked, it was messiness.

But now that he thought about it, last fall in Miles City, he'd seen her foreman, Ralph Tomlinson, going into the building that served as the bank and land office. Was Amelia buying land from Doyle—or helping him in some other way? Maybe she was setting something up for Mason whenever he was due to return.

Either way was a long shot. But next time he was in Miles City it might be worth his time to check. Bank accounts were private, but land transfers and titles were public information. If Amelia was buying vacated homesteads from Doyle, perhaps for Mason, it should be possible to find out.

But with tensions rising every day between the settlers and the hired raiders, anything he did might be too little too late.

Hanna sat in the parlor with her baby on her lap, watching the expressions change on his exquisite little face—pink lips puckering, forehead wrinkling in a baby frown, then a tiny yawn. Never had she imagined that a child could be so enchanting.

There was little, if any, of Mason—or even her—in the baby's appearance. His coloring was all Joe Dollarhide. But that didn't matter. She would have loved him regardless; and the miracle was that Blake seemed to love him, too. Maybe some higher power had meant for Blake to be the one to usher her baby into the world. In the three weeks that had passed since that moment, Blake had become everything a proud, protective father should be.

But now that she was recovering from the birth, what kind of husband would he be?

And what would he expect of her as a wife? So many questions. So many fears.

Did she want him? But why even ask? Since the baby had come and she'd begun to get her strength back, she could scarcely look at him without feeling a surge of desire in the depths of her body.

But did he want her? Blake had been tender and considerate, but that told her nothing. Maybe he was getting satisfaction elsewhere. Maybe when he looked at her, what he felt was contempt because she'd been with Mason first.

The weeks ahead would answer those questions. But Blake had promised not to touch her unless it was what she wanted. And Blake was a man of his word. It would be up to her to put her pride on the line and make the first move.

The sound of a footstep on the stairs broke into her thoughts. Hanna looked up as Kristin came into the parlor. Her violet eyes were laced with red and swollen with tears.

In a week's time, she was due to leave by train to join her great-aunt in Kansas City for the grand tour. Her bags were mostly packed, her ticket and passport arranged. Everything was in readiness for a journey any young girl would envy.

So why did she look as if she'd been crying her heart out?

Cradling the baby against her shoulder, Hanna made room

on the settee. "Come and sit down," she said. "You look as if you could use someone to talk to."

"Thanks." Kristen sank onto the cushioned seat. "I'm sorry. I know I should be dancing with excitement, but I'm thinking that I shouldn't go. If I wire Aunt Elvira tomorrow, she should be able to find another companion. Then I could spend the summer here and leave for school in the fall."

"But think of what you'd be missing," Hanna said. "You may never have an opportunity like this again."

"Oh, I know . . ." More tears welled in her eyes. "But it's Alvar. We both know that when I leave, we'll likely be saying goodbye for the last time. And I love him, Hanna. If I didn't take this trip, we could have three more months together."

As Hanna weighed her answer, the only sound in the room was the baby chomping on her collar, making little sucking noises. She and Kristin were close in age, but because Hanna was a wife and mother now, it was as if she were years older.

"And how does Alvar feel about all this?" she asked.

"I haven't told him that I'm having second thoughts. He's encouraged me to go and have a great adventure. But I can tell how much he's hurting. When I go away to school, I'll most likely be gone for years. Anything could happen. We know we can't promise to wait for each other. But three more months with Alvar would mean more to me than three months in Europe with an old woman I barely know."

"I know this is a delicate question," Hanna said. "But I need to ask. Have you and Alvar . . ." She let the sentence hang when Kristin began to blush. There was no need to say more.

Kristin shook her head. "There were times when I wanted it to happen, but Alvar is stronger than I am. He wouldn't hear of it. So no, I'm as virgin as the day I was born."

"You know that another three months might make things even harder, for both of you."

"That's what I've told myself. But there's something else. Something that worries me. I haven't wanted to mention it to you, with the baby and all, but—"

"There's no need to protect me, Kristin. If it concerns Alvar, I need to know."

"Alvar and your father, and some of the other men, have formed a vigilante group to fight against the raiders—not just to defend their homes but to punish those men. Franz Kreuger is the leader, and you know what a hothead he is. He goads them into taking dangerous chances with his talk about going up against the raiders, beating them, even killing them. I've tried to talk Alvar out of pushing things too far, and I like to think he's listening to me. But if I leave now, the situation could get out of control. He could get end up getting himself arrested, even killed—and if I were half a world away, I wouldn't even hear about it."

Hanna stroked the baby's back to soothe him. "Kristin, I'm no older than you are. I can't tell you what to do. But there's one thing I've already learned about men. You can try to make them listen, but in the end they'll do whatever they want. I know you love Alvar. I love him, too. But you can't hold yourself accountable for the decisions he makes. And you can't let his actions control yours. You have to do what's best for you."

"But it's so hard, and I'm so afraid for him."

"I know. But I know what Alvar would tell you to do. He would never want you to miss out on an experience that would enrich your life. He wants the best for you—but this has to be your decision."

"I just wish I didn't love him so much. But this trouble with the raiders is changing him. He seems almost angry, almost like he's trying to drive me away."

"Maybe he's just trying to make it easier for you to go, and easier for him to let you."

"Well, I can't say it's working." Kristin sighed, stood, and walked outside to the porch. The baby had fallen asleep on

Hanna's shoulder. Rising carefully, she walked back to the bedroom and laid him in his bassinet.

Kristin's words lingered in her mind. She hadn't seen much of Alvar lately, but like Kristen, she'd noticed a change in him. He seemed conflicted and on edge, even when there was no evident reason for it. Was it because of the raids, because Kristin was leaving, or both? And how much did Blake know about what was going on?

Blake had been working long hours at the lumber mill these days, coming home tired and out of sorts. Hanna knew that the fomenting violence had him worried. He probably knew about Alvar's involvement as well. But he'd said nothing of it to Hanna. Maybe, like Kristin, he didn't want to worry her. But Hanna was no longer a child, and she wouldn't stand for being treated like one. If the raids and reprisals involved members of her family, she needed to know.

That night Blake arrived home at suppertime, a deep weariness lining his features.

"What's wrong?" his father asked him. "Is there trouble at the mill?"

"Not at the mill. But Hans Peterson, whose boy works for me, got hit by the raiders last night. They burned his barn, shot two milk cows, and then rode over the wheat fields, smashing the new sprouts and shooting their guns in all directions. Hans's five-year-old son was almost hit by a stray bullet."

"Oh, no!" The exclamation came from Hanna. "I know that family. My father and Alvar worked on their barn. They're good people."

"I take it the drylanders are pretty riled up over that," Joe said.

Blake nodded. "Alvar told me something in confidence, but I can share it with you. There's a girl on one of the ranches who's seeing Christian Sorenson's son. She warned him that the raiders will be hitting the Sorenson farm in the next few nights. Kreuger's vigilante band will be standing guard waiting for them. I tried to talk Alvar into staying away, but he said that he and Lars would be standing with their neighbors. He says that if they don't fight back, the raids won't stop until every homesteader is gone."

Kristin had gone pale, but she didn't speak. Hanna knew how worried her sister-in-law must be. She was worried about her brother and father, too.

"I don't like it," Joe said. "Sooner or later somebody's going to get hurt again."

"I don't like it either," Blake said. "But you can't argue with their right to defend their families and property. The only way to stop this mess from becoming a war is to shut down the raids. I've asked the Calders for help, but even if they're not supporting the raids, they're all for the settlers leaving."

"So what can you do?" Sarah asked.

"I've been trying to find out who's paying the raiders. So far, I've got my suspicions, but no evidence. I may go to Miles City tomorrow and see what I can find out about the property Doyle's been buying up. Something tells me he's involved, but there's nothing to connect him with the raiders."

"Knowing Doyle, I'd guess he's paying a go-between," Joe said.

"That's what I think, too." Blake buttered a fresh biscuit. "Find the go-between, and if he talks, we've got Doyle. Maybe that will stop the raids."

Hanna lay in the dark, the baby asleep in the bassinet next to her bed. From the other side of the hanging quilt, she could hear Blake stirring in his bed, making restless sounds, tossing and shifting. Was he as worried as she was? Did he feel as helpless as she did, with a range war hanging in the balance and her loved ones in danger? She sat up, the bed creaking as she rearranged her bedding.

"Are you all right, Hanna?" His low voice came through the quilt.

"Yes." She kept her words to a whisper, not wanting to wake the baby. "I'm just scared, that's all. Why do people have to do terrible things to each other?"

"That's a question for the ages, and we're not going to answer it tonight. But if you want to talk, come here."

Her pulse lurched. Was he asking her to join him in his bed, if only to talk? She slipped her feet to the floor and lifted a corner of the hanging quilt. The room was dark, but she could make out the narrow bed, the covers thrown back, with Blake, clad in his drawers, lying on his side to leave a place for her. She knew where this could lead, and she knew it was what she wanted. But what if something went wrong? What if she made a fool of herself?

The room was chilly. She was shivering.

"Come on, I'll spoon you," he said. "We can keep each other warm."

Holding down the hem of her muslin nightgown, she eased into the bed beside him, her head sharing the pillow and her rump resting in the hollow between his belly and his thighs. His body was warm and, like the sheets and pillow, smelled of fresh pine and clean sweat. As she inhaled the comforting man scent, her tense body began to relax. Blake always made her feel safe.

"Better?" He laid an arm across her waist.

"Warmer, at least. But I'm still scared. Anything could be happening out there, with my father and Alvar standing up to those raiders."

"The raiders will be looking to terrorize helpless people. Tonight, the settlers are showing the kind of grit even the Calders have to respect. If the raiders see armed men guarding the place, they won't chance it."

"You're sure?"

"Nobody can be sure. But listen, Hanna. Close your eyes, be still, and you'll hear it."

When Hanna closed her eyes and held her breath, she heard it—the roll of incoming thunder and the spattering sound of rain against the window.

"There'll be no barn-burning tonight." His arm tightened around her. "With luck, the rain will keep everybody indoors."

She began to breathe again, her senses opening like flower petals to his warm nearness, his heart beating against her back, his legs lightly tangled with hers. After the uncertainties of their marriage, it felt right to be here, snuggling close, in the same bed. It was like coming home.

I love you, Blake. Let me be a wife to you. She wanted to say it aloud, but her courage failed her.

She lay still against him, eyes closed, feeling the raw need in her newly healed body, the pulsing sensation in its sensitive depths. Her swollen breasts tingled. Once she'd heard a friend of her mother's say that nursing a baby made a woman want her man. At the time, she hadn't understood. Now she did.

His breath was warm against the back of her neck. Hanna's pulse skipped as he nuzzled a spot behind her ear. A moan of pleasure rose in her throat. Driven by nature, she moved her hips and felt the jutting rise of his arousal through her nightgown. She felt no fear. Just a woman's need to touch and be touched, to feel her husband inside her.

This man had willingly married her, taken her child as his own, honored her as his wife, cherished and protected her. But over time, the respect and gratitude she'd felt had warmed into a blazing desire that roused in her every time she looked at him or heard his voice.

She turned in his arms, meeting a kiss that released all the need he'd restrained for so long. His hands pushed up the skirt of her nightgown and moved over her body, her breasts swollen and aching for his touch, her belly still soft from pregnancy.

"Yes," she whispered, as if he needed to hear. "I want you, Blake. I'm yours."

His only response was a breathy mutter that sounded something like, "*You're damned right you are.*" He had shed his drawers and was fully aroused, his erection hard against her hip. His hand moved between her thighs, parting the sensitive layers with a touch that sent shimmers through her body. With every part of her alive and glowing, she opened to him like a flower, wrapping him with her legs as he mounted her and pushed inside. The tenderness from the birth only heightened the feel of him inside her as he began to thrust. She gasped with wonder at the shape and size of him, pushing gently at first, then with an urgency that carried her to a shuddering climax. Waves of sensation rippled through her, sweeter and more powerful than anything she could have imagined.

He laughed softly as she lay quivering beneath him. Then he moved again, and she felt his release break inside her. She sighed with the pure joy of it. He was her husband now, and she was his wife in every sense of the word. The emotion that swept through her was so powerful that it brought tears to her eyes. This was what she was born for—to belong to this man, to share his life and create their future family.

"I love you, Blake," she whispered.

"I love you, too. And I'm talking about forever." He withdrew gently and gathered her close. "Now, Mrs. Dollarhide, what do you say we get some sleep?"

When Hanna woke to the sound of her fussing baby, Blake was gone. The first light of dawn glowed through the window as she lifted her son out of the bassinet and settled back against the pillow. Her breasts were sore and swollen, the tiny boy hungry and eager for milk.

After last night, she'd looked forward to waking in her husband's arms. But he'd slipped out of the room without disturbing her or leaving any clue to where he'd gone or why he'd left.

By the time she'd finished nursing Little Joe, the room was lighter. She could see that Blake's clothes and boots were missing. Maybe he'd gotten word of some emergency at the mill or on the cattle range.

After settling the baby in his bassinet, she dressed quietly, walked out through the parlor, and onto the front porch.

The rainstorm had moved on, leaving the air fresh and sweet with the fragrance of damp earth. The sky was clear with a pale moon setting in the west. Except for the sound of waking birds, the dawn was peaceful, with no sign of movement anywhere, and no sign of Blake. She could check the stable for his horse, but she would most likely find it gone. She could only conclude that Blake had left on some mysterious errand of his own making—and all she could do was wait and hope it didn't involve danger. Now that they'd made love, everything seemed more precious.

As the sky paled, Blake rode across the pastureland, taking the shortest route to the wheat farms that lay north and east of Blue Moon. In spite of last night's rain, there could have been a clash between homesteaders and raiders. He knew that Hanna was worried for her family and neighbors. He was worried, too. He wouldn't be able to tell her what had happened until he saw for himself. If he found everything quiet, he could return to her with the news that all was well. If there had been violence, especially if the news was tragic, he wanted to bring it to her himself.

Now, as the sky lightened with dawn, he could see across the fields to the Christian Sorenson farm, where the planned raid was to have taken place. Raising the binoculars he'd brought, he made a sweep of the property. The house and outbuildings were all standing, with no sign of damage. A thin column of smoke curled upward from the chimney of the house, where someone was probably making breakfast.

A man in overalls moved about the yard, doing chores.

Blake allowed himself a long exhalation of relief. Either because of the rain or a change in plans, the raid on the Sorenson farm hadn't happened—at least not yet.

The Anderson homestead was two miles to the west. Blake rode that way, not planning to visit Hanna's family, but to make sure, from a distance, that nothing was amiss.

When he scanned the property with his binoculars, nothing seemed out of place. He recognized Lars's tall figure hitching up the wagon, and there was Alvar, coming out of the shed. Both men looked fine.

Grateful that he could bring good news to Hanna, Blake turned the horse for home. A narrow wagon trail led south across the pastures to cross with another trail that led into town. The distance was longer than the way he'd come but he could make better time on the trail than cutting through pastures.

The crossing was marked by an ancient dead tree. As a schoolboy, he'd heard stories about the tree being haunted. He remembered those stories as he took the wagon road and nudged the horse to an easy trot. At least, he could laugh at them now.

His spirits lightened as he rode along the trail. Last night he'd made Hanna his true wife. The two of them, with Little Joe, had become a real family. That was something to celebrate.

Maybe later, when Hanna was able to leave the baby with Sarah, he could take her back to Miles City for a real honeymoon—a fine meal at the hotel and a night in one of its luxury suites. She could enjoy the bubble bath to her heart's content. But this time she wouldn't need to close the bathroom door. The thought made him smile.

By now the golden rim of the sun had risen above the mountains. Raindrops from the storm glittered like diamonds on the grass blades. Meadowlarks trilled their songs across the pastures.

Blake was dwelling on thoughts of a happy future when

he came to the crossroads. What he suddenly saw made his throat jerk tight, as if he were being strangled. He fought back a wave of nausea.

Black vultures perched in the tree, squawking and flapping. Below them, hanging by nooses from the limbs, were the bodies of two men. Their bloated, discolored features weren't easy to look at, but Blake recognized them. They were the two men who'd tried to rape Hanna, two of the gang who'd dynamited Ulli Swenson's house, killing his little girl.

He remembered their names—Sig Hoskins and his scrawny sidekick, Lem.

CHAPTER 18

*A*LVAR HAD SHOWN UP FOR WORK AS USUAL THAT MORN-
ing, looking strained but behaving as if nothing had happened. After Blake had returned to the house, let Hanna
know her family was safe, and gulped down some coffee, he
went back to the mill and took the young man aside.

"I saw the bodies of those two raiders, Alvar," he said. "I
know I can trust you to tell me the truth. Were you there?"

A troubled look crossed Alvar's handsome face. "We am-
bushed them on the way to the Sorensons'," he admitted.
"There were just three of them and nine of us, so we had
them outnumbered. The big one called Hobie got away, but
we caught the other two. We knew for sure they were the
ones who'd killed Ulli's little girl, so we gave them what they
deserved. We executed them. Franz Kreuger and Stefan
strung them up. I held one of the horses while my father
watched. And if you're wondering, no, I'm not sorry. It
needed to be done, and the law wouldn't do it."

Nothing he'd said surprised Blake. "I understand," he
said. "But you need to know that you haven't ended the trouble. From here on, things are bound to get worse."

"I know that. We'll be ready for them. So are you going to report us?"

Blake shook his head. "Whatever you've told me, I'll keep it in confidence. Beyond that, I can't promise anything except that I'll try to keep you and your family safe." He paused, giving Alvar a stern look. "That will be your responsibility, too. You know you've put your family in danger."

"They were already in danger. This is why we need to fight."

"I understand. Now get back to work and don't make any trouble."

Blake watched Alvar walk away, his blond head held high in defiant pride. Kristin was scheduled to leave on the train three days from now. It would be just as well if she didn't know what he'd been involved in. She would only worry. So would Hanna.

For now he would keep Alvar's story to himself, as he had promised. But he couldn't waste any more time getting to the land office in Miles City. Tracking down the source of payments and finding proof might be the only way to stop the raids before more people died. But first he had to speak with Garrity. Finding the old man, he told him about the hangings. Without mentioning Alvar's part, he warned Garrity that people might be coming by, and the three boys who worked at the mill could be taken in revenge.

He left that morning, arriving in Miles City about 11:30. The clerk at the land office recognized him and gave him free access to the property transfer records he requested. The transactions were listed in a thick book with entries going back to the early settlement days. Each entry included a legal description of the parcel, the names of the buyer and seller, terms of sale, the date, and the signature of the person submitting the deed to be stamped with the official seal.

Most of the recent land transfers were from departing homesteaders to Doyle Petit. No surprise there. But a closer inspection revealed something that rocked Blake onto his heels. Most of the deeds had been submitted and signed, not by Doyle, but by Ralph Tomlinson.

Amelia's foreman and lover working with Doyle? Now there was a surprise. Could Tomlinson be the silent partner who was passing cash to the raiders?

Nothing Blake had found here was illegal. But it was proof of a connection between the two men, who were both connected to Amelia. Could she be involved, too? Blake would bet against it. Violence wasn't her way of dealing with problems. It was too ugly and messy. Subterfuge and manipulation were her preferred tools.

But Ralph Tomlinson—the more Blake thought about it, the more the idea made sense. For as long as Blake could remember, Tomlinson had shared Amelia's bed and taken her orders like a slave or a dog. At some point that must have grated on his manly pride. He was virtually a kept man, with no family, no fortune, no life except with the woman who kept him on a leash.

Doyle most likely saw Tomlinson as someone he could use—and he'd taken full advantage.

Blake was a long way from proving Ralph Tomlinson's connection to the raids. But fate had just tossed him the ball, for who should walk into the bank just then but Ralph Tomlinson.

Blake had no evidence of anything illegal the man had done. But one of the things that made him a good poker player was his ability to bluff. And right now, bluffing was the only option he had.

"Ralph." He walked out of the land office and gave him a nod of greeting. "Running errands for Amelia, are you? Or are you working for Doyle today?"

Surprise flashed across Tomlinson's face. Then he quickly assumed a blank expression. "I don't know what you're talking about."

"Sure, you do. I was just looking over the land transfers. You're the one who's getting Doyle's deeds recorded and probably handling a few other things, too. Does Amelia know you're doing side jobs on her dime?"

"That's none of your business."

Blake gave him a knowing look. It would be all bluff from this point. "Not even when I have reason to suspect you're doing more than recording deeds? Somebody's paying a bunch of thugs to scare homesteaders off their land. Doyle has the most to gain, since he's buying their land. But knowing Doyle as I do, I realize he doesn't like getting his hands dirty. You, on the other hand, could be fed up with working for a woman who mostly pays you in bed and board. Being Doyle's go-between with the raiders would make you feel more like your own man, if that's what you are. Right?"

The color rose in Tomlinson's face. "I don't have time for this," he growled, glancing around at the people in the bank as if to see who might be listening.

"Then you might want to make time. I paid a visit to the U.S. Marshal. He agrees that Doyle is probably the one behind the raids, but if you're helping him, you could be charged with conspiracy in the death of that child. He's looking to talk to Hobie. That galoot would turn on you in a heartbeat to save his hide. But if you'll go to the marshal and give him Doyle, you should be able to cut a deal."

Tomlinson had gone rigid. "Again, I have no idea what you're talking about."

"Tell you what," Blake said. "I'll go down the street and tell the marshal that you're here and that you're willing to talk. That way I can let you know if he's open to a deal. If he gets to Doyle first, or even to Hobie, they might put all the blame on you. Think about that. You wait here. I'll be right back."

Blake strolled down the boardwalk and slipped into the recessed entrance of the hotel. From there, he saw Tomlinson come striding out of the bank, climb into his buggy, and head for the railway station, a few blocks away, where a train was unloading passengers.

After that, Blake lost sight of him. But when the train pulled out again, minutes later, the buggy stood beside the platform, abandoned.

Blake left the horse and buggy at the livery stable, with instructions to notify Mrs. Amelia Dollarhide that her property was being kept there for her. Then he mounted his own horse and rode back to Blue Moon.

Passing through town, he was tempted to stop for a beer at the saloon to see if word had spread about the hangings. But he decided against it. Trouble could be waiting inside. He felt the same misgivings about confronting Doyle at the bank. Until he had solid proof, he'd only put the banker on alert. And right now he needed to get back to the lumber mill.

Garrity was waiting for him when he rode through the gate. "I thought I'd better let you know right away," the old man said. "Some men came by—Hobie Evans and some of the hooligans that ride with him. They were lookin' for Alvar and the other two. When I seen 'em comin' up the road, I sent the boys to hide in my cabin till they rode off. But the bastards made some ugly threats while they was here."

"What kind of threats?" As if he couldn't guess.

"They said that if you throw your lot in with them honyockers, hirin' their men and marryin' their women, you'll get treated the same as them."

"Let's hope it's all talk. I may have just cut off their money connection. Let's hope that takes care of the raids."

"I got a feelin' that this wasn't about the money. Those galoots was mad as hell. All they wanted was to get the folks that hanged their buddies."

"You're probably right," Blake said. "We could have a range war on our hands, starting right here. Keep a sharp lookout. Let me know if you see anything suspicious. I'll do the same. Meanwhile, keep the boys out of sight. I'd send them home now, but they're probably safer here."

Leaving the mill, he rode home and turned his horse over to a stable hand. He found Hanna in the bedroom, putting Little Joe down for a nap. Her bodice was open from nursing, her face softly flushed. She looked so desirable that he was tempted to fling her onto the bed and take up where they'd left off last night. But this wasn't the time for it.

"How was your visit to Miles City?" She kept her voice low, as they'd both learned to do when the baby was sleeping.

"It was worth the trip. I discovered that Amelia's foreman, Ralph, was working with Doyle, and probably passing money to pay the raiders. Last I saw of him, he was catching a train out of town. Unfortunately, he got away before he could pin any blame on Doyle."

"And what else is going on? When I spoke with you this morning, I could tell you were keeping something from me. I'm not a child, Blake. You don't need to protect me. I'm your wife, and if I'm to be a partner in our marriage, I need to know what you know."

So he told her—the hangings, the threats, the danger to her family, all of it. By the time he'd finished, she was pale and shaken. She reached for his hand, gripping hard. "I won't tell Kristin," she said. "She's already distraught enough about leaving Alvar the day after tomorrow. It will be better if she goes without knowing how much danger he's in."

"I agree." He gathered her close, feeling her strength and her love as he held her against him. "We'll get through this hard time," he said. "We'll be fine, you and I and Little Joe. We're a family."

But nobody could guarantee the future. Blake could only hope he was right.

The next night, after midnight, Kristin slipped out of the silent house and walked partway down the road to where Alvar had promised he'd be waiting. As he stepped into the open, his tall form lit by the moon, she broke into a run that ended with her flinging herself into his arms.

They moved back into the trees, where he'd tethered his horse. She couldn't help wishing that she could climb on its back with him, and they could race off somewhere, awaken a justice of the peace, and get married. But they were both sensible people. It wasn't going to happen.

Tomorrow she would be leaving for Miles City, with a first-class train ticket to her exciting new life. This was the last time they would be together, and her heart was breaking. Why had she talked herself into going ahead with her travel plans when all she really wanted was more time with him?

He held her close, his strong arms almost crushing her. "I'll write," she said. "And you can write back as soon as I know where you can send letters. But it won't be the same. I love you, Alvar. I don't want to go."

"Hush." He kissed her. "I've always wanted to go off and see the world. Maybe someday I'll have the chance. But for now, you can see it for me. Go and enjoy yourself. Then come back and become a wonderful doctor."

"And you? What will you do?"

"You never know. Maybe I'll find you again, like the story about your father finding your mother. Anything can happen in this crazy life."

"Oh, Alvar!" She kissed him, weeping in spite of her resolve not to cry. "What will I do without you?"

He eased her away from him. "Walk with me," he said.

She took his hand, and he led her back through the trees to an open space where they could look up to the starry sky and out over the plain below. "As long as we are under the same stars, I'll be with you," he said. "What you see, you'll be seeing for me. And what you do—" He broke off, suddenly alert. "I smell smoke."

Inhaling, she went rigid. "So do I! From down below!"

A few steps more and they could look down to the lumber mill, which was tucked against the bottom of the hill, in the mouth of a canyon. Leaping flames glowed against the darkness. The lumber mill was on fire.

"No!" Alvar sprinted for his mare and sprang into the saddle. "Run to the house, Kristin! Get help!" He kicked the mare to a gallop, heading downhill, toward the fire.

"Alvar! No! Come back here!" she screamed. But he was already out of earshot.

Kristin wheeled and raced back up the road. By the time she reached the porch steps, her lungs aching, she could see a red glow beyond the hilltop, where the flames rose skyward. She could smell the fire, even hear it.

As she plunged across the porch and into the house, the sound of a single gunshot was lost amid the roar of the flames.

"Fire! Wake up!" Blake woke to Kristin's frantic shout. He shot out of bed, grabbed his clothes, and raced into the parlor. The first thing he saw was a faint crimson glow through the front window, then his sister, wild-eyed with terror. "It's the mill! Alvar went down there!"

Blake threw on his clothes, yanked on his boots, and strapped on his pistol. His parents were coming down the stairs. Hanna emerged from the hallway, the faint sounds of the crying baby coming from the bedroom behind her.

"Kristin, run back and wake the boys in the bunkhouse," Blake said. "Tell them to bring all the buckets they can find. Then come back here and wait. You're not to go down there. I'll be heading out now."

"I'll be right behind you," his father said as Kristin darted away.

Blake saw the look of alarm that flashed across his mother's face, but she didn't speak. She knew that no words would hold her husband back.

"Be careful, Blake." Worry was written on Hanna's face. "Look for Alvar."

"I'll find him." Blake left the house, bridled his horse

and, without taking time for the saddle, sprang onto its back and flew down the road at a gallop.

The gate had been pulled down, probably with ropes and horses. Inside the fence, the burning sawdust had gone up fast, igniting the logs and the cut boards under the roof. The metal saw, boiler, and tracks wouldn't burn, but the timbers supporting the open shed that covered them were ablaze, pieces of the metal roof glowing red as they fell to earth.

Blake knew he needn't have bothered telling the men to bring buckets. The whole operation was going up like a torch. Buckets of creek water would be useless to save it.

Leaving his horse safely outside the fence and drawing his pistol, he rushed into the mill yard. The raiders were gone. Blake could see the fresh hoof prints of their mounts in the dirt. But so far, there was no sign of Alvar.

Garrity's cabin and the stable for the two draft horses were on the creek. Hopefully, they'd been spared. Blake splashed through the shallow water. The stable was untouched, the horses safe, though frightened. But where was Garrity?

Blake's ears caught the faint sound of barking. He followed it and found the old man lying between his cabin and the creek. The dog standing over him growled at Blake's approach.

"It's all right, Custer. Good boy." Blake moved in cautiously. The big yellow mutt was protective and could be dangerous. But the dog seemed to recognize a friend and backed away.

Garrity was wounded but alive. "Bastards got me in my good leg," he said as Blake leaned over him. "At least they could've shot the bad one. After I got hit, I played dead so's they wouldn't finish me off. And Custer guarded me. I was scared they'd shoot him, too."

Blake stripped off his shirt and bound the old man's bleeding leg. "Stay quiet and you'll be all right," he said. "I'll send somebody to help you. Have you seen Alvar?"

"No. But I heard some shootin' a while back."

"Hang on. I've got to look for him."

Blake walked back the way he'd come. He could hear riders coming down the road, but they'd be arriving too late. The place had gone up like a torch. By now most of the sawdust and much of the dry wood had burned, leaving the metal skeleton of the saw blades, tracks, and boiler. The stacked logs, delivered days ago, had fared better. Left damp by the recent rainstorm, they might be salvaged. But the lumber that was cut and ready for delivery would be a total loss. Doyle's lumber business in town would be booming.

But right now none of that mattered. He had to find Alvar. The young man would almost certainly have come on horseback. But there was no sign of his mare. What if the raiders had taken him? What if it was Alvar's body that would be found hanging from the ancient tree at the crossroads? At the thought, Blake felt a nauseating chill.

But that wasn't to be. Minutes later he found Alvar next to the fence, not far from where the gate had stood. He was lying facedown, a crimson circle staining the back of his shirt, with a bullet hole in the center. He was dead. If he'd had a horse, it had bolted or been taken.

Damn! Blake's eyes stung with smoke and tears. He gulped back the raw lump in his throat as he stood over the young man. Why Alvar? And for nothing?

The riders, with Joe among them, rounded the last bend in the road and pulled up outside the fence where Blake had left his horse. Kristin was with them—he should have known she would be, even though he'd ordered her to stay behind.

Seeing him, she dropped from her horse, ran to where he stood, and flung herself down alongside Alvar's body, cradling his head and sobbing.

Joe dismounted. Favoring his lame hip, he walked over to join them. "I'm so sorry, girl," he said, laying a hand on Kristin's head. "Oh, God, I'm so sorry."

The fire was slowly burning itself out. Two wagons had been spared from the flames. After ordering two men to stay and watch the fire, he helped hitch the team to one of the wagons to carry the injured Garrity and Alvar's body back to the house. Kirstin sat beside Alvar on the wagon bed, with his head in her lap. The dog, refusing to be parted from his master, jumped up beside Garrity for the ride.

Blake drove the team, knowing that more heartache waited at the end of the ride. Hanna would be shattered by her beloved brother's death—and the Anderson family had yet to be told. Alvar had been their golden promise of the future. Now he was gone, and with him his someday wife, his descendants, and all that he might have become in this world.

The next day, Joe and Sarah drove Kristin to the train in Miles City. She was still distraught about Alvar's death and would grieve for a long time to come. But her parents had persuaded her that there was no point in her staying for the burial. She had already said goodbye to the man she loved.

"It was my fault," she whispered as Blake gave her a farewell embrace at the house. "If he hadn't come to say goodbye to me, he would have been safe at home."

"You didn't start this trouble," Blake said. "You didn't start the fire or pull the trigger. Alvar would never blame you. He would thank you for loving him. And he would want you to have a happy life. Do that for his memory."

"I'll try." She hugged him fiercely before she climbed into the buggy with her parents, her tearstained face raised to the sunlight.

Blake stood with Hanna and the baby and watched the buggy disappear around the first curve in the road. "She'll be all right," Hanna said. "She's strong."

You're the strong one. Blake didn't voice the thought. He knew his wife wouldn't want praise at a time like this. Alvar's death had broken her inside, but she was determined to keep her composure for him, for her baby, and for her family.

Now that Kirstin had departed, they would drive the wagon, with Alvar's body wrapped in sheets, to the undertaker in town and continue to the Anderson farm, where Hanna and Little Joe would keep her mother company while Blake and Lars dug the grave. The next day they would hold a simple burial service with the family and any friends who'd heard the news and chosen to come.

Earlier that morning, before dawn, an exhausted Blake had made the long ride to carry word of their son's death to Lars and Inga. They had taken the news of his loss like the stoic people they were, but Blake could imagine the depth of their grief.

Like Kristin, it was natural for him to blame himself. If he hadn't hired Alvar to work at the mill, this tragedy would never have happened. But the chain of events that had led to the death of a promising young man was something no one could have predicted.

"We will bury him on our own land," Lars had said. "I will dig the grave today. As long as my son lies here, we will never leave."

"Wait for me to come and help you dig," Blake had replied. "Alvar was my brother."

"But what will we do about the men who did this terrible thing?"

"We will find a way to make them pay," Blake had promised, even though all he could see ahead was a chain of bloody reprisals. He may have gotten rid of Doyle's secret go-between, but the conflict would no longer be about money or even about Doyle. It would be about vengeance heaped upon vengeance, and he felt powerless to stop it.

Only the Calders had the manpower and influence to prevent a bloodbath, and Blake had already asked for their help and been refused twice. He knew better than to ask a third time. All he could do was protect the things that were his and the people he loved.

Now, with the team hitched to the wagon, he laid a canvas

tarpaulin over Alvar's sheet-swathed body, helped Hanna and his son onto the wagon seat, climbed into the driver's place, and started down the hill.

At the bottom, they passed the lumber mill. Blake hadn't taken time for a thorough inspection, but even from the road, he could see that, except for the biggest logs and the metal parts of the saw assembly, the place was a total loss. At least he'd had the foresight to buy insurance; but even so, the mill wouldn't be operational until midsummer.

In any case, the mill would have to wait. Right now, other concerns were more important.

The day was bright and clear, the fields and pastures green from the spring rains. Wildflowers, in shades of yellow, violet, and white, dotted the rangeland. Cattle and horses grazed on the fresh grass.

Blake glanced at Hanna. She sat quietly beside him with Little Joe asleep in her arms.

"Are you all right?" he asked her.

"I will be in time. But I'm worried about my family and all that's to come. Losing Alvar . . ." Her voice caught as her throat jerked. "Losing Alvar could be only the beginning."

"I'll do everything I can to protect them—and you, and Little Joe," he said. "You're a strong woman, like your mother, Hanna. As long as you're with me, we can be strong together."

Hanna and her mother sat at the table in the Andersons' tar paper shack. They were alone. Axel and Gerda had gone to visit friends who lived nearby. From the grass-covered knoll at the rear of the property came the sound of shovels as Lars and Blake dug the grave that, after tomorrow, would hold Alvar's casket.

Inga held the baby on her lap, her fingers playing with his dark curls. Her face showed the ravages of a mother's grief, but when she spoke her manner was composed.

"Thank you for bringing this little one. Seeing him helps remind me of how life goes on from one generation to the next."

"It reminds me, too, Mama," Hanna said. "But I'll never stop missing Alvar. He was like our angel, the best part of our family."

Inga gave her a sad smile. "He was my firstborn. When I held him for the first time and looked into his eyes, I had the feeling that God had sent me one of his angels, and that I might not be allowed to keep him long. I forgot about that as he grew up—he was never sick. But I remembered it when Blake came and told us he was gone.

"Sometimes I think, oh, if he hadn't met that girl, he would still be here—but no, I think it was fated. I think maybe God missed him and wanted him back."

"Kristin is a good girl, Mama. She loved Alvar and he loved her. She made him happier than I ever saw him in his life."

"Then I suppose I can be glad that he knew love in his life. And you, *kära,* are you happy with that husband of yours?"

Hanna nodded. "I am so happy. Blake is so good to me, and now we have Little Joe. I count my blessings every day."

"And what about the other one? The brother?"

"He left. He is out of our lives. And so is his mother. She wanted nothing to do with me or the baby."

"Then all is as it was meant to be."

"But I worry about you and Papa and the young ones," Hanna said. "What will you do without Alvar, especially with so many terrible things happening?"

"We will do as we've always done, and as you must do— the best we can. And we will love the people we have while they are with us, knowing that every day is precious. Come here, *kära.*" Inga reached out, encircled Hanna and the baby with her arms, and held them close. "In this sad life, love is the only thing worth keeping."

* * *

Alvar was laid to rest the next day, atop a grassy knoll where wild violets grew and rabbits had their dens. Attending the burial were Blake and Hanna, Joe and Sarah, the Anderson family, and a handful of neighbors who'd brought food to the house.

There was no clergyman to offer a religious service, but Blake had been asked to say a few words. Standing beside the open grave, he glanced around the circle of faces—Lars, fighting tears, Inga, lips pressed tight, her arms around her younger children, Sarah and Joe, looking somber, and Hanna, clasping her baby as tears trickled down her face. He began to speak.

"Alvar was the kind of man I'd want my son to become. He was intelligent, curious, respectful, and not afraid of hard work. And he always put others ahead of himself. He died trying to protect my family's property—a senseless, tragic death. We're all better people for having known Alvar. My sister loved him. My wife loved him. And I loved him like a brother . . ." Blake's voice broke as he stepped back from the grave.

An older man in the group offered a prayer to end the service. As the dirt clods thudded on the lid of the coffin, Blake laid an arm around his wife and son and led them away. Joe and Sarah followed him. That was when they saw the shiny, black buggy drawn by matched bays, pulling up to the grave site.

On the front seat sat Benteen Calder, his wife, and Webb.

Webb climbed down from the buggy and helped his parents to the ground. With his wife on his arm, Benteen, looking even more frail than Blake remembered, walked toward Blake and Joe.

"I hope we're not too late to pay our respects," he said.

"It's never too late," Joe said. "It was good of your family to come, Benteen."

"We heard about the fire and the death of this young

man," Benteen said. "But that's only part of the reason we've come. Between that and the hanging at the crossroads, we've come to agree with what you said to us, Blake. The situation is spinning out of control, and it's going to affect all of us. We need to stop the raids and reprisals before the whole county becomes a war zone."

Blake's pulse quickened. "So what are you proposing, sir?"

"I'm already talking to the other ranchers. We're prepared to send out a band of cowboys to either catch the raiders and put them in jail or chase them out of the county—and to make regular night patrols until things settle down. We're hoping you'll join us."

"Certainly. But the homesteaders—will they be left alone?" Blake asked.

Benteen nodded. "We figure those folks will have enough challenges without having to worry about being burned out or shot. As long as they keep the peace, they'll be left alone." Benteen coughed, turned his head away, and spat in the dust. "The first thing that has to happen is to make sure neither you or Mr. Anderson will retaliate for the damage that's been done."

"I'll talk to him. But we'll need to involve Franz Kreuger and the other leaders of the vigilante group."

"I understand," Benteen said. "Do whatever you have to. This valley needs to be a safe place for our families, our livestock, and our crops, and that's going to take all of us working together."

Blake exhaled in relief as Benteen shook his hand and Joe's, then walked with his wife toward Alvar's family. The struggle wasn't over. There was a lot to be done, and it might take time. But at last there was hope.

Far to the south, a train steamed its way across the vast midwestern prairie, the steady *click-clack* of wheels on the tracks whispering in Kristin's ears. *Alvar . . . Alvar . . .*

Alone in her compartment she gazed out the window at the endless sea of grass and wiped away tears. The world was waiting for her at the end of the tracks, but she could only think of what she'd left behind, the love she'd felt, and the words he'd spoken to her before the smoke reached them.

As long as we are under the same stars, I'll be with you. What you see, you'll be seeing for me. And what you do . . .

She closed her eyes and tucked him into her heart.

EPILOGUE

Eleven months later

*A*NOTHER SPRING HAD COME AFTER A LONG, HARD WIN-
ter. The pastures were greening. The wheat fields, those that
remained, had been plowed and planted and would soon be
thrusting emerald shoots above the soil. The ducks and
geese that had flown south in the fall were returning to the
wetlands to raise their young.

The air smelled of fresh earth and new life.

Blake stood at the porch rail at the end of the day, watching the sun set in a fiery ball, leaving ribbons of purple
across the indigo sky. He'd spent most of the long day at the
lumber mill, which he'd modernized after the fire, adding a
new band saw that could cut bigger logs with more preci-
sion, as well as electric lights and power. Orders were coming in from Miles City and the new settlements springing up
around it. With business booming, he'd hired more young
men from the homesteads. With the raiders gone and the
land at peace for now, they were eager for the work. Even
Lars, a skilled carpenter who was getting more jobs in Blue

Moon, had helped with the rebuilding. And Garrity, his leg healed, had been there to keep an eye on everything.

The harsh winter had driven more families to leave. Doyle Petit, who'd emerged from the debacle of the raids with no proof of any wrongdoing, was still buying up their properties. But thanks to the Calders, the harassment of the settlers had abated.

Gazing down the road through the twilight, Blake was relieved to see the buggy coming around the last bend in the road. Hanna had spent the day visiting her mother with Little Joe, an active toddler now, running everywhere and starting to talk.

Leaving her driver to put the team away, she climbed out of the buggy and released her son at the top of the steps. The little dark-haired boy raced across the porch toward Blake. "*Dada!*" he shouted. The word tugged at Blake's heart as he swept his son up. Little Joe was all Dollarhide, the image of his grandfather. Only his green eyes betrayed the missing part of his lineage.

Hanna laughed as she crossed the porch. "This little rascal wore me out today. Give me a few minutes to put him to bed. Then I'll come out and join you. It would be a shame to waste such a lovely evening."

She took the squirming boy in her arms and vanished into the house. Sarah and Joe had taken the train south to visit family and spend time with Kristin, who was at the top of her class in school. Except for Shep, who wasn't up to babysitting, Blake and Hanna had the house to themselves. They were enjoying the privacy but missed the extra help with their active little son.

A few minutes later she was back, stretching on tiptoe to kiss him. "How was the visit to your family?" he asked.

"Good. Mama always enjoys Little Joe. And we planted some flower seeds on Alvar's grave. Britta says she's going to be a teacher, and that she might not ever get married."

Blake chuckled. "That sounds like Britta. She'll do whatever she wants. How's their new house coming along?"

"The framing's done. But Papa's been busy with the wheat and his carpentry jobs. He's promised to have it finished by fall. Mama swears she won't spend another winter in the shack, listening to the wolves howl outside."

"When he's ready, I'll send somebody to help him." Blake slipped an arm behind her waist, pulling her to his side. "I went to town today—ran into Amelia in the bank. We talked, but only in passing. Now that Ralph's gone, she's managing the ranch by herself. Doing fine with it, I guess. But she's starting to show her age."

"That's probably just her meanness coming out," Hanna said. "I'm surprised she hasn't brought Mason back to take over."

They rarely mentioned Blake's half brother. The subject was still painful. But it was no secret that Joe still missed his other son. "Maybe he doesn't want to come back," Blake said.

"Do you think he ever will? After all, he's heir to that ranch."

Blake shrugged. "It doesn't matter. Let him come. You and Little Joe are mine. Nothing's going to change that—ever."

"Oh, but something's going to change." She gave him a mysterious smile. "We could use another boy in the family, don't you think? Or maybe even a little girl."

Pulse leaping, he gazed down at her beautiful face. Her blue eyes were twinkling. "Really?" he asked, scarcely daring to believe what he'd heard.

She laughed. "Really. About November, I think."

With a whoop of joy, he swept her off her feet and waltzed her around the porch.

Please read on for an excerpt from Janet Dailey's next novel, *Blue Moon Haven*.

BLUE MOON HAVEN
The New Americana Series

New York Times **Bestselling Author**
Janet Dailey

Can the good old-fashioned warmth of a rural small town make a broken family whole again? **New York Times** *bestselling author Janet Dailey explores the healing power of love and the enduring allure of the drive-in movie theater in the latest novel in her New Americana series . . .*

Kelly Jenkins heads to bucolic Blue Moon Haven, Alabama, believing a new life will heal the two orphaned children in her care. Signing on to revive the drive-in theater seems like a worthy venture, until she discovers the property is in deep disrepair. Still, spurred on by the elderly owner's plea to bring back the theater's good old days, Kelly takes on the renovation, beginning with an ancient tree that needs to come down—and unexpectedly bringing on the wrath of her reclusive neighbor . . .

Seeing Kelly take an ax to his little girl's favorite tree is like being struck in the heart—whatever heart Seth Morgan has left after losing his daughter. With his own attempt to buy the old drive-in thwarted, Seth reluctantly steps in to help Kelly, even offering her and her kids shelter in his home, a place that hasn't seen a woman's touch—or a child's joyful laughter—in far too long . . .

Soon everyone is bound up in the fate of Blue Moon Haven's drive-in—and the new family taking root in town. Because it looks like the love blooming between Kelly and Seth just may rival any found on the silver screen . . .

CHAPTER 1

AT AGE TEN, KELLY JENKINS DREAMED SHE WOULD LIVE in a quaint two-story country home with a red roof, operate a highly successful cotton candy business in her spacious backyard and fly fighter jets in air shows on the weekends (part-time, of course!) to the cheers of adoring crowds comprised of thousands.

At age thirty-four, Kelly, homeless, stood in a field of knee-high weeds in Blue Moon Haven, Alabama, with seventy-one dollars in the pocket of her ripped capris and two abandoned siblings—one of whom despised her—at her side.

Life had always had different plans than Kelly did, and the world hadn't always been kind, but deep down, she still clung to the secret hope that things might one day improve.

"It has wheels." Todd Campbell, ten years old, with the shrewd gaze of a middle-aged litigator, frowned up at her. "You said we'd never live in a place that had wheels again. You said when we moved here, there'd be a house." His eyes narrowed. "You said—"

"Yep." She nodded vigorously. "Yep, I know exactly what I said."

And two weeks ago, when she'd emailed her (sorely lacking) résumé to Mae Bell Larkin, owner of the Blue Moon Haven Drive-In, and accepted a management position, that's exactly what Kelly thought she would acquire—a home. That, along with a thriving drive-in–theater business exuding nostalgic appeal.

Instead, the massive sign, fourteen feet high and forty-eight feet wide, marking the drive-in's entrance, was covered in moldy grime, and the large letters comprising BLUE MOON HAVEN DRIVE-IN were faded or dangling precariously. And the lot itself was even worse. Weeds and briars were everywhere; patches of them rustling in succession as though small, unseen creatures scurried about. Two massive projection screens, one obscured by the sprawling branches of a pecan tree, had gaping holes and seemed to be covered in the same grime that slicked the entrance sign they'd passed earlier. Leaves, cigarette butts, beer bottles and other debris littered the concessions building and one of the two tall projection booths slumped to the right as though it had a bum leg.

But the worst—the absolute worst—was the ancient, poky trailer slumping at the back edge of the lot, its metal surface glinting beneath the early-spring Alabama sun, heat rolling off it in hazy waves despite the morning chill still lingering in the air.

"'Living quarters,'" Kelly said quietly. "'Homey living quarters.'" She twiddled her fingers by her sides. "*Homey* to me meant *home. House.* Not a mobile home." Cheeks heating, she winced. "I guess I should've ask—"

"Yeah, you should have." Todd crossed his arms over his chest. "You should've asked about the structure, how many rooms, where it was located. You should've asked how much you'd be paid, if you'd get health insurance, bonuses, retirement." He stamped his foot. "You didn't ask anything, did you?"

Gifted. Kelly grunted. That's what the school psychologist had told her six months ago when she'd been called to Todd's elementary school to discuss his unruly behavior. Behavior that had strangely involved Todd dressing down his new seventh-grade teacher (Todd had recently skipped two grades) for having made an absentminded mistake in a mathematical equation on a worksheet he'd given the class to complete. Todd had thrown his math worksheet and laptop out of the classroom window, then marched to the principal's office, reported the teacher as incompetent and demanded he be reassigned to another class.

All of this had happened because Todd was intellectually gifted far beyond his years, the school psychologist had said. He possessed an unusual combination of creativity, insight and innovation. Unfortunately, according to the psychologist, Todd's personality also included extreme sensitivity, a keen sense of justice and a volatile temper.

Kelly shook her head. Too bad empathy and politeness didn't seem to be in as plentiful supply at the moment.

But . . . considering all Todd had lost over the past year, most especially his mother and father, his anger was to be expected and easily forgiven.

"I did ask, Todd. I'm not completely inept." She breathed deep. Choked back her pride. Counted to ten. "I asked how many rooms and where it was located. I asked about all those things, except for the structure part. But the simple truth is, I had no choice but to move on from where we were. You're incredibly intelligent, and I know you'd understand if you knew all the details, but there are some grown-up things I can't discuss with you."

Like the fact that her former boss had been a micromanaging dictator with no heart, focused on dollars and cents instead of compassion and rewarding hard work. Of the twenty-five job applications she'd submitted, only one job—this one, in fact—had resulted in a callback. With no income and two extra mouths to feed, she'd had no choice but to . . .

"I need you to trust that I made the only decision I could for us at the time," she said softly.

A soft breeze rolled over the empty lot, ruffling Todd's thick hair. His brown eyes glistened, and his chin trembled.

Heart aching, she reached out, smoothing back his bangs with her fingertips. He flinched and jerked away.

"I'm sorry," Kelly said. "I know this isn't what you expected. What either of us expected, really. But it doesn't have to be bad. It can be whatever we make it." She studied his rigid back, then set her shoulders and smiled. "All we have to do is look to the birds."

He eyed her over his shoulder, examining her from head to toe as though she were a piece of crap stuck to the toe of his well-worn tennis shoe.

"From the Good Book," she prompted. "Birds are always provided for and never worry about tomorrow. Your mom used to say it all the time. We just gotta be optimistic."

Pain flashed in his eyes. He scowled, lifted his chin, then bit out, "This place is abandoned. There aren't any birds out here."

She laughed. "Of course, there are. There's"—she tipped her head back and scanned the blue sky—"well, there's . . ."

Nothing. Absolutely nothing. No wings, no beaks, no chirps. Not even a cloud.

A small hand tugged the hem of Kelly's T-shirt. Daisy, Todd's six-year-old sister, blinked her thick eyelashes and crooked her small finger. Over the past year, she rarely spoke, and when she did, it was only to Kelly or Todd. Daisy's words were as precious and valuable as she herself was to Kelly.

Kelly bent, placing her ear close to Daisy's mouth, and waited for Daisy's little lips to brush her cheek.

"Over there," she whispered softly. So softly, Kelly barely caught it. Then Daisy, clutching her well-loved doll named Cassie to her chest with one hand, pointed toward the tree line in the distance.

Lo and behold, a black-and-gray figure emerged, leaping

from the towering tip of a pine tree, flapping its wings and ascending high above the weedy lot.

"Hot dog!" Kelly kissed Daisy's cheek, nudged Todd with her elbow and bounced up and down as if her exuberance alone would ignite a spark of interest in Todd. "Daisy spotted one right over there. Look at that beauty go. She knows how to live. Spreading her wings, soaring without a care. A strong red-tailed hawk who has tossed away her worries and is poised to conquer the world."

Todd glanced at the bird, then smirked. "That's a turkey vulture."

Kelly stopped bouncing. "Oh."

The vulture circled them twice on the swift breeze, then glided away over a thick clump of trees in the distance. The spring wind picked up, whistling over the abandoned lot, and the weeds started rustling again, the strange scratching sounds of creatures hidden among the overgrown grass growing closer and closer.

Biting her lip, Kelly hugged Daisy close to her side. "I think we need to pay our new boss, Mae Bell Larkin, a visit."

Visit our website at
KensingtonBooks.com
to sign up for our newsletters, read
more from your favorite authors, see
books by series, view reading group
guides, and more!

BOOK ┃┃┃┃ CLUB
BETWEEN THE CHAPTERS

Become a Part of Our
Between the Chapters Book Club
Community and Join the Conversation

Betweenthechapters.net